A Longing for Impossible Things

JOHNS HOPKINS: POETRY AND FICTION
WYATT PRUNTY, GENERAL EDITOR

A Longing for Impossible Things

stories by
DAVID BOROFKA

JOHNS HOPKINS UNIVERSITY PRESS
BALTIMORE

This book has been brought to publication with the generous assistance of the
John T. Irwin Poetry and Fiction Endowment Fund and the G. Harry Pouder Fund.

Johns Hopkins University Press
2715 North Charles Street
Baltimore, Maryland 21218-4363
www.press.jhu.edu

Library of Congress Cataloging-in-Publication Data

Names: Borofka, David, 1954– author.
Title: A longing for impossible things / David Borofka.
Description: Baltimore : Johns Hopkins University Press, 2022. | Series:
  Johns Hopkins: poetry and fiction
Identifiers: LCCN 2020057377 | ISBN 9781421442136 (paperback ; acid-free
  paper) | ISBN 9781421442143 (ebook)
Subjects: LCGFT: Short stories.
Classification: LCC PS3552.O75443 L66 2021 | DDC 813/.54—dc23
LC record available at https://lccn.loc.gov/2020057377
A catalog record for this book is available from the British Library.

The epigraph that appears on p. vi is taken from Fernando Pessoa, *The Book of Disquiet*,
edited and translated by Richard Zenith (Penguin Classics, 2002). It is reproduced here
courtesy of Penguin Random House.

*Special discounts are available for bulk purchases of this book. For more information, please
contact Special Sales at specialsales@jh.edu.*

For Deb

For our girls, Katie and Mara, Krissie and Amanda

And for Everson Philip, the apple of all our eyes

The feelings that hurt most, the emotions that sting most, are those that are absurd—the longing for impossible things, precisely because they are impossible; nostalgia for what never was; the desire for what could have been; regret over not being someone else; dissatisfaction with the world's existence. All these half-tones of the soul's consciousness create in us a painful landscape, an eternal sunset of what we are.

—FERNANDO PESSOA,
The Book of Disquiet,
ed. and trans. by Richard Zenith

CONTENTS

A Longing for Impossible Things

My Life as a Mystic

ONCE UPON A TIME, I was very religious. I saw angels in my bathwater, and when I opened the front door birds would roost upon my shoulders!

Well, no.

I can't tell you that, not truthfully.

I was *prepared* for it, however—the birds, the angels, God speaking to me in a hushed and confidential tone, me and Him, He and I, with secrets to share— that was the life I had envisioned for myself. Now and again, driving to work on a bright and sunny day in early spring, I was sure that God would step out onto the highway and flag me down, illumination as hitchhiker. In those moments my head would get so light, my mood so euphoric, I feared for my sanity, but a doctor friend, a shrink, claimed that these incidents were nothing more than a manic phase. "Wait a bit," he told me. "It's early yet." My wife, on the other hand, insisted that I was experiencing an electrolyte imbalance. "Drink some Gatorade. You'll feel better."

I felt fine, I insisted. The air was nectar, the sky ambrosia. God was dancing in the peach blossoms.

She patted my hand as though consoling a stroke victim.

"Jesus," I said, "give me a break."

"Not now, dear," said my wife, assured of her hold over me. "Maybe later."

• • •

This went on year after year. If I saw two sides of an oak leaf dancing back and forth on its branch, I knew God lived on the other side of the breeze. Surely. But He always stayed that one breath away.

On occasion I acted less than responsibly. According to my wife, at least. One evening, I drove into a pasture by accident while looking at the moon. A fat, silver disk swimming in aquamarine twilight, it looked like a doorway into another dimension. Then the car went up and over a barbed wire fence and tipped, nose-first, into an irrigation ditch. My head hit the steering wheel, and the lights went out. When I woke, water was lapping at my feet, and the car, a Buick, my father's last before he died, was beginning to shift against the current. His displeasure—with what I had done to his inheritance—was palpable, the taste of blood coating my mouth.

"I was distracted," I said, scrambling out of my seat belt. The bank was packed dirt, but wet and slippery, and climbing it was no easy matter. A primitive form of life rising from the ooze, hands and feet, elbows and knees. Three cows stood placidly by, thoughtfully observing from the other side of the ditch bank. Thank God for cell phones.

"Moron," I heard my father say. "Space cadet."

"I'm open to new experience." I spit out a tooth. "Is that such a bad thing?"

"You never could focus. Always lost in your own little world. Nothing but fantasies."

"I could never figure things out. Not like you could."

"Ha," he snorted, one of the courtroom tactics calculated to rattle me, his most recalcitrant witness. "You just didn't apply yourself."

An old argument, my failure in law school, where I couldn't get through the most elementary course in contracts. I sat in classrooms late at night, surrounded by the drone of precedent and statute but listening for a melody no one else could hear. I lasted most of the first semester until I started having breathing problems. The classroom door closed, my chest tightened, and I'd have to get away, a prisoner escaping his keepers and cell.

"You had the mind," my father grumped.

A tow truck idled next to the ditch, red lights blinking above the cab, the driver hooking cables to the undercarriage of my father's former car.

"But not the heart," I said. "I never did."

The one decision that pleased my father was my marriage. Jenna, he said, had enough gumption for both of us. My mother approved of Jenna as well, for similar reasons.

"She'll keep your feet on the ground, Charlie," my mother said. We were sitting on the patio across from each other, our drinks on the glass-topped table serving as intermediaries. "You need that, you know. Otherwise you're liable to float away. I've been afraid one of these days I'd look up at the sky, and it would be: 'Oh, look, there goes Charlie.' Jenna won't let that happen."

A tax attorney for Nieboldt, Brand, and Marcus, Jenna spent that first evening tossing back slugs of Johnnie Walker with my father and trading stories about the worst judgments they'd ever received while my mother started a preliminary guest list for the wedding. I wandered the backyard, watching the shadows of the palm trees make fingers along the back fence, before taking off my shoes, rolling up my pants legs and sticking my feet into the swimming pool, hoping the water would be more than just wet.

It wasn't.

No matter that it chucked against the tiles like laughter, the pool lights playing hide-and-seek in the folds of its surface, or that it burped in the skimmers, the water was only wet.

No more nor less than the water that poured from my father's Buick when the tow truck lowered the back end down in our driveway. Why should I have expected anything different?

Jenna watched from the front door, her hands on her hips. "Forget to look at the road again?" she said. "Take the turnoff for the highway to heaven?"

• • •

Which is not to say I was so otherworldly that I neglected everything, Jenna's feelings notwithstanding. I'm not some kook who, certain that the end of the world will happen on January 17, sells his house and heads to the mountains to wear buckskin and eat berries. As you know, I had a wife, but I also had a job, a mortgage, and after this last incident, car payments. A life like any other. Maybe that was the problem. The ordinariness, the conformity. Maybe I was just looking for something to make life different.

I drove to work every day. I paid my bills. Did I mention that I'm an appraiser of vineyards and orchards, ranches, and other small farms near the foothills of the Sierra? No? Forgive me. After my failure in law school, I went to work for a bank. I was supposed to become the assistant appraiser, but the man assigned to train me had a heart attack and died. There were several mix-ups in the wake of his death, and to make a long story short, the bank manager sent me to evaluate an orchard in Sanger. This, in spite of my protests that I knew next to nothing. I tromped through the trees and in and out of barns for three hours, I sweated rivers, and I was no closer to an appraisal than I was when I arrived. I totaled estimates twelve different ways and never arrived at the same answer twice. Finally, at my wits' end, a figure popped into my head with more authority than any of the numbers at the end of any one of my columns, and I penciled it in with a shaky hand, deciding I could update my resume later.

Imagine my surprise when no repercussions were forthcoming. The manager nodded to me the next morning and each morning thereafter, and within a month my paycheck included a substantial raise. Herein the other part of the problem: the bank and those who employ me believe that my assessment is based on acreage, soil quality, condition of the outbuildings, equipment, etc., but in reality, I rarely do more than step over a fence and sniff the air and run my fingers through the field grass. It doesn't take long to know whether or not an acre of Thompsons is worth the investment. The verdict announces itself in the air. It sounds rather precious, I know, and I can no more explain my method to myself than I can to anyone else, but after fifteen years, although they can hardly be called rational analysis, my appraisals have become the standard by which other appraisals are based. I am successful—*wouldn't that be a surprise to my father?*—an accomplishment without intention.

So day after day, I drive into farmland, an expert who knows nothing but his own intuition, and risk losing consciousness over the sight of a brown horse foraging in the green tufts of spring, certain that something essential is about to be revealed. (Though, to be honest, I have always been disappointed.) And at night, I drive home, tracing the rocky course of the Kings River, and watch the sun set, a deflated old basketball disappearing into the purple veil of dust and haze. Is it any wonder that some evenings I come home convinced that I *almost* saw something beyond the thing itself?

• • •

And yet this is what's puzzling: sometime last year, I had an appointment with an elderly widow. She was buying an orchard from the grandson of old friends, Nathan Albright. I knew Nathan. We had gone to high school together, where he was known as something of a shmuck and a fool. He burned off his eyebrows in chemistry class—twice. His girlfriend turned up pregnant our junior year. He quit school, got a job, and his girlfriend gave birth to twins. His grandfather died, and with the inheritance, he bought a doughnut shop which went bankrupt six months later. His mother died, and he bought an orchard, although he knew nothing about farming. Mrs. Caldwell had no interest in the orchard. She was only buying it so she could lease it back at a fraction of its true cost. He needed the money; she needed the write-off. What could be better?

However, she insisted that I meet with her before doing the appraisal, an irregularity that caused Jenna to raise her eyebrows.

"The old lady has her hooks out for you," she said, laughing. "You'll be hanging onto the doorknob and she'll be throwing bedsheets over your head."

"She's seventy-two," I said.

"And you are naive."

"She has a dozen grandkids."

"All the more reason," she said, snapping shut her briefcase. "Be careful. Be very careful."

I backed out of the garage in my new tank of a Navigator, Jenna's gift to me, the peal of her laughter ringing in my ears.

Mrs. Caldwell's house was in Fig Garden, an unincorporated area within the city limits of Fresno. Dwarfed by its tall, unmanaged cedars and without the severity of sidewalks or curbs, Fig Garden does not resemble the cookie-cutter neighborhoods elsewhere in town. The houses, set back from the street by deep lawns and thick hedges of oleander, have aged gracefully, slumping a bit at the corners, perhaps, like your uncle's mustache, but managing a cheerful senescence nonetheless.

A note on Mrs. Caldwell's front door informed me that she was in the backyard, and that I should come through the gate by her detached garage. From somewhere deep inside the house a dog began to bark. I stepped off the porch and around to the back where a radio was playing and water was running.

Mrs. Caldwell was swimming laps in a black keyhole-shaped pool, a slow water-churning stroke followed by an arthritic flip turn at each end. I let myself through the gate and sat in one of the Adirondacks on the patio, watching her plow the water. Back and forth, back and forth. The robotic nature of the exercise seemed somehow futile and without hope.

"Oh, Charlie, you made it. So good of you to come. And so far out of your way."

She stepped out of the water, nearly six feet tall, and pulled a robe around her shoulders. Once considered elegant, she was now, however, only skeletal, with gray, gun-metal hair clipped schoolboy short. Seeing her, I might have been looking at a preview of Jenna thirty years hence. Have I mentioned that Jenna was once a model? That her posture is always correct? No? Forgive me yet again. Jenna was once a model. Which means that, like Mrs. Caldwell in her prime, she is tall for a woman and extremely thin, a narrow waist and hips, and if it weren't for a surgical enhancement, little more to her bust than there is to mine. She can wear anything, and if shoulder pads are incorporated into the design so much the better. You should see her, thing of beauty that she is, in front of a judge; with her high cheekbones and her honey-colored hair pulled back, she appears severe, ethereal, but she has a way of turning her attention over to others in a way that hands over her beauty as well. Impossible to resist. She was once a model, until she encountered a tax problem that cost her five thousand dollars in tax money and twenty-five grand in legal fees, and then she became a lawyer. A ferocious one, so I've been told.

We met during my brief stay in law school. She had given a lecture on the history of tax law, and there was a reception afterwards in the faculty commons. I should mention, by the way, that not only is she three inches taller than I am she is nine years older, and although she has no more illusions about my abilities than my parents had, she has a tolerance where I am concerned that must be love. Of some kind anyway. I had been hired for the evening to serve hors d'oeuvres, and she saw me in my white waiter's jacket, standing in a corner of the room by myself, eating the canapés before I could circulate among the guests.

"Hungry?" she asked.

My mouth was full. I nodded, offering her the tray.

"Well," she said, "this has been a lovely event."

I had not attended her lecture, and my sense of imprisonment was in full gallop even here at the party. There was no way I could have faked agreement. And then there was this surreal creature accosting me in my corner.

"I hate law school and every single one of these people," I swallowed. "It's choking the life out of me."

"A common reaction. We all suffer from it."

As it turned out, the lecture had been anything but lovely. The audience had been dull and uninterested, and the professor who had invited her to speak, an old boyfriend from whom she had parted unpleasantly, had acted badly, and if he started anything at the party, she swore there would be consequences.

"Let's get out of here," she said. We had polished off the last of the shrimp, and she handed me a napkin. "Wipe your mouth. Do you have a car?"

"Sure."

"Dickhead picked me up. He probably knew I'd bail out of here otherwise. Let's go."

We left through the kitchen; I kept my jacket, she left her coat, not quite an even trade, but there was no way in hell she was going back to retrieve it tonight.

I unlocked the passenger door of a Buick Regal, just one of the many cars my father gave me over the years.

"This is your car? This is something Nixon would drive. Jesus Christ, Nixon's car."

"My father gave it to me."

"Of course he did. And he's never owned a convertible, has he? Here, give me the keys. I'll drive."

We barreled north on 99 as far as Merced with the windows down and the chill February air pouring in. The only reason we stopped was Highway Patrolman Cardenas, who had clocked us doing one hundred and ten and watched us weaving back and forth among the semis and tractor-trailers. Jenna pulled to the shoulder, rolled down her window, and beamed a smile into the darkness. Soon enough we were on our way south, albeit more slowly, with only the mildest of warnings.

"Would it surprise you to know I've never gotten a ticket?" she said. "How old are you, anyway?"

"Twenty-two."

"A baby," she sighed, "who hates law school."

"Yes."

"Poor little snookums."

Once off the highway, she stopped the car in a new development on the north end of town. Hers was the only completed house on the street, and the framed skeletons of houses-to-be stood outlined against the dark sky like the aftermath of disaster. Earth movers and backhoes posed like museum dinosaurs underneath the streetlights.

"Well, you are coming in, aren't you?"

There was something a little frightening about the insistence of her invitation. "It's pretty late."

"Oh, please. There's a hot tub on my back deck and a beautiful view of the stars." She threw me the car keys. "I could use a little pick-me-up, but it's your choice."

Is there anything more flattering than being seduced? To be wanted by someone else, in this case, someone so beautiful I found myself rubbing my eyes lest she disappear.

I followed her into the house. She led me upstairs to her bedroom, where she tilted my face up to her own. The kiss was sweet, but—forgive me, Jenna—tainted by the tired breath of a long evening.

She disappeared into the bathroom, and I inspected the books by the side of her bed, paperbacks in glossy, metallic covers that one buys in supermarkets then throws away half-read, while on her dresser was a litter of make-up—tubes and jars, little pots and squeeze bottles—a graphic reminder that even the most angelic creatures must leave their gross residue behind.

Emerging from the bathroom in a thick robe, she indicated with yet another kiss that it was my turn, that she would be waiting for me out on the deck.

Unbuttoning my clothes, my fingers shook. I ran water in the sink and splashed my face, yet nothing relieved my sense that I was about to faint or that my next breath would be my last. Think what you will. I stumbled back into the bedroom, my eyes straining to make out the bed, the dresser, the frame of the sliding glass door now opened to the deck outside.

Her disembodied voice murmured against the darkness: "Lose the boxers, please. We don't need to stand on ceremony, do we? I thought we were friends."

Obedient to her wishes, I shrugged off my shorts and stepped into the spa aware only of the tingle of cool air and hot water on skin, but to watch Jenna rising from the steam and the dark circle of water was a revelation beyond the capacity of language, my senses cascading toward meltdown. I couldn't have told you whose mind I was in, never mind the hot tub, the stars, my own stiffening flesh, and although the sensation did not and could not last, fifteen years later, I catch myself on occasion disbelieving my good fortune, even if I can now admit to myself that Jenna's choosing me was closer to a random act than otherwise; I was simply the first male who wasn't pursuing her, my foolishness so awkwardly displayed. Despite the power she wields over others, she believes such effects dubious, a counterfeit of the truth, her faith reserved for anyone but herself. How else to explain this permanent rendezvous, a one-night stand of fifteen years' duration?

When she straddled me that night, she did not understand that in our coupling I was prepared for translation, hers or my own, that the air like opaque glass might shatter, revealing heaven for itself. We yelped and trembled, quivered and moaned under the patient dome of inky night sky. But even I knew that, although nearby, God would remain safely disguised.

Jenna herself provided the coda for the evening. We were spent, drowsing in her bed, when she yawned, saying:

"You are a very nice boy, yes, very nice. And very much a boy. I'll never need to have children."

And if over the course of the years we have disappointed each other by what we hope or expect to see, it is no one's fault, neither one of us to blame.

We are, after all, only human.

· · ·

Where was I? Jenna, yes. And Mrs. Caldwell, who, upon rising from the water of her pool, reminded me of my wife.

"I apologize for bringing you all the way out here, but there was something we need to discuss before you inspect Nathan's orchards."

"Mrs. Caldwell, I really can't talk about an appraisal before—"

She waved one hand in the air. "Of course not. I wouldn't presume. But I'm not asking to benefit from the situation, Charlie. Nathan is the grandson of my best friend, and sometimes I think he must have been born under a dark star. Everything falls apart for the poor boy. But he's something like a godson, and although he's a terrible farmer—so terrible, even I can tell he's terrible—and I would like to do as much for him and his family as I can within the bounds of business. Charity is not good for a friendship. You do understand, don't you?"

She was asking me to be as generous as possible with regard to my evaluation of his property.

"I know Nathan," I said.

She sighed. "You don't have to warn me about the possibilities. Or the consequences. I will be an absentee landlord with unimproved property, and Nathan will not know who owns it."

"The higher my assessment, the higher your taxes will be. You can pay whatever price he'll accept, you know."

"I'm aware of the ramifications, but I'd rather I was compelled to pay his price."

"I'll have to be reasonable."

"Of course. And remember: Nathan is not to know."

"I'll see what I can do."

Nathan would not realize that his godmother was not the fairy variety, but flesh and blood. Or he might suspect Mrs. Caldwell's role, but choose to believe in good fortune instead. Either way, metaphor is a lie, clouding instead of illuminating. I left Mrs. Caldwell's backyard, assuring her of my best intentions all the while harboring a sense of oppression. A sense that was not lifted by the sight of Nathan's orchards. I could tell you that the loveliness of the spring day was replaced by dark clouds and the threat of rain, and that the weather acted in accordance with my mood, but that would only be a convention and untrue. The sky was blue. One cloud, a lustrous white, sailed like a balloon above the mountains.

But standing along both sides of the highway were orange groves whose floor was carpeted with the damaged fruit of last December's freeze. The temperatures dropped below freezing for a week and thousands of laborers were left without their usual subsistence. And on the southwest corner of Nathan's orchard there was the blackened hulk of the former owner's house; consistent with Nathan's luck, the house had burned down three weeks after he and his family moved in. Faulty wiring, investigators said. They have neither knocked it down nor have they rebuilt—there was some problem with the insurance—and they have lived for the past five years in a single-wide trailer in the opposite corner of their parcel. One reaches their door only by a dusty, two-track path that leads a half-mile away from the ruin that was all too briefly their home.

I stopped the car before I was one hundred feet down Nathan's driveway. Dust billowed around me on all sides. Without my opening a window or a door, without a single look at soil or branch, a number, impossibly low, was already suggesting itself. Mrs. Caldwell would not be pleased. On one side of the car track were peaches, on the other nectarines. Both sides were equally neglected, poorly pruned, nearly wild, their blossoms in this time of noisy color looking impossibly glum. Even the bees, hovering above their boxes, seemed dispirited, uninterested in the mean fare above their heads. Ahead through the trees, I could see the trailer and hear the piping of high voices. Besides the twins, who are long past high school, Nathan has two more children under the age of five, and I could imagine the scene: the children at play, their dilapidated trailer the backdrop, rusty farm tools their props, acting out roles their lives would never offer.

I backed out onto the road; if anyone saw me, I was just a stray motorist who had made a wrong turn. I stopped on the shoulder of an orange grove littered with damaged fruit and filled out the appraisal form, including an estimate of worth that was at least twenty-five percent higher than the truth. Even at that, the figure would not entirely satisfy Mrs. Caldwell's wishes, but it would have been impossible to do more. Generosity has always seemed to me to be a noble thing, but the gesture gave me no pleasure.

Near Nathan's farm, Riverbend Road runs up and over the fingers of the Sierra foothills. The orchards here are well-tended, beautifully cultivated despite the undulations of the topography. In a valley so flat as ours, deviations from the typical landscape are welcome and inviting, and teenagers take advantage of these minor hills to race their cars where—on the downhill side of the crest—it is possible to get all four wheels off the ground. I understand the impulse, the sense of freedom, of translation, when one loses contact with the earth, but every spring there is some bloody accident involving a cheerleader or a member of the debating society or student body secretary, some child in a ten-year-old Camaro with primer spots who for one moment listens to his or her blood rather than parental caution. The newspaper will run a photograph of twisted, jagged metal against a backdrop of fruit trees or vines. A body bag may or may not be seen, but the message is clear.

No doubt my brief visit to Nathan's farm was the reason behind my particular impulse: I floored the heavy Navigator, and we were airborne. My own cautions were alerted for an instant, but only for an instant, and then it was too late. Visions of tragedy appeared unbidden: a retired farmer crossing the road to check his mail; a dog warming himself on the asphalt; a pickup two feet over the center line; a car turning left into an orchard driveway. A price would be exacted, I was sure.

But as it turned out, my visions were only the shadows of reflected fire, nothing realized. My only witness was a young woman with a bright yellow knapsack, her mouth agape, watching my flight from the safety of an orange grove, a young woman who waved her arms at me, running after me to flag me down, until the Navigator, bouncing on its stiff springs, skidded to a stop.

"That was beautiful," she shouted when she reached my door. "You were flying. Really flying."

"I don't know what came over me." The landing had left me a bit breathless, and perhaps I was more truthful than I had intended. "It was a stupid thing to do. I'm usually very cautious. I'm not a good driver."

"Oh?"

"I sometimes forget what I'm doing."

Below the knees, her blue jeans were full of orchard mud, and her jacket was ripped at the shoulders and elbows, fiber fill leaking out like the Scarecrow's straw in *The Wizard of Oz*.

"Listen," she said, "I don't suppose you're heading to town, by any chance? I was just about to start walking, but then you came over the hill."

"I need to sit here for a moment."

"That's fine with me. You just say the word, I'll sit all day long. Inside, that is."

She walked around to the passenger side and climbed in, muddy boots and all, threw her knapsack into the back and closed the door. Cut short, her dark hair stuck up in dirty spikes around her face. An angel made out of mud.

"There," she said, folding her hands in her lap, "all set. My name is Maria. And who might you be?"

• • •

Shortly before he died, my father asked that I come see him. In the last stages of liver disease, he had fired off orders and issued directives, bullying everyone equally: doctors, nurses, my mother, myself. He had rejected the idea of a transplant ("You must be joking"), refused hospitalization, and forced my mother to set up a sickroom in his study downstairs. He sat up in bed and wrote threatening letters to the doctors who cowered and catered to his whims. The only person who was allowed to touch him was a three-hundred-pound hospice nurse by the name of Orlando.

"Look," he said, "don't get me wrong. You're my son all right. But you're nothing like me. And I want to know why."

I sat down next to his feet. "Jenna says I have your nose."

"Big deal. A schnozz is a schnozz."

"We share other qualities."

"Oh, come on."

"Seriously," I said, but any comparisons I could think of were pretty far-fetched.

Who was I? My father had wanted to know, and I couldn't tell him. An immortal soul encased in flesh? Or was I merely a genetic mutation, the mysterious sum of my parents' determined parts?

A few weeks later my father died, remote and furious to the very end. I inherited his Buick, which I drove into a canal. So when Maria, this little slip of a dark-haired, muddy-headed girl, asked for my name, I heard my father's voice reproaching me by the light of a wintry moon, and the question seemed more complicated than normal. The silence that followed was unbearable.

"I'm a seeker," I said at last, my voice constricted by the sensation that I was about to choke. "A watcher of the skies. A pilgrim and a wanderer. I don't know, I couldn't stand law school."

"You're a nut," she said, "but that's okay. It's sweet."

"Charlie. It's Charlie."

"We all have to take a part, you know. Take me, for example. I wanted to play for the oranges. The trees were hurt so badly, they were weeping for their children. They make a very high, keening song. Have you heard them?"

"Now who's the nut?" I said. "You're speaking metaphorically, I assume."

She sat up straight and squared her shoulders. "I have never lied to anyone," she said.

"I spend every day out here," I said, trying to keep the hurt out of my voice. "They've never sung to me. And I don't expect they ever will."

"You never know, Charlie," she said as though promises could be made. "It's so beautiful out here, so lovely. We wept together and sang together, and they thanked me for sharing their grief. Then you came flying over the hill, and I knew it was the right time to leave."

I started the Navigator, and we pulled slowly away. It was so unfair! All my life I had longed for some sort of affirmation that connections could be made, that a certain rapport might exist between myself and the spirit of God. My passenger, Little Ms. Doolittle, was singing to the trees as part of the choir, whereas I had ruined an entire, fully-functioning American car for the sake of the moon!

She retrieved her yellow knapsack from the back seat and pulled out one of those wooden flute things. A recorder, I guess they're called. "They particularly liked this," she said, "and they suggested some different arrangements."

I can't tell you the melody she played. I'd never heard it before; I've never heard it since. I didn't hear much of it anyway since about three bars into the piece I began to cry. Like the orange trees? I couldn't tell you. However, my weeping grew so violent that I had to swerve off the road and into the parking lot of a little country store that seemed to leap suddenly out of the ground in response to my need. In front of the store was the stuffed and padded figure of a man, dressed and painted as an Indian, the waves of political sensitivity having missed this backwater, his stoic countenance the witness to my unraveling.

Maria patted me on the shoulder. "Listen," she said, "I'm going inside to get a couple of things. I'll be right back."

"Fine, fine," I sniffled. What she might need I couldn't possibly guess.

"You'll be all right."

God's choice is capricious and without regard for fairness. I knew I would never be all right. I've seen *Amadeus*. I know how Salieri ends up.

• • •

Would it sound naive if I said it was my first taste of true bitterness? It's the truth and nothing but. I have been a good-natured and honest seeker my whole life. As a child, my mud pies might become birds if only I imagined them so, but I wasn't offended when they didn't rise and take wing. In college, I read all the oracular literature I could get my hands on—the Vedas, the Kabbalah, the so-called Hermetic writings—and although baffling and mysterious, such works held me in their sway. My mother was probably right: without Jenna I might have floated off for good. Not the best training for law school.

In the second book of the *Corpus Hemeticum*, Poemander, the mind of the Great Lord, the most Mighty and absolute Emperor, answers the narrator, young aspirant and seeker, who "would Learn the Things that art, and Understand the Nature of them and know God":

> "Have me again in thy mind, and whatsoever thou wouldst learn, I will teach thee." When Poemander had thus said, he was changed in his Idea or Form and straightway in the twinkling of an eye, all things were opened unto me: and I saw an infinite Sight, all things were become light, both sweet and exceedingly pleasant; and I was wonderfully delighted in the beholding of it.

Likewise, when Maria had played her recorder, I had understood—*straightway, no less!*—that nothing had been opened to me, and in all likelihood nothing would ever be revealed: sweet, pleasant, or otherwise. I would be muddling along for a lifetime, a blind man without a stick.

Maria returned from the store with a bulging grocery sack and a worry line denting her forehead.

"Here," she said, opening a container of orange juice and a box of Saltines. "You look like your blood sugar's a little low."

"Thanks," I said. It had been a bad winter for oranges, but you would never know it by the juice, so cold and sweet; I could feel it spreading through me like light in a dawn sky.

"Better?" she said.

"I think so."

She gave me a handful of crackers and an address in a neighborhood not far from my own—"If it's not too much trouble," she said—and lightly touched the keys hanging from the Navigator's ignition.

"Yes," I said. "We're going."

Whereupon she promptly fell asleep. As soundly and immediately as I have ever witnessed in another human being. Her head tipped back, her mouth dropped open, and a gentle snore issued forth. Her shoulders and back turned to jelly. She must not have slept for several days, and she was making up for lost time.

There is something quite profound about driving while another human being, riding alongside in the passenger seat, sleeps. A measure of trust in the good will of fellow human creatures. Putting one's fate in the hands of another. I had never spoken with the trees in anything but the most metaphorical of ways, and yet Maria saw me as the one selected to carry her home. I flew, then landed at her urging, part of God's divine order for her life. The miles slipped by. Orchards gave way to horse farms, horse farms gave way to tracts and strip malls. When I was a boy, these fields had been barren, and now they were teeming with middle management and Little Leaguers. I was ten minutes away from Maria's address when a phone began to ring, a chirping that emanated from Maria's yellow knapsack. Ordinarily, I wouldn't think of answering another person's phone, but this day had been filled with contrarian impulses.

"Yes," I said, while Maria slept on.

"Lisa?" a cigarette-roughened female voice replied.

"No," I said, "I'm a friend of Maria's, this is Maria's phone."

"Maria?" the voice said.

Other voices murmured in the background: "He says he's with Maria."

"Listen, mister, if this is some kind of game, you don't know the rules."

"What game would I play?" I was becoming annoyed, and traffic was growing heavier. I should have turned the phone off. "You must have the wrong number."

"You're with Maria?"

"That's what I said. She's asleep. Maybe you should just call her later after she gets home. She'll be there in a couple of minutes."

The line went dead. The call was unsettling, to be sure, made more unsettling by the fact that I shouldn't have answered the phone in the first place. But ahead of me was the university with its beautiful ball fields. Then shops and those medical complexes that cater to the well-to-do. Turning north, I realized that Maria was staring at me—for how long I couldn't have told you.

"What are you doing?"

"I'm sorry," I said. "You were asleep, and I didn't want to wake you. But I shouldn't have answered your phone. Normally, I'd never do that."

"Where in the hell are you taking me?"

"Home. I'm taking you home."

"Ah, shit. Shit." She began to pull at the irregular spikes of her muddy hair. "Home. He thinks he's taking me home."

We were stopped at a traffic signal one block from her address, and she began to hit me with the sides of her balled-up fists, nothing that really hurt, mind you, but difficult to understand. She slapped at my face, and my glasses flew off.

"You cocksucker," she said. "Asshole. Son of a bitch."

"What's the matter, Maria?" I said. "What did I do, what did I do to you?"

"Maria," she said, practically spitting, then resumed her work with her fingernails. "That little bitch."

The light had turned green, but blue lights were revolving behind us, and a cop was tapping his stick against my window. Maria was peeling a layer of skin from the side of my neck.

"I think," the officer said, "it's time to exit the vehicle. You're about to be filleted."

· · ·

All was straightened out after a fashion. Maria—or Lisa, Julianna, Sophia, or Diane, she had as many names as she had personalities—was escorted into one of the two waiting squad cars, to be taken back to her room at the psychiatric hospital from which she had gone on the lam. The woman on the other end of the cell phone was Maria's ward nurse, whose responsibility it was to call every three or four hours in the hope that one of Maria's better selves would respond. After speaking with me, she had alerted the Fresno police, one of whose officers put two and two together when he saw a man in a jacket and tie being beaten by a girl made of mud.

So my latest contact with the divine was nothing more than the inspiration of the mental health ward, and as such should be considered suspect. Of course, the *Corpus Hermeticum*, that supposedly ancient treatise attributed to Hermes Trismegistos, is also something of a fraud, composed as it was in the second or third century rather than being the product of our darkest past. Its evocation of wisdom and transformation is the offspring of a wish, older maybe, but no more powerful than our own. But as my father, that old fart, was fond of saying, Wishing doesn't make it so. If wishes were fishes . . . But you know the rest.

Thank God for cell phones.

• • •

Which reminds me: I once saw an old man wearing beautiful shoes. This was in front of the opera house in San Francisco following a performance of *Tosca*. "I have lived by art, I have lived by love," Tosca sang. I have lived on illusions; is that so much different? Tosca leaped to her death from the parapet, and Puccini's dream ended. We applauded, the lights came on, we moved slowly, Jenna and I, still in Rome, postponing our retreat into the mysteries of an ordinary night.

Shepherded by a young man and woman with walkie-talkies, the old man was among the last to exit. I don't know who he was—a former senator, perhaps, or maybe the retired CEO of a multinational corporation; I suspect, however, that he only had money. Eighty years old if he was a day, he was, nonetheless, dressed immaculately—a beautifully cut gray suit, snowy shirt, silk tie—but his shoes, ah, his shoes were perfect, and although he was obviously frail, he stepped from the theater toward a waiting limousine with the light, balletic feet of a deer. I half-expected that metamorphosis to occur in a bloom of fire. But no—he merely ducked his silver head into the darkness of the limousine, settled his rump into the cushions of the rear seat, and said something to his driver, one moment nearer the blossom of death.

High School and the Mysteries of Everything Else

1. Adult Behavior

"Leanne," Mrs. Novatny says, "would you mind taking this to the office?"

Her English teacher holds a manila envelope containing forms or reports or God knows what other serious adult nonsense. Her fingernails are brightly polished with a color the shade of a stop sign, and the layers of her many skirts swirl and flutter.

"Sure." Leanne stands, and a low wave of laughter sweeps the room from side to side, a slow roller for no apparent reason other than her own embarrassment. It is in such moments that she becomes so aware of her body that she doesn't quite know how to stand, where to put her hands, how to keep the blood from rushing to her face and throat. It is in such moments that she curses the bottom drawer in her bedroom where she keeps the bag of assorted delights: Hershey's Kisses, Reese's Pieces, M&Ms, and the seven pounds she will never lose.

"You want me to go to the office."

"The counseling office, not the attendance office. With this." Her teacher shakes the envelope.

"Okay."

Mrs. Novatny crosses her arms over her chest. "Don't take too long. No cavorting," she says. Mock stern. "No cavorting or frolicking."

"No," Leanne says, "no cavorting."

"Or dawdling."

"No."

"Okay," Mrs. Novatny says, "off you go. See you soon. The Bard and Hamlet await. Ta-ta."

Mrs. Novatny waves and the plastic bangles on her wrist sound like dime store wind chimes, while the low growl of laughter sounds like real derision.

Why is it, Leanne wonders, that English teachers, the women especially, like to think of themselves as hippies of the might-have-been? Why are they always so weird?

The door closes behind her, and she is alone. The breezeway between the buildings is absent of students, teachers, administrators, or staff of any kind. The breezeway is filled with breeze.

And isn't that a pleasant thing?

2. Concrete and the Learning Environment

East High School is one of those concrete monstrosities built about the time Leanne started elementary school; the architectural model might have been that of an enlightened prison. Classroom blocks three stories high. Wide cement walkways. Windows that do not open. Gray walls and concrete zero-scaped planters. Surveillance cameras in the breezeways and the classrooms. Loudspeakers on light poles around the quad. A barely discernible hum from fluorescent tubes starting at six in the morning and lasting until ten at night.

Which is when the custodians come and, with blowers and pressure hoses, wash the concrete clean of the day's debris. After more than ten years the school looks as it did the day it opened, as though no teenager has ever been present or passed through its doors. No one associated with the school ever mentions ivy or hallowed halls. The principal's office is filled with athletic trophies, an inflatable six-foot-high hula dancer, and a sign reading, "We put the _fun_ in dysfunction." Some wit has posted a second sign which reads in smaller letters: ". . . and if you don't get to class on time, we'll put the _fun_ in funeral." Ha, ha. _Funny._

Leanne has attended East for three years but she doesn't think about it much, and she never thinks about the classrooms or the teachers in any serious way. She is conscious only of the passing periods, the jostle in the walkways, the sideways lean to get to her locker, the nonstop chatter and smash and clang to which a studied obliviousness is the only sane reaction. She often wonders if she is deficient in some regard. Most other students of her grade and age do not seem to feel as though they are on the outside looking in; instead, they seem to be so completely inside a sphere of belonging that they aren't even aware of those like her who have been relegated to the outer orbit. The outer-outer orbit. To be sure there is the odd assortment of misfits, but their presence seems to be another form of indictment, and their collective exile another tribe that Leanne is not interested in joining.

Her mother, who is blonde and rail thin and beautiful even in her forties, would not understand; her experience of high school included football pep rallies and bonfires and the homecoming court. Leanne went to one football game her sophomore year but only because her Spanish class rode on a float depicting Zorro, and Señora Millhouse required the entire class to attend. They chugged around the track once, Leanne made sure that her name was on the class sign-in sheet, she watched as the players slammed into one another and the pep squad jumped around like fools, and everyone else seemed to think that there was nothing more important to do on a Friday night.

Big deal.

3: We Are All the Roles That We Play

Outside the counseling office, a groundskeeper is working in one of the concrete planters. His shirt has an embroidered nametag that reads "Oscar" and he is elbow deep in a hole.

"Hey, Oscar," Leanne says. She has recently decided that she needs to change her personality, to be more outgoing, more assertive around strangers. A resolution is a resolution.

The man in the planter stares at her. He seems to be trying to decide something.

"My name is Felix," the groundskeeper says. "I just borrow his shirts."

"Oh."

"And sometimes it's good if people think I'm Oscar."

"I see," she says, although she doesn't exactly.

"I like a low profile."

"Okay, Oscar/Felix," Leanne says. "Keep your head down."

"You know it, girl. You do the same."

In the counseling office, Leanne hands the envelope to one of the student aides, a girl with big hair and multicolored eye shadow that she recognizes from her Spanish class. Maria. Who speaks Spanish in the hallways with the other Mexican girls, and yet is failing Spanish class. Why is that?

"Hey, white girl," Maria says. "You can go now."

"I'm going," Leanne says.

"Don't make me tell you again."

"I'm not stupid," she says. "I'm out of here. Bright and sunny day like this, you don't have to tell me twice."

"Jesus Fernando Christ," Maria says. "Crazy white girl."

She leaves the office, but she doesn't go back. She dawdles, if not cavorting and frolicking, taking the long way back to her English class. Walking in the opposite direction, she circles the athletic fields and the automotive shop. From the shop come sounds of clanging and banging, shop tools hitting the floor, a muffled expletive. Goddamn, son of a bitch. Shocking, the language. On the practice field several gym classes mill about in some semblance of activity. A couple of ninth grade boys throw rocks at each other while other boys take turns launching themselves into the long jump sand, and a gym teacher makes notations on a clipboard. A tangle of legs protrudes from the pole vault pit. Can a tangle of other parts be far behind?

The sun does that to people, she thinks. Makes them drowsy. And stupid.

As she edges around the outfield fence of the softball complex, she hears her name. Leanne, Leanne. Behind the backstop, she finds one of those groups of misfits whose attire and accessorizing has, by now, become stereotypical: two girls with hair of colors not found in nature, three boys with bad skin and baggy pants and chains dangling from every pocket and belt loop. They all sport metal protruding from lips and tongues, nostrils and eyebrows, ears and ears and ears. But the one who has called out to her is not like any of them; he is like her, unmarked and unremarkable. Except for the Bible he carries in his left hand. Aaron, who sits one row over and one seat back from her in her advanced algebra class. Who, on occasion, looks at her with more interest than seems necessary or desired. He is one of the outspoken Jesus heads, but unlike the majority of the Christians in this enclave of the Fundamentalists, he takes the publican-and-sinner bit seriously, much to everyone's annoyance.

"I was just telling Marcus that the self-destructive impulse doesn't hurt anyone but himself."

"Fuck off," Marcus says. He's not particularly angry nor is he terribly interested.

"There are more productive ways of being rebellious. You could work at a soup kitchen or volunteer at the hospital."

"You are friggin' nuts," the girl with fluorescent orange hair says.

"I'll get right on that," Marcus says. "Right after my latte."

"I'm just saying how confused everyone would be if you did that. Embraced God, I mean, by embracing your responsibilities to other people. Leanne knows what I mean."

"What?" Leanne says. She hasn't realized that she has a part to play in this conversation. "Sorry, Aaron, but I'm probably closer to Marcus's view on this one."

"You can't go around telling people what to do," the other girl says.

"Yeah, fuck off," Marcus says again.

"I mean," Leanne says, aware that she's repeating what's already been said, "I mean, you can't go around telling people what to do."

"See?" Orange Hair says.

"All I'm doing," Aaron says, "is making a suggestion."

"Maybe," Marcus says, "maybe you oughta keep it to yourself."

"Even if you mean well," Leanne says.

"I can't not say anything," Aaron says.

"Oh?" Leanne says. "Shutting up is not that hard."

4: Okay, So There Might Be Impediments

Mrs. Novatny is disappointed, distressed, upset. She feels betrayed and deceived. All because Leanne has been cavorting and dawdling and frolicking. Late. She was late. Actually, she has been absent for the entire period if one doesn't count the first five minutes and the last five when she made her unfortunate and belated re-entrance. And now, due to this conversation, she will be late for her Spanish class. Mrs. Novatny's next group of literary scholars is already milling about and making no great effort to hide their interest in the conversation.

"I was interrupted," Leanne says by way of explanation. "I was detained."

Which is the truth of a sort.

"Detained."

"Yes."

"By whom, may I ask?"

Aye, there's the rub . . . Rub-a-dub-dub.

5: To the Marriage of True Minds

After Leanne left the softball fields and the backstop with its rebels and the one reactionary, she became aware that Aaron had not stayed behind with the metal spikes and studs and the colors not found in nature. He was at her heels, like some small, barking dog.

"I didn't mean to put you on the spot," he said.

"Oh? I think you did."

She stopped, turned, faced him, fully aware of the moment and its theatrical quality. Her own power beckoned. She had something to say and a tone with which to say it, but then . . . He wasn't that bad looking, you know? No, not that bad. His eyes were hopeful, his mouth gently amused. His earnestness lent gravity to his features that most boys his age lack. From one angle that gravity might have been seen as pompous and laughably dogmatic; from another, he seemed driven and purposeful. By silent agreement, they pushed past the corner of the gymnasium into a shadowy niche. Classes were in full sway, and they were alone.

What was one to do?

She pushed him against a wall and kissed him. Hard.

Take that.

His eyes went from hopeful to glassy in a second. One hand blindly reached for, and touched, her hip.

"Maybe," he said, panting a little. "Maybe you'd like to come to Youth Group."

Oh, boy. Would she?

"You're kidding, right?" she said. She kissed him again and felt his lips respond. His legs pressed against hers.

Now who is the evangelist?

• • •

How is she to explain *that* to Mrs. Novatny?

6: Mirror, Mirror

When she thinks of herself she imagines a small girl with an imperfect smile, limp hair, and a mole on her neck the size of a goiter in one of those films about Africa. Reflection is delicious torture, one that she visits hundreds of times a day, in bathroom mirrors, and sliding glass doors, and car windows. "Hag." Denunciations flit through her mind like pinpricks. "Witch. Crone." In truth, and she knows this in those moments of utter honesty that go beyond the limits of language, her teeth are only a little crooked, the mole at the base of her neck is no more than a beauty spot, and her hair can only be called limp on those mornings when she threatens not to take a shower. She is five pounds heavier than she wants to be and ten pounds heavier than what some so-called beauty magazine call ideal, but she cannot stick to a diet, and since she hates throwing up—hates it passionately—she can no more imagine sticking a finger down her throat with those other girls in the bathroom than she can imagine gouging out her own eyes. Those five extra pounds, she figures, will have to take care of themselves, and in the interior conversation that she often carries on with herself, she has named them Fred; although Fred rarely listens and never answers, she often finds herself pleading and cajoling: "Don't you think Barbados would be nice, Fred? You could visit, get a little sun, and buy me a bikini. Or, if you don't want to travel that far, how about moving from my waist to my boobs? Huh? Wouldn't that be a nice change, for you and me?" So when Aaron put his hand on her hip, her first thought was for Fred. C'mon, Fred, she thought. Keep a low profile. Please?

More to the point are those features she recognizes in herself from her mother, father, and her mother's mother, the only grandparent she has had the opportunity to know. Her eyes are her mother's, her nose that of her absent father, her chin her grandmother's. A mutt. It's enough to make her wonder what other traits she's inherited and what the years will bring. Her mother's temper is enough to light fire at twenty paces, her father is a delinquent and has a knack for refusing all commitment, and her mother's mother, well, that's another story altogether.

Take this afternoon—and what a day this has been after all—her mother has gone to the nursing home where her grandmother has lived for the past five years. Her grandmother's dementia has deteriorated to the point now where she rarely leaves her bed. Caring for her is a 24-hour-a-day proposition. Her grandmother lived with Leanne and her mother for several years, until the old woman's decline—her paranoia and wanderings—became too much for her mother to handle. The deterioration of her grandmother's condition has been precipitous and frightening, and now Leanne can't remember a time when she wasn't demented. The final straw occurred when her grandmother opened the front door and skedaddled into the peach orchard a mile away from the house. They found her drinking water from a stand pipe and muttering dark curses in Russian, a language she hadn't spoken in sixty years. After her mother moved the old woman to Oakdale Pointe, Leanne made it a habit of stopping by the nursing home and her grandmother's room each afternoon after school, but after a year or so, she began to find reasons to skip. Now, days go by between visits. Weeks, even. The old woman was a dancer once upon a time and then a secretary and then a real estate broker, but now she lies in bed and stares at the stains on the ceiling. She lies for hours with one wasted arm over her eyes. When Leanne visits, her grandmother does not acknowledge her presence. Leanne holds her grandmother's hand for half an hour or so, and then tiptoes away when she falls asleep. Leaving is a guilty relief. Is this what lies in store through the years? At what point will she be the one in bed?

Leanne finds her mother's note on the dining room table. "I've gone to see Nana." That's all. No "Love, Mom"; no "How was your day?" Well, one can't be too judgmental. She has learned that from Oprah, who today is listening to people talk about their wild and uncontrollable behavior following gastric bypass surgery. These people have lost hundreds of pounds and now can't stay out of strange beds, go home before midnight, or drink something other than Manhattans and Cosmos. Everyone has a problem, and the world is a mess. This is what Leanne has learned. It's all a big fuck-up. This is why she can't kiss Fred goodbye. The test of character, she has decided, lies in one's ability to accept those circumstances which are unwanted and unlovely and embrace them however one can. Fred will just have to be voluptuous.

Leanne turns up the volume on Oprah and listens to yet another tale of lost fat gone bad.

7: Transformations

So the days pass, and Leanne gets used to the idea of having Aaron around. During lunch he sits with her and eats her granola bars and apples while she eats the sub sandwich that Aaron's mother, the preacher's wife, buys for him every evening the night before. The Fundamentalists like meat, and she can't say no to the daily offer. After school, Aaron walks her home the long way. They stop at the park on Leonard Avenue to swing on the swings and pretend the innocence of elementary school. They push the merry-go-round until they both feel sick. Their dizziness is an effective means by which they can fall on top of each other. Aaron has taken to carrying his Bible in his backpack instead of under his arm, and they are both more comfortable with his newfound freedom of movement.

Last Sunday, she attended Aaron's youth group at the First Church of Something-Something, its full name escaping her then as now. As she suspected, Matt Birkland, the youth pastor, is completely insane, a former druggie who met God while going through withdrawal from heroin. He plays guitar, he sings using a heartfelt falsetto, and he raises his hands in prayer. When he gets going on a subject, like the believer's need to achieve unconditional surrender to the Holy Spirit, spit flies from his mouth. But, when he talks about his own conversion, his voice gets very low, his eyes close, and he seems to relive the moment. There were lights, a still, small voice, and a revelation. He doesn't wish for anyone to go through what he did, but two things are clear: he's proud of his experience, and Aaron has set him to the right hand of Jesus. When Aaron introduced her, she had the sense that Matt was gauging her potential to be among the chosen. She also suspected that, since she was wearing a skirt, he was checking out her legs.

Oh, those meat-eating and horny Fundamentalists.

• • •

In her second period government class, Mr. Schuster announces that each student will be placed into a group and each group assigned a community service project. Groans dominate the room, although Leanne is secretly pleased. She imagines reading stories to small children whose innocent faces will shine while she reads. She will find stories that touch their hearts. She will read with fervor, and they will love her.

The universe—or Mr. Schuster—conspires, however, and luck of the draw prevails. Leanne's group draws the nursing home where her grandmother lies staring at the ceiling. She will do the right thing. She will visit her Nana, take flowers to brighten up her room, but don't ask her why. An examination of motive will not bear scrutiny.

• • •

A postcard arrives in the mail from her father, whom Leanne hasn't seen in three years. Since the divorce, he has moved around, chasing his own tail. Chasing tail, if you believe Leanne's mother, although Leanne has a hard time believing that her father could be so ambitious. Hi, Leanne, baby. That's how it begins. From her own father. More twaddle follows, about where he's living now (some hamlet in the Midwest), what kind of job he has (he doesn't), the woman he wants Leanne to meet (she will have three kids by three different men and tattoos in various locations, of this she's sure). The picture on the back of the card is a wet kitten climbing out of a toilet. No caption, thank God. She'd expect more from Aaron. The only thing to give Leanne pause is the postscript: I'm so sorry, baby girl, not to be there for you. The very bottom of the card in tiny, tiny handwriting. She throws the card into the kitchen trash, then retrieves it from the junk mail and egg shells and coffee grounds and reads the postscript again. Throws it away again and pulls it out. Again. Goddamn it. Why can't you make up your mind, Dad, whether or not you want to be the adult?

8: Allies of the Unnatural

Leanne's mother has an intermittent and occasionally hectic social life. Normally she dates men she's met at the bank. Owners of local businesses, a hobby store, a café. A loan officer or two. They are almost universally horrible: nose pickers, fingernail biters, cuticle chewers. They dig around in their ears, and then look at their fingers. They wear glasses and bad clothes. One or two of them have had wives. "What do you see in these guys?" she asked her mother, who seldom bothers to respond. But recently, she has gone out with a man who works at the high school. He's not a teacher, and he's not someone Leanne sees very often. He's in charge of maintenance, so when he's outside his office on campus, he's usually talking to one of the custodians or groundskeepers, telling jokes around an open hole in the ground. In the fall, he roams the football stadium on Friday afternoons, making sure that the bleachers are clean and the field chalked and ready for that evening's production. How Leanne's mother met him is a mystery.

Pete seems hearty and eager and a little loud, the sort of man one might expect to run into at a used car lot or in a neighbor's backyard around a barbecue. Not at a school. He was probably one of those teenaged boys who went into the Navy after his junior year. He wears polyester, short-sleeved shirts and bright, moronic ties that feature hula girls or cartoon characters. "What do you see in him?" Leanne asks. Her mother smiles inwardly and doesn't take the bait. "He's a decent guy," she says. But Leanne smells trouble and the truth the first afternoon she comes home from school and sees her mother's bedroom door closed and hears what she hears. Aaron wasn't able to walk with her from school, and so she's arrived an hour earlier than usual. Her mother is normally at work until five o'clock except for those days when she's at the nursing home visiting Nana. How long has this been going on? And how gross is that? She goes outside and waits on the curb across the street until she sees him back his car out of their driveway. She takes pleasure thinking about sin and judgment and the fires of hell, but that's just an echo inside her head of Aaron's church and nothing she truly believes. Even she can see that. It's just one more thing she'll have to accept.

The first time Pete sleeps over Leanne finds him in the kitchen at breakfast. She hasn't realized he's there until she stumbles to the refrigerator for some orange juice. She's in her nightshirt, and her skin tingles when he clears his throat. "Well, look at Little Miss Sunshine," he says behind her. "Who made you so big and bright?" He is sitting at her mother's dinette set, drinking a cup of coffee while wearing nothing more than a pair of red boxers at least a size too small and one of her mother's moth-eaten robes, which even worn open grabs at his shoulders and under his arms. His belly rolls the waist band of his boxers over onto itself. His chest is covered in uneven patches of hair like the pelt of a mangy dog. He's staring in a way that makes her uneasy.

The best she can do is to pretend he isn't there.

"Good morning," he says. "I didn't mean to be cheerful."

"Whatever," she says. Whatever? That's the best she can do?

"Cheerfulness in the morning is a curse. I always wake up early, and I'm always happy. Don't take it the wrong way."

How is she supposed to respond to that? What way would be right? She shrugs.

"Your mother is still half-asleep, and I know if I wake her up, she won't be happy."

"No, I don't suppose she will."

School starts in an hour. She has to shower, put on a little make-up, and rifle through her closet for something she hasn't worn in the last two weeks. Then she'll think about how she might frame this story for Aaron. As a conversational tidbit rather than the subject of moral outrage. But not now, not now. Now, she's late.

As though he knows what she's thinking, Pete says, "I'll drive you."

"What?"

"I'll drive you to school. I'm heading there anyway."

"That's okay. I have feet."

"Suit yourself." He yawns and stretches, and the robe shows off more of his belly and chest than she needs to see. "Maybe I'll risk it with your mother. See how awake she is."

"Good luck," Leanne says. "It's your funeral."

"Yeah. So it is."

He excuses himself from the table more politely, more formally than she could have imagined under the circumstances. Courtesy from a pair of boxers and a woman's bathrobe.

Later, while in the bathroom, she will marvel at the mechanics of her life: it's true, isn't it, that no one can predict how things will turn out. Who could have guessed that she would have a Fundamentalist boyfriend? Or that her mother would find Mr. Manager of Open Holes? She imagines introducing Aaron to Pete. Won't they make a pretty pair? But not even in her most earnest daydreams can she rid Aaron of that Bible or Pete his mangy pelt of gray hair. No more than she can imagine Fred taking a permanent vacation. She gets a funny, hollow feeling in the pit of her stomach when she thinks about Aaron, a pain that she nurses even as it lingers, but Pete . . . the jury is still out on Pete. Normal guys don't wear women's bathrobes in the kitchen the morning after, do they? And talk to a teen-aged daughter as though she's the one who's underdressed?

That, she decides, is her mother's problem. She can't think that far ahead. She turns on the shower to scalding hot and locks the bathroom door.

Coincidence

IN THE BEGINNING, Cole Jensen did not understand the latitude of his particular gift. But then, no one did, so I suppose he should not be faulted especially. The ways of Providence are mysterious and their appearance innocuous and easily missed. He who has eyes, etc., etc. It is difficult enough to see traces of the divine in a rose; who would think to look in a badly managed suburban high school, in the back row of an afternoon trigonometry class?

This happened some thirty years ago, before our schools masqueraded as battlegrounds. Although early fall, the day was warm. Mrs. McHugh, an elderly Scottish Presbyterian, nearly deaf and as forbidding as a clock tower, was lecturing about sines, cosines, and tangents. She punctuated her shrill, high-pitched explanations by stabbing angle A and side c with her chalk. 1:55 p.m. In fifteen minutes, Cole, along with the twenty-six other nodding heads, would be released to the final period of the day. One more right angle of time to endure. A pair of flies buzzed back and forth, crossing the threshold of the opened door. The occasional lowing of a cow could be heard from the last farm holdout across the street. We know, Mrs. McHugh said, that the sum of the angles of any triangle is fixed, 180 degrees; that fact is immutable, and the trigonometric relationship of the sides of a right triangle is likewise absolute.

In his drawing of triangle ABC, Cole saw only the triangle formed by the crossing of Lydia Robledo's long brown legs. Three seats ahead and two rows to the left, Lydia sat with her head tilted into one hand, unaware of the likeness. The outline of her bra showed clearly against the thin white cotton of her sleeveless blouse and the suggestion of a lace cup brushed the inside edge of one perfect arm. She twisted her dark hair around her pencil while Cole sketched pubic hair in angle c and felt his own meat stiffen. Circles D and E, courtesy of last year's geometry class, grew nipples, and concentric circles F and G became lightly shaded areolae. From his seat in the next row, ferret-faced Buddy Williams leaned over and tugged at one corner of Cole's paper, intent on bettering his own view. Without thinking, Cole stabbed at the intruder, breaking the pencil along with its lead in the back of Buddy's hand.

"Well, shit," Buddy said. He looked at his hand. The remains of the pencil rose between his knuckles and wrist like a stump. He yanked the yellow stub out of his hand, leaving behind a bright bubble of blood. Buddy squeezed his hand, and the blood ran down his fingers. "Thanks a lot."

"I'm sorry, Buddy."

"Sure you are."

"Mr. Jensen. Mr. Williams." Mrs. McHugh stood between them in the aisle. "Am I to assume that you're discussing the function of angle A?"

"No, ma'am." Tears glazed the blue of Buddy's eyes. "He stabbed me, Mrs. McHugh," he said, holding his bloody hand in evidence. "The lead's still in there. I'm gonna have lead poisoning."

"I didn't mean to hurt him," Cole said, then stopped. "I mean, he was pawing all over my desk. That gets annoying is all I'm saying."

Mrs. McHugh ripped two hall passes from the pad on her desk. "You, Mr. Williams, to the nurse's office. And you, Mr. Jensen, will speak to Mr. Kessler, please. Assault with a No. 2 Faber-Castell may not be an offense worthy of headlines, but it is breach of the promises we make to one another in community. Please, the both of you, depart."

"Mrs. McHugh," Cole began.

"Go." The elderly teacher pointed to the opened door. "No more nonsense, now. I mean it."

They gathered books and papers. Mrs. McHugh ushered them outside. "I don't understand the two of you whatsoever," she said. Her belief in the natural depravity of man meant that she was never much given to surprise; even so, she was no stranger to disappointment. "I expect better of you, you know."

The door closed behind her. They heard her lecturing the rest of the class about the dangers of unruly behavior.

They walked through the main locker hallway and a knot of football players in their letter jackets who, for no apparent reason, were punching the doors of lockers with their fists.

"I'm sorry, Buddy. Really."

"Midway between the third and fourth metacarpal," Buddy said, flexing his fingers. "No damage to bone or tendon. None that I can see anyway. The lead's a problem. Might need to open up the puncture to clean it out."

A dogged student, Buddy would fail to be accepted into a single medical school after college. Eventually he settled for a dental school in the Caribbean desperate for American dollars. He accrued huge debts for school and equipment. He was married three times, twice to married chairside assistants with whom he had affairs, and the legal paperwork, testimony of his entanglements, filled a dozen boxes in his garage. The realization of happiness eluded Buddy in a particularly mean-spirited way, and over the years, Cole would often wonder why good fortune favors one and not another. He would further wonder if somehow, in some absurd way, he might not be responsible for the other's poor choices and missed opportunities.

"Let me see," he said. "I'm really sorry."

"I believe you, okay?" A sly look crossed Buddy's narrow face. "Who were you drawing?"

"No one," Cole said, inspecting Buddy's hand. He corrected himself: "A girl. Lydia Robledo, maybe. I don't know."

"Lydia. Good choice, nice legs. Now, me, I prefer my women a little bustier if you know what I mean."

"You've never had a date in your life." Cole turned Buddy's hand over, compared both of them together. "Buddy," he said, "do you notice anything odd?"

"What?"

Cole passed the flat of his thumb over the back of Buddy's right hand, as smooth and unblemished as the back of his left.

"There's nothing here. There's nothing wrong with your hand."

Buddy looked, then turned, as though by accident he had dropped his injury and left it behind on the sidewalk.

• • •

Cole Jensen told me this while grilling hamburgers and linguiça. His wife and mine had become quite chummy following our move into the house next door. Cherry, Cole's wife, seemed truly fascinated by the stories we told about our time in Japan as lay missionaries in the Made in America English Language Institute. She couldn't get enough of it.

"Cole, honey," she said, "can you imagine? Honestly, go someplace that foreign and that crowded, where they eat fish heads and rice by the bucketload—just to sucker some poor sap about Mr. Jesus? I don't think so. You think you could do it?"

"Not in a million years, hon," Cole sang. He turned the meat and a billow of smoke rose straight into the still hot air of a July afternoon in Fresno.

Cherry was a brassy redhead, the color of which came only in a bottle. Her forearms jangled with thin gold bracelets and charms. I told Linda she looked like a gypsy. Or a hooker with better-than-average taste in clothes.

"I like her," Linda said after their first meeting while we were unloading the U-Haul. "She's honest at least. She says what she means." Linda bit her lip. "She's honest," she repeated.

Cherry showed up at our door the next morning, bearing coffee cake, apple fritters, and a chocolate torte. "I never cook," she warbled, "but I bake like a crazy lady. Now tell me again about them Oriental fellows." That was three weeks before. Now, Cole and I studied the barbecue while Linda embellished her story about Toshi, the sixty-year-old businessman who planned to open a dude ranch in Colorado following his retirement. His karaoke rendition of "Happy Trails" could make you believe that the West would have to be fought for and won all over again. Cherry drank her Rum and Coke and clucked her tongue when Linda described the salarymen at play.

We never would have had a place of our own except that Linda's aunt died. In her will, Aunt Cecily, a fright and a menace during her seventy years, left Linda her house and thirty thousand dollars, which meant that the opinions we had harbored during her life had to be revised now that she was underground. I met her once not long before we went overseas. This was on the occasion of her birthday. Linda and I were not married yet, but we had announced our plans; we were to be married a week before our departure, and our honeymoon would be spent in service to the Lord. Until then, we lived in a shabby pink duplex—she in her side, I in my mine—suffering our engagement and our chastity like proper Christians. Our respective roommates, friends from college, thought us stupid for waiting and didn't mind telling us so. They even offered to live together for our sake.

Aunt Cecily met us at her door wearing a red velour housecoat and a new pair of bunny slippers with thick, floppy ears. She carried a water glass of bourbon. A thick coat of lipstick painted the rim. In her other hand she held a cigarillo, its fragile column of ash hanging in defiance of logic and nature.

"Hey, Bobby," she yelled into the back of the house, "the Holy Family's here."

"Happy birthday, Cece." Linda gave her aunt the birthday present and a peck on the cheek.

Cecily put her drink down, stubbed out her smoke. "What do we have here? I told the boys no presents."

"Just a little something," Linda said. She had spent the better part of two days debating whether or not we were to go, and at the last minute wrapped a thrift store jewelry box with a copy of *The Four Spiritual Laws* inside.

Cecily untied the bow and pursed her lips as the paper fell away. "Now aren't you two the thoughtful little Bush people? I finally have a place for my pearls."

Her boys, Bobby and Eddie, had organized the party, and by the time we arrived everything was catch-as-catch-can. The kitchen counter was awash in bottles, beer was spilled, and the card table holding chips and dip had been the victim of ravenous hordes. There was as much food and drink on the floor as on the table. A motorcycle was parked in one of the bedrooms, and coats were hanging off the handlebars. Cecily saw us looking.

"We ate the finger sandwiches before you got here. Sorry."

"I'm sorry we're late," Linda said. "The car wouldn't start."

"It's true," I said. "And I just took it in for a bunch of repairs, too."

Technically, I suppose, we had not told a lie. I had spent fifteen hundred dollars getting the head replaced, money I didn't have, but the only reason the car wouldn't start was because neither one of us had been sure we wanted to turn the key. Two years later, however, we were happy to call Cece's house our home, and if we had known that we would be living here that day of Cece's party, we might have noticed Cole Jensen, squatting next to a broken sprinkler or scraping old paint off the eaves of his house. Almost thirty years older now, his hair thinner and going gray around the temples, a little paunchy around the middle, he was a homeowner and a husband if not a father, his parents having bailed out, moved to Arizona, deeding the place and the family hardware store over to him and Cherry. The last of the family line.

• • •

So what happened following Cole's discovery? I would like to report that Buddy's miraculously recovered hand was dismissed as an odd phenomenon, an aberration for which there was no explanation. I would like to report that the two of them looked at one another, laughed nervously, then vowed not to speak of it with a soul. However, within moments of the event, Buddy Williams had told everyone on campus that the same person who had stabbed him with a pencil was also responsible for healing him without a trace. It was a miracle, he said, an honest-to-God miracle. Mrs. McHugh was doubtful. What proof could he offer? She hadn't taken a very close look at his hand. How did she know that he hadn't used make-up to simulate the stabbing? Buddy was just the sort of boy to pull that kind of stunt. Even those most accepting of strange tales by nature, the science fiction and fantasy freaks—the Trekkies, the Heinlein junkies, the Castaneda potheads—did not for a moment buy the story. They were conditioned to believe only those details reported in paperbacks with broken spines and dog-eared corners. Cole was likewise a skeptic. He was there, it was true, but he hadn't felt a thing, and wouldn't it follow that, if he had been the responsible party, he would have felt *something*? Whatever happened to Buddy, he sure as hell wasn't the cause of it. And if Buddy Williams was publicly mocked and reviled as an idiot, a nerd, a moron with glasses and a GPA only slightly better than average, well, so be it. It wasn't his fault.

But a week later, Amanda Burton broke her ankle while playing volleyball on the blacktop during third period P.E. Coach Taliaferro had seen her share of injuries, and she knew what she was facing. The girl's ankle looked like a sausage casing. She told Cole and another boy to carry Amanda to the girls' locker room. Amanda put her arms across their shoulders while she hopped on her good leg. But before they reached the gymnasium, she was putting weight on the bad leg and five minutes later she was walking again. She kissed Cole on the cheek and did cartwheels in the parking lot. Coach Taliaferro hugged Cole, and two months later—after throwing up three straight mornings—her doctor told the forty-year-old coach that she was eight weeks pregnant. Altogether improbable, given the anguish and expense caused by fifteen years of unsuccessful fertility treatments. And ironic. After all, Cole was born the same year as Donna Taliaferro's first prescription for progesterone. The coach reported a burning sensation in her womb (the coach started to say uterus, but by that time the poetics of the experience had taken over); Amanda recalled that her leg had grown icy cold. The school newspaper carried a front-page article about Cole's gift, and the story was subsequently reprinted by the *Bee* and picked up by several of the wire services. Such was his notoriety.

In the wake of the publicity, Cole's parents—pale, private people who favored plastic slipcovers and refused deductions on their tax return—disconnected the phone; even so, within hours their address became common knowledge. Mothers holding babies rang the doorbell at six o'clock in the morning. Doddering veterans in wheelchairs maintained a vigil on the sidewalk. Crutches and splints, hearing aids and glasses littered the lawn and flower beds. An ace bandage drooped from a Chinese elm like the last remnant of a teenager's prank. There were unconfirmed reports that infants had been cured of ear infections, hip socket deformities, colic, and heart irregularities. A seventy-year-old man wearing a campaign hat claimed that he had been healed of forty years of emphysema merely by Cole's glance from across the street. The claims multiplied. A woman, blind since birth, saw a sunrise. Broken bones were mended, infirmities cured.

Three news vans were parked in the street around the clock, the news crews competing for the first exclusive taping of an actual healing. One reporter attempted to force his way into the house through an opened bedroom window—he had sliced open the screen—and refused to leave until the police were called.

The last day that Cole attended school, he had walked no more than a block before he had been mobbed by those wishing that his hand only graze their clothing.

• • •

One Saturday morning, a week after the newspaper articles, the minister from the Four Square Church of His Shekinah Power showed up, only to be told by Cole's father that his presence was not necessary. The young man stood on the Jensens' front porch in a pale blue seersucker suit, freshly pressed, thumbing the doorbell. A large black Bible rested against one eggshell-blue thigh. "Mr. Jensen," he called, "I'm only anxious to ascertain the legitimacy of your son's gift—you don't want to live with Satanic forces in your midst, I'm sure."

"Go away," Cole's father yelled through the door. Under other circumstances he was the politest of men, but since this onslaught of attention, he had found a rudeness in his language bordering on the aphasic—a development as frightening to him as it was exhilarating. "Get your ass off my porch, goddammit. Can't you see we're surrounded?"

"You have an obligation," the minister shouted, "to know the truth. Only the truth can set you free."

Hearing no further response, he turned to go, slapping the Bible against his leg. He waved to the news vans and spoke briefly to those waiting respectfully on the sidewalk.

"They have a right to their privacy," the minister shouted, loud enough for the news people to get a reading on their sound equipment. "I respect that. But this kind of gift belongs to everyone. It belongs to the ages and needs to be shared."

Those on the sidewalk cheered, and one of the wheelchair-bound yelled, "Fucking A!"

Sitting at the kitchen table with his mother and silver-haired Dr. Hartley, the minister of St. Stephen's Episcopal, Cole heard the electric murmur of the crowd intensify.

"You don't think that this could be some kind of coincidence," Dr. Hartley was saying, one finger running around the rim of his clerical collar. "Some sort of fluke?"

"*I* don't know, that's for sure," Cole said.

"We can't answer our own door any longer," his father said. "I can't piss in my own toilet without a reporter looking in through the window."

"Roger," Cole's mother said, "please." She got up to pour coffee from the percolator into a cup for the minister.

"It's true, and you know it." He turned to Dr. Hartley. "You ever tried to piss with a stranger watching you?"

"Only at football games," the minister smiled. "And I try to pretend no one is there."

"No one has been at our bathroom window, Roger."

"Well, if I want to fetch my morning paper, I have to hurdle three cripples, a pregnant woman, and the morning reporter from Channel 47." He ran his hands through his thinning, sandy-colored hair. "To go to work I have to sneak out the back door and climb the fence. This isn't normal. You think it's normal? I don't think it's normal."

"This has been a very unsettling situation, I realize," the minister soothed. "Distinctly *not* normal."

"It stinks, it's so not-normal." Cole's father slumped over the table. "I hate it."

"But we appreciate your being here." Cole's mother rose from her chair, shredding a paper napkin in her hands. "It's just that we're going a little crazy from all this. I know we're not regular attenders, but I thought you might know what to do."

The minister remained seated, sipped his coffee, then pulled a pack of Marlboros from his shirt pocket, "You don't mind, do you?" He tapped the filter end against the table while Cole's mother and father shook their heads. They were a bit cowed by the minister, and they would not have thought to protest had he brought out a bong and a baggie. Cole's mother found an ashtray in the cupboard and set it in the center of the table.

"Perhaps I could speak with Cole in private. Just for a moment."

The three adults turned to Cole as though aware of his presence for the first time. His mother cleared her throat. "Of course," she said. "That will be fine."

A moment later, the sound of the television echoed from the living room. The minister looked at the cigarette as though thinking better of it before using a stainless-steel Zippo. He exhaled a stream of smoke toward the ceiling with a sigh.

"I know I should quit," he said. "Health reasons aside, you'd be surprised how many church members have an idea about what a minister should and shouldn't do. Some days, though, it seems like it's the last pleasure left."

"That's up to you, isn't it?"

"Right. And that's not why I'm here, is it? Whether or not I should smoke. We need to find a solution to *your* problem."

Cole nodded. His parents had never particularly trusted Dr. Hartley, and their declining attendance at St. Stephen's dated from the time of his arrival five years before. Although the minister dressed in accordance with the guidelines of the diocese, there was something a bit shifty in his habit of wearing golf cardigans over a black clerical shirt and collar. Cole's father, who never left the house in the morning without a coat and tie, no matter how mismatched, had never entirely forgotten or forgiven the church picnic at which the minister had arrived in a Hawaiian shirt, flowered surfer shorts, and flip-flops.

"My problem," Cole said, "is that I didn't *do anything*. I did not do a goddamn thing. Something good may have happened for a few people, but it's not my fault,

I had nothing to do with it. I can't even go to school anymore; I haven't left the house for two weeks. My mother calls the school office every morning saying I'm sick."

"You're absolutely sure? That you didn't do anything, I mean? You didn't feel anything, you didn't do anything that you're aware of?"

"No," Cole shook his head. "Nothing."

Something like a sneer passed across the minister's face. "You didn't even pray?"

"Was I supposed to?"

"No. Not necessarily."

"Would that have changed anything?"

As a seminary student, Dr. Hartley had once visited Lourdes. He had been impressed by the pilgrims he had met there, by the sincerity as well as the hopelessness of their quest. He sighed: "I doubt it very much."

"You know," the minister continued, "your situation is rather ironic."

"I don't care what it is," Cole said. "I just want it to be over and everything back to what it was. I never thought I'd dream about going back to school."

"You're like Jesus but without the self-awareness."

"Give me a break," Cole said. "What am I going to do?"

"I wish I knew what to tell you. Go outside, heal everyone who's waiting. Why not? Send them home happy."

Outside the living room window the news trucks had edged forward onto the lawn, and Cole's father was shouting about the clematis while a reporter did a live feed on the doorstep.

"That's easy for you to say. How do I know what's going to happen? What if I go out there and nobody gets better?"

"Get the hell off my porch," Cole's father was yelling through the screen of an opened window. "Get the hell off now before I call the police."

"Then they'll stop coming. This isn't about you, after all. Not really. You're merely the vehicle for what they want."

"Roger," Cole's mother said. "Roger, dear." Through the kitchen door, Cole and the minister could see her tugging at her husband's shirt while he dialed the phone. "Do you want to have a heart attack?"

"Fine," Cole said. He looked at the minister, whose shave that morning had evidently included two or three mishaps along his jaw line and throat. "But you have to go out there with me. If I go by myself, they'll tear me apart."

"Deal."

The minister extended his hand, and Cole shook it, feeling as though some sort of shady business had been transacted.

"That's right," Cole's father shouted into the phone. "The street is blocked. We're surrounded by bloodsuckers and cripples. We need crowd control. It's a riot here, for God's sake."

. . .

I suppose confession is in order, and now is as good a time as any.

Linda and I didn't last in Japan. We were prepared. We'd read the brochures, we'd watched the tapes, we had endured weeks of orientation sessions and classes. The Baptists took our training seriously, and we were willing disciples. We were ready to experience our newlywed life together as strangers in a strange land. We were ready to serve Jesus and American culture. But we no sooner stepped off the plane at Narita than we knew we weren't going to make it. Why? I'm still at a loss. Too many people, too foreign, too . . . something. Maybe we were trying to manage too many changes in our own lives. We got married, we had sex, much to the amusement of our respective roommates, and then we flew to Japan to grant succor to the alien and the pagan. After our first sexual experience, no longer virgins, missionaries who had tasted the pleasures of the flesh, we understood the joke had been on us all along. Our eyes were opened, and we saw color and chaos; our ears were opened and all we heard was noise.

So this was what we had been saving ourselves from and for?

We were clumsy and shy, we couldn't even enjoy ourselves properly, and it called everything else in our lives into question.

We managed three months out of our two-year commitment, and we came home embarrassed and ashamed, different people than we had been thirteen weeks earlier. We discussed divorce. We drank at night. Linda cried every night that we were there, and she cried for six months after our return.

I wasn't any better.

If anything, I was worse.

We were crying because we'd intended to dedicate our lives to a higher good and a more noble purpose as we turned away from the familiars of home and dogma and tracts-in-a-box, and instead, we discovered that, after a twelve-hour flight, Jesus had become remote and unknowable. We were true believers, remember? Little Bush people, according to Linda's Aunt Cecily. But before we knew it our true belief had transformed itself into something different, like a tire that goes flat overnight. We stepped off the plane only to realize that we'd lost our souls, and that, truth be told, they'd gone missing for quite some time.

. . .

Dr. Hartley led Cole through the front door. There was a moment when the sound grew ominous—like that pause before the collapse of a building, perhaps—and they thought they would be overwhelmed by the crush of people hoping to get close to him: the lame and the infirm, the camera crews and the reporters. Cole's father and mother watched from the living room window in genuine fear for their son. But gradually, as the minister and the teenaged boy stood still on the front porch, the crowd grew quiet, stepped back and gave them a respectful distance.

"Ladies and gentlemen," the minister began, "we appreciate your patience and your curiosity, but if we can maintain order and decorum, our young man here will do what he can." He paused and looked at Cole. "Do you want to say anything?"

Cole shook his head. "Not really," he whispered. "Tell them I'm nothing special, and they ought to go home."

"You need to tell them that yourself."

Cole looked stricken, but he spoke regardless: "I've told everyone I can tell. I don't know how some of these things have happened, but I do know that I didn't have anything to do with it. What I'm saying is that this whole thing is a mistake, and I don't think anything is going to happen now. I'm sorry."

A man wearing a camouflage jacket stepped forward. "That's all right, son. No apologies are necessary. Lots of us are more than willing to be helped by accident."

"Amen," said a woman whose wheelchair was stuck in the apron of the driveway.

"Now," Dr. Hartley said, "if everyone would be good enough to form a line, Mr. Jensen will do what he can. And if he can't, no one's the poorer."

For six hours, a line of supplicants marched past Cole. There was no jostling or pushing or shoving. No taking cuts in line. No bad behavior of any sort. He asked each person his or her name, he put his hands on each person's shoulders, he asked what was wrong. They talked. But no one was suddenly healed; there were no miracles. No one who came in a wheelchair left with a hop, skip, or jump, and yet each person said thank you. By one o'clock that afternoon, the last of the hopeful, a young woman whose right cheek and neck were bruised from where her husband had hit her, was gone. The news crews had left hours before when it became clear that no one was casting aside his crutches today.

"You see?" Cole said.

"Well," the minister said, "you showed them." He lit a cigarette and sat down on the porch steps. "Maybe you'll get back to a normal life now."

"Maybe." Cole sat next to the minister and batted away the smoke when the breeze shifted. For a week he had run from this sudden bout of notoriety, fleeing the idea that somehow he had been given a gift he had never asked for nor wanted. What seemed so odd was that he was now so disappointed.

"That's a good thing," Dr. Hartley said. "Peace and quiet. Your father's flower beds are safe. You can go back to school. Although I've yet to meet a teenaged boy who thought that was a good thing."

"School's all right."

"Of course it is. It beats being trapped inside your bedroom twenty-four hours a day."

"Yes, sir. It does."

"Listen, Cole," the minister began, "I'd like you to think about this experience. Think about it honestly, and then, after you've done that, I want you to come and talk with me about it. Deal?"

"Sure. One more deal." Cole shifted to his feet. Above him the sky was blue and cloudless, ordinary details that had escaped him during the past week. "But I doubt I'm going to have any big insight."

"That's okay," the minister said. He likewise struggled to his feet and shook Cole's hand. "Little ones will be just fine."

• • •

I would be happy to say that three months later, Cole knocked on the door of Dr. Hartley's office, and together they explored what it means to perform a miracle without any knowledge or underlying belief. Dr. Hartley would have offered Cole a soft drink while the minister would have smoked one of his forbidden cigarettes. I would like to say that, but three months later, Dr. Hartley was offered a position at a monastery near Santa Barbara, where he conducted spirituality workshops and encounter groups. A year after accepting the position, he died—not from lung cancer, which would make a pat and ironic ending, but in a hang gliding accident, which was also ironic, but in no way a moral judgment. And thus Dr. Hartley's role in this story comes to a close.

Or maybe not quite. Since Cole didn't have any other pastor or minister in whom to confide, he never had the opportunity to talk about his experiences. Life happened and thirty years went by; he took over his father's business and his parents' house, and he married Cherry. They were ambivalent about children, so he had a vasectomy. Easy enough to forget that, for a brief moment in time, he was regarded as the Jesus of northeast Fresno. He was happy to forget it ever happened. But then Linda and I moved in next door. The former missionaries, no matter how muddled our qualifications. He seemed to think that we had had the proper training, that we might somehow be able to supply the answers to questions that had eluded him so many years earlier.

So as we talked, the sun flattened into the haze, a breeze kicked up, and the heat of the July day began to lift. Cherry and Linda went inside to bring out plates and silverware. Cole reached into a cooler and handed me a beer without asking if I wanted one. I wanted one. And I hadn't even realized it.

And I realize now that I've never gotten round to telling you how we came to own Aunt Cecily's house in the first place, what with her despising us proportionate to the amount that we despised her. If we were little Bush people, then from our perspective she was Satan's high priestess. Or something to that effect. I mean, you're probably wondering why she would will us her home and her life savings when she had her own children, her boys, they of the motorcycles in their bedrooms, and she had no use for us. The answer to that is as ironic as anything I've ever heard, and if you don't believe me, I won't blame you. It's harder to credit than Cole Jensen healing broken ankles and making the barren fertile. You remember that jewelry box with Linda's copy of *The Four Spiritual Laws* tucked inside? Here's the weird part: Aunt Cecily actually read the tract the night after her birthday, one thing led to another, and a week later she had committed her life to Christ and was baptized by the minister of the Four Square Church of His Shekinah Power—the very same seersucker-clad minister who showed up on Cole Jensen's doorstep that Saturday morning. Thirty years older but just as certain of his beliefs. God works in mysterious ways . . . I know, I know: it's too much coincidence for anyone to believe, so let me put your mind at rest—you don't have to believe it if you don't want to. It's not that germane to the story anyway other than to explain how we came to live in an overgrown tract house with lousy insulation and paint peeling from the trim. Besides, it's only going to get worse.

Aunt Cecily was baptized in a mass ceremony at the Kings River near Centerville. After the minister had covered her nose and mouth and then tipped her back into the water, her sins clinging to her like vines, she had come up smiling and clean, this seventy-year-old one-time doyenne of bikers and outlaws. Too much to believe, right? It seemed so, even to us, when we read her letter our first week in Japan. We thought she was putting us on. We were suffering the malaise of doubt and despair and reading letters from Linda's reprobate aunt about the salvation of her immortal soul. But we received a letter from her each day for the next two months, and by that time we were already defeated and despondent and making our plans to come back home, where Jesus had once lived for us.

We never saw Cecily after our return, however. The night before we landed at the Fresno Air Terminal, she went back to the Kings River, apparently under the belief that if one baptism was good for what ails a soul, a second immersion would be twice as beneficial. She slipped into the water at Centerville (her car was parked in the gravel turnout above the water), lost her footing, and didn't come up again until her body was trapped against the pilings of the Reedley bridge.

We didn't know any of this until several weeks later. We had called Cecily several times, but her phone rang and rang and rang. But then Cecily's lawyer called us with the news. House, bank accounts—all ours, in gratitude for our care and concern. I was lost but now I'm found; I was blind but now I see, she wrote. Seventy years old and I never knew.

It beggars belief, I know. I'm not sure I believe it either. Even now. All for a gift of a tract and a secondhand jewelry box and a birthday party that we almost didn't attend. Her boys were hopping mad about the loss of their inheritance, let me tell you. She had changed her will the week before she died, and if we hadn't been in the air when she died, there might have been a criminal investigation. I've seen movie murders with less motive. Thirty thousand dollars in IBM stock, who knew?

We didn't get the house or the money right away, of course. Linda's cousins hired lawyers, Cecily had her lawyer, and we had one of our own. We didn't want the house or the money—maybe I should say that we weren't coveting them until we knew they were potentially ours; we were embarrassed by Cecily's largesse— but they were her wishes. Then Bobby was busted selling crank, and Eddie was caught holding up a liquor store, and their suit against us was thrown out as having no legal basis. Cecily's will was in order, she was in her right mind as far as it was possible to determine, and the judge was not sympathetic to their pleas—two felons against the nice Christian couple and the salvation of their aunt and her longsuffering soul. We may have been confused evangelists, but we had the blessing of a permanent address. We were homeowners.

• • •

Cole's healing gifts disappeared as suddenly as they had shown themselves, and his life slowly returned to what it had been. He went to school. He doodled geometric fantasies in the margins of his notebooks. He walked home alone. His house was no longer surrounded by news vans and the desperately optimistic. His father, without the hubbub to distract him, fell back upon his usual complaints, grousing about the government and the price of things, while his mother crocheted doilies and listened to her husband. Now and again, someone who hadn't heard about the outcome of that Saturday would appear on the Jensen doorstep. If Cole's father answered the door, that person was met with a swallowed burst of profanity and a closed door, whereas if Cole happened to open the door, he explained the situation, placed his hands on the supplicant's shoulders, apologized, and sent him on his unhealed way. Cole tried to remember the tone that Dr. Hartley had used—light and self-deprecating, but attentive, to show respect for the need that had driven someone to his door, but with enough irony at his own expense so that no one would think he was taking himself too seriously. He couldn't rid himself of the disappointment that nothing miraculous had happened since that one week at school and likely never would again. The sense that the failure was somehow his fault. That nothing about his life would ever again match up to those puzzling and terrifying and awe-inspiring moments.

On the other hand, Linda and I came home completely unhinged. Did you know that there are psychologists and mental health groups who specialize in debriefing returned missionaries? Yes, we were hardly the first to go crackers in the name of Jesus, and we are not likely to be the last. Our counselor, Dr. Gerald Geffen, who was supposedly on the cutting edge of missionary re-acclimation research, refused to let us refer to him as either Doctor or his given name, Gerald. Instead we called him Jerry, and spent our hour each week talking about how Jesus had failed us. We already knew how we had failed Him.

• • •

"So, what I'm saying is this," Cole Jensen said. "I'm saying that God must have a serious sense of humor if he's going to be healing people through me. I mean, I don't go to church, I swear when I'm upset, and I met my wife in a bar."

"Hey," Cherry said as she and Linda came outside with a bowl of potato salad and platters of corn on the cob and garlic bread. "No giving away the family secrets."

"It was a nice bar," she said to Linda, "and I was there with my mother."

"God has a sense of humor," I said. "No question."

"And then, after everyone gets excited—*pffft!*—nothing, *nada*, zip. I couldn't even work a Band-Aid. Even Dr. Hartley was disappointed."

He shrugged, speared the hunk of beef on the grill and dropped it absentmindedly onto the platter that Cherry held out for the purpose. The sun flared one last time, then dropped completely behind the haze hovering above the mountains sixty miles away to the west. Night fell. With the darkening sky came the hint of a breeze. A true miracle.

"Look," Cole Jensen said, "you can tell me. What do you think happened?"

"Cole, honey," Cherry said. "It was a long time ago. What can they tell you?"

"You had a gift," Linda said. "But it was temporary. It wasn't yours to keep. Having a gift like that isn't necessarily permanent."

"Well, it could have messed me up big time. Maybe it did."

"God doesn't need us," Linda said. "We're the ones who need Him. What would He need us for?"

"That's cheap," Cole said. "Cheap and shabby, if you ask me."

Time stretched in front of us all.

We would never be so blessed as we had once thought.

"'They also serve who stand and wait,'" I murmured.

"What?" Cole said. "What was that?"

"Nothing," I said.

Cherry passed out the steak knives, and the platters began to go around.

"Nothing," I said again. "A bad joke. That's all."

Spies

BALLARD'S ROOMMATE during the spring of Watergate was Iranian, and according to rumor a member of SAVAK, the Shah's secret service. A picture of the Shah's wedding party adorned Ali's desk, and his demeanor—Ali's, that is—was watchful, suspicious, and seemingly available for confidences. The Shah, on the other hand, whose Pahlavi Dynasty had once seemed so unassailable, was pictured smiling broadly, escorting his bride underneath a bower of drawn swords, confident that this third marriage would produce the requisite heir. Unlike Ali, he would not prove watchful enough.

Ali was noticeably different from the rest of the Iranian students who drove black Trans-Ams, partied every evening into the early hours, and seemed desperate to establish their reputations as libertines in the grand European style. Instead, Ali worked dutifully at his built-in desk, drawing schematics and diagrams for his engineering courses until midnight each day. Then he rose at five each morning to work in the campus dining hall before his day-long schedule of classes and labs. Ballard once caught a glimpse of him in the dish room standing at his position next to the commercial dishwasher, wearing a rubber apron and long, black rubber gloves. Given his slight stature and hollow expression, he looked like a weary young boy in a photograph illustrating the abuses of child labor laws.

Ballard, indifferent at best to his classes, left campus each evening at midnight for his job downtown, where he cleaned the offices of his great-uncle Leo's collection agency, Loss Finders ("No bad debts, only bad debtors"). The offices were extensive, and although one might think that white-collar workers could not make that much of a mess, the job kept him busy until six Monday through Thursday. He stayed awake long enough to attend his classes, all of them morning seminars, then went to bed. He did not see Ali except in the early evenings, when he woke to find his roommate in his characteristic pose: hunched over his desk and his drawings, holding his breath, his lips hidden beneath his heavy mustache, his desk lamp shining down like an academic third degree.

"Good morning, Sleeping Beauty," Ali might say, twisting around in his chair, while Ballard stumbled into the shower.

Often enough, Ali would be gone by the time Ballard returned with a towel around his waist, dripping water on the tile floor. To a study carrel in the library or a table in the student union. Ballard wasn't offended; Ali needed privacy and concentration. So he was surprised one Saturday evening when he returned to their room to find it filled with other Iranian students. Ballard realized with a start that he had never seen Ali with them before. Ali was sitting in his chair, his elbows on his knees, and the others were standing around him in an attitude that resembled nothing so much as some sort of fraternity hazing. Or an interrogation.

"I'm sorry," Ballard said. "I'll be out of here in a second."

There was a certain amount of awkwardness as Ballard, clutching his towel, searched in his drawers with his free hand for, well, a clean pair of drawers that he could wear under his least dirty pair of jeans. One of the girls snickered. Zari, he thought, though he couldn't be sure since they all wore the same style of black silk blouses and skintight black pants, their only ornament the heavy gold chains looped like gorgeous ropes around their necks. He could hardly think of them as girls, though, since they possessed not only more money than God, they were also possessed of more experience than he could ever hope to acquire. They spoke with ease of skiing trips to Biarritz and shopping expeditions in Paris, New York, and Rome. Since coming to college, Ballard had met many wealthy students, but the Iranians seemed always to go one better in their lavishness and casual disregard of how much things cost. And although he had been Ali's roommate for nearly a year, he had yet to get to know any of them.

"Ballard," Rahim said, "we were trying to get your roommate to come with us, but he insists that he must study."

"He studies a lot."

"Too much," Zari, definitely Zari, said.

Rahim placed a hand on Ali's shoulder as though to hold him in his chair. "What can we do to persuade him? We would like to go out and have a nice time, but he refuses all our invitations. It is hard not to be offended, if you know what I mean. No one can study all the time, can they?"

Ballard did not know them well—they obviously had different expectations of life now as well as life later, and they moved in such different circles as to be planets in other orbits—but he understood that at some level coercion was being administered. Against Ali. Why, he couldn't say. "I can't study all the time. But I should, I guess. I should study a little more. A lot more. Still it's hard to turn down a little bit of fun."

Standing behind Rahim, Maryam said, "Poor Ali needs a break. Even Ballard understands the value of fun." Maryam, quiet, with sleepy eyes, pushed half a dozen gold bracelets up one slender forearm. "But all poor Ali says is no, no, no. Baby needs to have a little fun." She crouched beside his chair, put one manicured finger to his lips. "Don't you, baby?"

"I have a test on Monday," Ali said evenly, "and I'm a full chapter behind."

"Poor baby."

"Just think how much better you'll study," Rahim said, "after a little break. We won't keep you out very late. Just enough to refresh your thought process."

"I cannot."

"Such pessimism."

"I am not so gifted that I can play at night with my friends. At night is when I learn what I failed to understand during the day."

"Poor baby." Maryam clucked her tongue in some approximation of sympathy. "Poor baby."

"Yes, he is a poor, poor baby."

They all crowded around him—Rahim and Maryam, Zari and Pasha, Houri and Mohammad.

Ali rose from his chair, the weary laborer, pushing them away as though for air. "Okay, maybe. Okay. If Ballard comes, then I'll come. For an hour, no more, then I come immediately back. Agreed?"

"Wonderful," Rahim said. "That's all we asked. A little diversion from work, work, work."

Ali turned to Ballard who was still struggling with his towel and clothes. "You'll bring me back?"

"Sure. Just let me get dressed."

"Wonderful," Rahim said again. "But we're already so late. I'll give you the address. It's a club on the east side. A Persian club, you understand, but you're our guest. Here, I'll write it down, and you can join us later, okay?"

He tore a page out of Ballard's economics notes and wrote the address down, obliterating the Keynesian ideal of government's role in employment. "You won't need any money. Just ask for us at the door, and they'll let you in. We'll buy you a drink when you arrive."

It was a remarkable moment, to be addressed by these fabulous creatures, invited to their personal playground. "Okay," he said. "Sure."

They left then, herding Ali out between them, Pasha, the weightlifter, the last to leave. Pausing, he turned to face Ballard, his short black hair bristling around his square brown face. "See you later, alligator," he grimaced, an expression that thickened his already thick neck, expanded his shoulders and deep chest.

"I'll catch up," Ballard said. "I'll be there in a little bit."

He dressed quickly, feeling the weight of some undefined tension, an urgency reinforced by Ali's mournful look back at his texts and schematics. The address was practically to Rockwood and took about forty-five minutes to reach. And then, of course, the address turned out to be a vacant field next to an industrial park. The name of the club, Ebrahim's, was not listed in the phone book. He looked at the paper again, wondering if he had made a mistake. No, this was the name and address, and instead of a line of young sultans extending from the door out onto the sidewalk, he was faced with a chain link fence and scraps of wind-littered garbage. What were they trying to pull? Not since the fourth grade had he felt so obviously snubbed. Told to get lost. What was going on? And what were they doing to Ali?

He found out three hours later. He had driven to Burnside and, watched by three envious winos, bought a gallon jug of Tokay and a sack of chicharones at a corner market, the pork rinds so greasy and full of fat that the paper bag was translucent before he left the store. The night would not be a total loss. He threw the stack of textbooks and notebooks under his desk and filled a coffee cup with wine, opened the window above his desk and, sitting on the sill, imitated the residents of the Burnside hotels. He drank steadily. Other students passed underneath the window, occasionally a couple holding hands, radiating the aura of their sexual heat. When the wind shifted, he could hear the sounds of the Saturday night band in the commons, the staccato of a drum set, the woof of a bass. He drank some more, nibbling the pork rinds. Ali came in a little after midnight. He unlocked the unlocked door, then stood on the threshold. His white shirt was ripped and blood-stained from a cut above his left eye, the skin around which was already turning the color of eggplant.

"What the hell?" Ballard said.

"I tripped," Ali said, "getting out of Rahim's car, you know, getting out of the back seat."

"That's pretty dangerous, all right."

"No, no. It is difficult getting out of Rahim's back seat. There were seven of us in the car. It was dark. Pasha was pushing me out. It was my own clumsiness."

"It looks like they pushed you out on the freeway."

Ali stripped off his shirt then threw it in the trash can between their desks.

"I tripped and fell against a fire hydrant. It was an accident."

"That fire hydrant must have been in a pretty bad mood."

"Yes," Ali said, an unfocused smile stitched across his face, "well."

"Well, here," Ballard said, holding up the jug. "I've been drinking. Very bad stuff actually."

"I see that. We missed you, you know. At the club. Everyone was dancing. There were many women. Ebrahim's. A very fancy place. Very fancy women. You would have liked it."

"There was no club."

"I think Rahim gave you bad directions."

"He gave me the address of a vacant lot. For a club that's not listed in the phone book. A club that doesn't exist."

"No, no, no. You don't understand. It's very private. The only people who go there already know how to find it. There's no need for a telephone listing."

"Listen, Ali. I don't know what the problem is, but I think Rahim and Pasha and Mohammad beat you up, not too badly, but just enough to let you know they mean business about something. I have no idea what or why. I don't need to know."

Ali shook his head slowly, like a draft horse tired of its yoke but still pulling nonetheless. "Everything is as I said. I am sorry for your inconvenience. Let me make it up to you." He opened his closet and rummaged behind his shoes, emerging at last with a bottle of Glenfiddich, the seal unbroken. "Put away that poison."

Ballard emptied his coffee cup out the window.

"You should wash that," Ali said. "It would be criminal to pollute such good scotch. And maybe you could bring back some ice."

The ice, as it turned out, was for Ali's eye and not for the scotch. Ice, according to Ali, would have been yet another pollutant. Ballard poured a little of the Glenfiddich into his mug and into a glass that Ali offered.

"Is it allowed?" he said.

Ali snorted and downed the amber liquid. "I am not one of the fundamentalists. Neither am I one of the dilettantes. I am what I am not. I also know what the rumors say, but I am no informant either. I'm poor. That's what I am. That's my crime. My father owns a greenhouse in Tabriz. Those others, they think that I am watching them to report to their families and to the government, but I don't care what they do. They're ridiculous. They can do anything, they can spend thousands of dollars, a million dollars, and it doesn't matter. Me, though, if I do not pass a test, I can be brought back anytime, a discredit to my family. I am grateful to the government which has allowed me to be here, but I do not owe them anything other than a good life and to use my skills when I return. I am not one of them. I don't care about the radical religionists either. At least they are concerned about something other than pleasure, but I am not one of them either. If they have their way, they would imprison us to save us."

Ballard, who knew nothing of Iranian politics or religion, said little while, using a washcloth dampened with a few drops of the scotch, he touched the cut on his roommate's forehead.

"Still, these friends of yours mean business."

Ali's wan smile reminded Ballard once again of a child in a coal mine.

"You mean fire hydrant."

"Right. That fire hydrant means business."

• • •

Ballard had no business being in college—not a good one at any rate—and the letter of acceptance and the terms of scholarship had come as a complete and unwelcome surprise. Harriet, his grandmother, was responsible. "If I hadn't done something," she said, "you'd just rot here. That place is ga-ga for the children of alums, and it's not like you can't do the work. Not if you put your mind to it." Secure in her belief that Ballard was the recipient of a superior gene pool—*hadn't his father, her son, gotten his start there?*—she ignored his father's dismal end and his equally dismal high school record. She wrote his application essay ("How World Peace Might Be Accomplished") aware that her grandson, when not emptying trash cans and scrubbing toilets at midnight, had spent the better part of one summer in his narrow room, staring at the ceiling above his twin bed until his eyes lost focus, tracing the cracks which, depending on one's mood, resembled a map of the Panama Canal or the profile of Raquel Welch, but she chose to believe that a young man's excessive time in his bedroom was an indication of hormones rather than a symptom of depression or fear. Wrong about most of his motives, his grandmother was right about one thing: there was little short of dynamite that could have gotten him out of his bed, out of his room, out of that house with its musty, mildewed smell. Ever since he and his sister had come to their grandmother's house, Lucy had done everything in her power to leave, while he could only imagine staying—waiting for Harriet to die.

But the real problem was knowing that he didn't belong. Not in his grandmother's house and not in this hothouse of privileged children. It wasn't a feeling so much as an article of faith that he was in the wrong place, as certain of that displacement as if he had stumbled into one of the women's dorms after midnight. The Iranians were an extreme case, but the other students seemed testimony to the fact that not only did he not know as much as they did, he also did not have as much money. Check that: he had no money. They were worlds apart, and while it was easy enough to hop in a car with others from his floor at two o'clock in the n orning as they made a pizza-and-beer run, he did so, checking his pockets for loose change, with the distinct impression of being an imposter. School bored him, that was a given, but—what was worse—his participation in it had turned him into a frightened spy on an assignment he didn't understand.

Other roommates in other semesters spoke with confidence about fraternities and thermodynamics, Kitzbühel, and Hegelian imperatives. He nodded knowingly, all the while wishing he could shout: *What in the hell are you talking about?* Was it any wonder that Ali seemed like a kindred spirit?

• • •

Once, not long after he and Lucy had arrived on Harriet's doorstep like an advertisement for foundlings, clutching their battered suitcases and wearing their best clothes and most guarded expressions, Ballard overheard Harriet lecturing her only child over the telephone: "They're young, I'm old. I'm sick, they're healthy. We're a match made in heaven, all right. If you think you've done me a favor, boy, oh, boy what a rotten son you turned out to be. They're little sneaks, these two, all eyes, watching all the time. Gives me the creeps." His father must have said something funny then, because the last thing Ballard heard before his grandmother hung up the phone was the sound of Harriet's laughter.

Which was Ballard's father's gift—making jokes—as well as his curse. Jokes and racquet sports, his twin legacies of college. In twenty years of competitive tennis, he had been renowned for his repartee with spectators, gaining more notoriety with his wit than his serve which, never better than mediocre, was also something of a joke. He had joked with Ballard's mother until she ran away with their next-door neighbor the airline pilot; evidently, she no longer felt like laughing, was no longer willing to be part of her husband's gallery, the imagery of flight more resonant than a loss in the quarterfinals of yet another no-name tournament.

So, their father had dumped them with Harriet. Temporarily, he said, not realizing that one night after a match at the Cow Palace in San Francisco, he would get loaded and walk in front of a Muni streetcar. Ballard was eight, his sister twelve, and Harriet's only comment was to lay down the law:

"I have a life, and I don't intend to give it up for two little snotmeisters. You have a room, you'll be fed and clothed, but otherwise you're going to take care of yourselves. We all have our rows to hoe, and some are longer than others. You'll go to school, you'll do your work, and you won't touch my stuff. Got it?"

Harriet's life was largely conducted across the river in Vancouver, where she earned the largest portion of her income playing poker at the five-dollar tables. If her career was a trifle odd, her "stuff" was bizarre: a dozen or more red wigs, never worn by anyone except the Styrofoam heads upon which they sat, stored on two shelves in the dining room. Bouffants, falls, beehives, Little Orphan Annie curls, you name it. At moments, Ballard could see them as harmless enough, eccentric collectibles; at other times, they seemed to be something more sinister, the remains of enemies propped up on stakes, their totem power sufficient warning against rebellion.

In high school, at the urging of a well-meaning teacher, Ballard once wrote a letter to himself: "I am the loneliest person I have ever met." This did not particularly cheer him, although he supposed his teacher felt better for having suggested it. By this time, Harriet had thrown Lucy out of her crooked, malodorous house; she had caught Lucy and her biker boyfriend fucking like jackrabbits atop a valentine of red wigs. So, his only ally had been vanquished, and the narrow room he had shared with Lucy became his to do with as he wished. To sleep, to stare at the ceiling. He wished to do nothing.

Enter fat Uncle Leo, Harriet's younger brother, who needed some slave labor, and Ballard was the very first person he thought of. He needed someone willing to get his hands dirty scrubbing toilets, emptying the trash, changing light bulbs down at the Loss Finders office. "Who knows? You get through with school and you're interested, you can chase deadbeats like me." Leo, all three hundred pounds if he was an ounce, scratched his belly between the straining buttons and gold polyester fabric of his shirt. "It ain't a profession for Pollyannas. You lose all respect for human nature, that's for sure. Not that anybody's so awful, you understand. They're just lousy. Lousy and weak. In the meantime, you need to get your butt out of my sister's house. Just for some fresh air if nothing else."

"Is there any chance," Ballard asked Leo, "any chance at all I was adopted?"

• • •

Ali left during midterms. Buried inside the library, Ballard might have merely assumed, but their room displayed the unmistakable signs of departure: Ali's books, his stereo, his picture of the Shah. All gone. He looked in Ali's closet and found only a few empty wire hangers which began to swing in sympathy when Ballard opened the door. The chest of drawers held nothing but nylon dress socks without mates. Besides them there was nothing except the rug, which lay in the center of the room; he had taken everything else. The other Iranian students were no help. Pasha only grinned and shrugged his massive shoulders, saying, "He moves a lot, you know." Rahim did not even acknowledge Ballard's question, apologizing instead for the mix-up about the nightclub: "I am so stupid sometimes. Stupid. Our little club is on the *south*east side, not the *north*east as I wrote down in the address. Ali told me about my mistake, and I felt terrible, terrible. You would think I was dyslexic or something like that. We will have to make it up to you some-how." Only Maryam was more forthcoming, but even that, he suspected, was at least partly a lie. "He did," Maryam said, "what he thought best, I'm sure. Rahim was trying too hard, trying to make him one of us, you see, and so he's gone. To keep his distance. As though we won't see him. As though we won't find him in the dish room or the library. He didn't have to do that, you know. We were only trying to include him, and what does he do? He hurts us. Like a brother who is spiteful and mean to his family." Her anger, like heat rising from asphalt, shimmered about her head.

But she was wrong. About seeing Ali around campus, that is. Ballard looked in the usual places. The next morning, he left work an hour early, the sky still bruised with night, and made his way down the hill from his dormitory to the dining hall. A side door was open for student workers: girls in hair nets grating potatoes, mixing batter, and frying bacon stood sleepily at the countertops and stoves. Ballard walked through the kitchen and into the dark, humid bowels of the dish room. Curtains of steam billowed from the dishwasher where, instead of the slump-shouldered posture of Ali, he encountered the back of a girl, her thick, corky hair twisted into a knot held in place by a wooden spike. Waves of noise from the dishwasher crashed against the stainless-steel surfaces of the dish room.

"Who?" she shouted in reply. Her fists were on her hips while moisture from the steamy air dotted her forehead and cheeks. "Who do you want?"

"I can't help you," she said an hour later in the downstairs coffee shop, sliding into a booth opposite Ballard. She pulled the spike from her hair, made frizzy from the steam, and shook it out. "He left. I don't have a clue why or where. Diana—she's the supervisor—called me, told me he didn't show up for work, and she could give me more hours. I didn't ask questions. Don't get me wrong, I'm sorry about your friend, but I need the money."

"He quit."

"That's what I'm saying."

"What about school?"

She waved her hands in the air like a magician releasing a favorite dove. "I wouldn't know."

As though he were one of Uncle Leo's investigators, following a trail of bad checks, false information, and less than noble intentions, Ballard next walked to the engineering building where Ali's lab partner, a haggard, gray-faced chain-smoker named Parker, glumly informed him that Ali had not been present for the previous four weeks.

"He kept sending me notes," Parker said, "and I kept turning in lab reports with both our names. They were bullshit, the notes. 'Please forgive my inexcusable behavior,' that sort of crap. Pissed me off."

Ballard could imagine the notes: Ali's fastidious printing, the courtly, excessively polite apologies revealing nothing.

"I'm sure he had his reasons," he said.

Parker lit a Lucky Strike. "Actually, since he's been gone, the work's been easier: no more triple-checking the results. He wants to bail, fine by me. He's so fucking anal."

According to the registrar, Ali had not withdrawn from school. Not officially. "People have their reasons," a secretary told him, "and after the deadline for refunds, they don't always bother to tell us."

That was that. Ali was gone. He had cut and run for reasons Ballard didn't entirely understand. Other than Ali himself, who could know for sure? It seemed clear that his treatment by the other Iranians was responsible, at least in part. The beating. The implied threat of more. What else could it be? Such barely concealed antagonism seemed as exotic as it was inconceivable. To be held in such regard. Such contempt. To matter that much.

• • •

"I don't suppose he told you we were to be married."

"No. He didn't tell me."

Another Saturday night and another entrance into his room clutching a towel around his waist only to find that he had an audience: Maryam stretched out on Ali's bare mattress, one slender forearm covering her eyes.

They had known one another in Tabriz, the children of poor families, and there had always existed an understanding between them. But when they were offered scholarships abroad in exchange for their loyalty to the Shah and SAVAK, their paths diverged. "I was smart enough to know there were other ways," Maryam said. "That has always been Ali's fault, he can't see with his imagination, he can only grasp what is in front of his nose. Rahim and the others—they are nothing but spoiled oil brats, they are not radicals or fundamentalists, there is no reason to spy on them. They are not about to undermine their money, their parties, their decadence for the sake of some ayatollah, some imbecile in a caftan. Can you imagine me veiled?"

Despite their differences, despite her role in his beating, Maryam and Ali had made up shortly before his disappearance. But he had lied to her about the state of their relationship. "Our reconciliation," Maryam had said. He had not written or called since he left, and she felt offended and deceived. He was a different person altogether from the boy she had known; he had accepted the culture of deceit as the manner of his life. "This rug, you see. The one thing he left was my present to him before we left our country. It is his way of leaving me behind after the promises we had made to each other."

"I don't know," she said, rolling off Ali's bare mattress and onto her lethal heels. "I could accept his choice if it were in the name of ideology, but for Ali it is only a practical matter. He wants a degree in engineering so he can build dams, so he can be a part of this grand design, as he calls it. He needed to be a part of something. So, he informs on others for the sake of his own life. A spy, with no moral compunctions. I see him sometimes, I think, watching me, but he would not be doing that for sentiment but for a report."

So maybe it wasn't that surprising when, following Maryam's visit, Ballard began seeing glimpses of Ali in the strangest places and at the strangest times: hunched over a desk in the collection agency at two o'clock in the morning, riding a bicycle across the Hawthorne Bridge at dawn, standing in line for dinner outside the Portland Rescue Mission. Each time he stopped the car or hurried to look, it turned out to be his mistake, a stranger's eyes, usually someone who, when viewed at close range, looked nothing like Ali. The mustache was wrong, the shoulders too wide. It was haunting, though, and Ballard could not rid himself of the feeling that Ali was not truly gone, that he was somewhere nearby, watching him.

And indeed, one morning while unlocking his car in the basement parking lot underneath the collection agency, Ballard grew so heavy, so uneasy with the sense that someone was watching, that he spun around, not at all surprised when a Volkswagen, faded blue and decorated with the pop art decals of a popular shampoo, sputtered away, the driver dark-haired and slump-shouldered.

"Ali," he cried, running after the receding car, "what the hell are you doing? Ali!"

He ran three blocks, the chain of office keys jangling at his side, but in the light early morning traffic, the VW ran one red light and was gone.

That was that.

• • •

The years passed, but not without their share of other disappointments, other illusions. Ballard graduated, and he fell in love, but following graduation, his girlfriend—the heiress of a gasoline pump manufacturer—decided that a life with those of her father's tax bracket was preferable to a life with someone such as Ballard, and her judgment seemed confirmed when, in the uncertain economy of the Carter years, he failed to find a job that paid more than waxing a relative's floors at midnight, his degree and half-hearted efforts notwithstanding. His basic unsuitability, it seemed, had been unmasked, showing him as the fraud that he was. In the text of Ballard's life, Ali's disappearance was a brief but provocative chapter.

Even so, Ballard thought that someday Ali would contact him, an expectation that persisted long past the point of reason. Ali might have wished to disappear, but he had to have sensed the sympathy and concern of his former roommate, the twinning of their experience. So went Ballard's thinking. A letter perhaps. Something on the order of "I profoundly regret the haste of my departure, but circumstances dictated an immediate withdrawal. Please forgive my rudeness, etc., etc." And yet, except for his few bills and announcements of campus events, his mailbox was empty. No letter, no phone call, no note slipped stealthily under the door—nothing came. Ever. But, even at that moment when Ballard waited with Susan for her boarding call, standing at the gate where she would board a plane to Ohio and home and the members of her class, and while she nattered on, hoping, she said, to remain such good, good friends for the rest of their lives, Ballard's attentions were drawn involuntarily toward those who sat on the margins of the waiting area, suspecting that somewhere among them Ali might be lying in wait.

Two years later on a chilly night in the fall, while driving home from work—he had, through sheer inertia, risen from night janitor to one of Uncle Leo's junior investigators—he passed a downtown church, its exterior dimly illuminated by the light of hundreds of candles, a demonstration in progress. Ballard parked in a side street, then walked around the police barricades to watch while robed and hooded figures marched silently back and forth in front of the church's gothic facade, in and out of the lights of the television news crews that had come out to cover the event. The marchers held no signs; no one addressed the growing crowd with bullhorn or microphone. But for a few hooded protesters distributing pamphlets, the purpose of the gathering would have been inscrutable; the participants just as easily could have been Klan members or monks bundled against the chilly night air. Printed on cheap paper, the pamphlets denounced the Shah's declaration of martial law, the crackdown on dissidents, the curtailment of religious expression, and the violation of the will of Allah. The shrill, inflamed rhetoric screamed for jihad and the imminent return of Allah's servant Khomeini. The protest was orderly, unnaturally silent, until a photographer began taking a series of pictures from the dark edges of the crowd, the camera's strobe freezing the marchers in still frames of blue light. A collective growl emanated from the marchers, and their ranks began to break.

"Traitor," Ballard heard someone in the crowd say. "SAVAK pig."

More rumbling among the demonstrators as well as those watching.

"He is taking names," someone else said, "as well as pictures."

"Our families will be ruined."

With a shout, the protestors, aided by confederates in the crowd, surged toward the flashes from the camera. The lone photographer—slight, his head drawn in to his shoulders—scrambled toward the haven of darkness. Candles were dropped, there were curses and screams, Ballard heard the soft sounds of flesh being struck, the whimper of pain. Something smashed against the pavement as the police moved to break up the disturbance. One of the robed figures howled as his sheet caught flame. Others reacted, rolling the poor unfortunate on the ground. Caught up in the crowd and carried toward the street, Ballard pushed his way out of the crush only to see Maryam, muffled inside an enormous greatcoat, kneeling over the shattered pieces of a camera. He watched as she picked up something from the pavement, placing it inside the pocket of her coat.

"Ah, you," she said, seeing him. "I remember you." She touched the side of his face, close enough that, even in the shadows, he could see the dark, finely textured skin along her cheekbones, smell her fragrance of jasmine and spice. "The world is chaos, and we are destroying one another, aren't we? Like a dog with a tail."

"That was Ali," he said, "with the camera. Wasn't it? And you were picking up the film. You're both in on it."

Her index finger traced the line of his jaw, tapped him lightly on the chin. "We shall have to get together one day. Have a little gossip. But that must wait for another time."

She kissed him then, neither an answer nor invitation to follow, and she slipped away, her hands in the pockets of her greatcoat. He would not see her again for years, by which time the Shah had fallen, Iran was a shambles of fundamentalism, and she would be seven months pregnant, her face sallow and rounded, the peacefully settled wife of a Swedish consular official. This happened at a chamber of commerce Christmas party; he looked across the serving line and there she was, wearing a sequined top over the swell of her breasts and belly and mounding a plate with crab salad and ham slices. It was the sort of event that breeds chance meetings, and after living a lifetime in one spot, even a collections investigator (and one-time night janitor) is bound to run into acquaintances. Her husband had excellent diplomatic connections, of course, and as his wife, she could travel anywhere—even Tabriz if she wished, though a modern woman like herself would never choose to wear a veil, now would she? "Can you imagine," she said, rubbing her sequined belly, "can you imagine me in a chador?" At various moments

during the course of the evening, he asked her about Ali, and each time she gracefully deflected the conversation to other topics. As she and her husband left, she
shook his hand with both of her own and whispered in his ear: "Life is what it is,
after all. Your imagination will not make it something else."

That was nearly the same time that he met Nadir. Nadi, as he preferred to
be called, answered the door when Ballard knocked, looking for the person who
had defaulted on payments toward a used refrigerator. The collections report
listed an address just south of downtown. A dilapidated three-story frame building, the gray paint blistered and peeling, the apartment house sat on a slight in-
cline at the end of a dead-end street. A date, 1918, was inscribed into the sidewalks,
and iron rings for the reins of one's horse were yet embedded into the curbs. From
the sidewalk, three steps descended to the locked front door. Ballard pressed the
buzzer by the apartment number listed on the paperwork, and when the front
door clicked open, he stepped into a hallway lit by one blue bulb, dust rising like
steam from the threadbare runner and into the gloomy aqueous light.

"Ali?"

"One moment." The stoop-shouldered man closed the door to release the
safety chain before opening it again. "I'm sorry. You must be mistaken. My name
is Nadir Mansur. Nadi to my friends."

The slight figure in the doorway was attired in a sleeveless tee shirt and a pair
of dirty work pants, his face broken and scarred around the sockets of his eyes,
the crooked path of his nose. At some time—maybe years before—he had shaved
off a mustache. Of that, Ballard was certain.

"I know it's you," he said.

"No," the other man said, shaking his head. "It happens very often. I am often thought to be someone else, but I assure you I am not."

The small man stepped away from the door, motioning Ballard inside.
"Please. I am about to have tea."

On the uphill side of the building, the one room apartment was essentially
underground. A narrow window near the ceiling admitted the muddy light of
an alley. The radiator hung from a bracket in the ceiling, the plaster of which
was crumbling and falling to the floor, a crazy quilt pattern of mismatched
Congoleum.

This apartment, with its crumbling ceiling and its patchwork floor, was precisely the sort of place Ballard had been running from for twenty years because
of its feeling of home. Living here—and he could imagine it all too well—would
constitute a kind of surrender from which he was not sure he would ever be able
to recover. Thoughts of Harriet's house, mowing Harriet's crabgrass lawn, tending

her garden and picking the fig tree, hearing the same lies about walking barefoot to school through snow and stubble fields in South Dakota, those moral lies about diligence, purpose, and hardiness of spirit—these ran in front of Ballard like a dying man's remembrance of a bitter life.

"I know the person you're looking for, this Ali. Ali Mussadegh. Yes. He has gone back to Iran, I believe. So he can build dams for Allah. Always the dams." This other man winced. "Please. My tea is nearly ready. Maybe you would join me."

Ballard ignored the offer, noticing for the first time a picture of the Shah on the table beneath the narrow window. "He disappeared quite suddenly."

"Yes. That happens."

"I think he was in a great deal of danger. People wanting to hurt him, maybe kill him."

"It's possible." Nadi pointed to the disfigurement of his own face. "But a car accident is even easier. I don't drink now. Allah—and the state of Oregon—forbid it."

"Ah." Ballard handed Nadi one of the agency's orange business cards, his home phone number written on the back. "If by some chance Ali didn't go home, have him call me, okay?"

"Yes," he said, and his lips seemed to be looking for what camouflage a mustache provides. "I will tell him. Of course. You were good friends."

Later, while sitting in his car, at the end of the dead-end street, Ballard wrote *Whereabouts Unknown* across the top of the agency file, knowing that by the next morning it wouldn't be a lie.

• • •

When he began working at Loss Finders, cleaning the agency's offices, he was fifteen and not unhappy to be away from Harriet's house several hours each night, though most days he was asleep by his third-period Algebra class. Sunday mornings, to the sound of various church bells, he picked up the trash from the Friday before, cleaned the bathrooms, and with whatever time he had left, waxed the hallways, shampooed the carpets, really cleaned. There was something soothing about the deserted offices while he danced with the electric buffer or swung a mop, the reverential quiet of papers stacked and squared away on desks, paper clips in their holders, staplers at the ready. Most of the desks also held pictures of families and loved ones: trips to the beach or ski slopes, graduations, birthdays, anniversaries. He knew something of their lives by their desks, and he sampled them vicariously. Mr. Montgomery, for example. One of his uncle's newest investigators, Mr. Montgomery kept a picture of his wife next to the phone. They had been married only for a short time. Mrs. Montgomery wore flowers in her hair while leaning against the trunk of a tree, her eyes nearly closed, and Ballard could imagine Mr. Montgomery, yawning away a slow afternoon and falling into that picture like a dream of love and belonging. Or Mrs. Harrington. One of the telephone agents, she had a daughter who had run away—she kept track of her daughter's movements, credit card transactions, that sort of thing, on a yellow pad underneath her desk blotter. Whereas his Uncle Leo kept a bottle of vodka in the lower right-hand drawer of his desk, a bottle that was replenished every three days. Ballard restricted his sampling between the first and second day, when his uncle's suspicions would be least likely aroused.

His lunches were similarly a potluck of whatever he found in the office. He looked through the cupboards and the office refrigerator for those items that wouldn't be missed—a soda, crackers from a box, an apple from a nearly full bag—and he rooted through the trash cans for whatever appeared not to be spoiled or dirtied. The night of Uncle Leo's sixty-second birthday, he came in to find the remains of an enormous sheet cake on the conference room table. The top had been decorated with a caricature of Sherlock Holmes, the two-billed hat and the bulbous pipe the unmistakable signs. *Happy Birthday to the Sleuth of Misfortune!* was written in script along the sides. Barely a quarter of the cake had been eaten, and a note had been taped to the table:

Dear Ballard,
Even the fat guy gets a birthday once in a while. There's ice cream in the
fridge, paper plates, plastic forks in the cupboard. Make yourself sick, you
lousy kid! Just kidding, ha, ha. Seriously, pretend you're one of us, okay? I
know it hurts. Forget the floors for tonight, we'll live in filth for a day. It won't
hurt us. Just stay the hell out of my booze, that's all I ask.

There was at least a quart of ice cream left in the refrigerator; he cut a slab of cake and dumped it into the container of ice cream, blessing his uncle and his uncle's birthday from the other side of midnight, grateful for the bellyache he was about to create, unable to believe how hungry he was.

Then again, he couldn't remember a time when he wasn't.

O Perfect, Perfect Love!

I

In high school, I played football for no reason other than to meet girls, not realizing that one runs into very few girls while playing football except on the rare sideline play. And I played right guard!

"Please, no deodorant jokes. I've heard them all," I used to say. My number was sixty-nine, that old symbol, so you can imagine the noise when we were introduced. "At right guard," *ha, ha,* "number sixty-nine," *ha, ha, ha,* "Ray Dante . . ." *Ray, Ray. Fucking Ray.* On game day, we wore our jerseys to school, and I wore mine like the stigmata in the hallways. Was I proud or ashamed? Before every game I threw up. During pre-game drills, my chest would tighten and my heart race. Afterward, my aches and pains were matched only by my relief that the game was, in fact, over. The games themselves I don't remember much.

My senior year, Mia and I became an item. After four years of helmet-induced pimples, finally, a girlfriend. Whoa, Nellie. You could say we met during practice. We ran a sweep right, I pulled, and one of our second-string linebackers decided to play tough guy. We rolled out of bounds like a couple of tumblers and took out the legs of the cheerleading and pep squads who were pretending to practice. Panties and legs, wool sweaters and ribbons, all in a heap. I had to push somebody's breast out of my cage. Much whimpering and crying. "Buck up," I said. "We do this every day." Betraying, I suppose, a fundamental lack of sensitivity to anyone's problem but my own. Coach Carmichael blew his whistle, his face flushed purple, the vein in his forehead pulsing with cartoon speed. Not good signs. So we untangled ourselves and restored order, an opportunity to dust off a cheerleader's backside. The gesture was not appreciated. Much tugging and repositioning of garments. On the top row of the bleachers there was a girl who wore overalls and a flannel shirt and a smirk she didn't bother to hide. "Hey, Ruthie," she yelled to the captain of the pep squad, "your butt's hanging out."

This is quite a girl, I thought. This is the one to know, overalls be damned. I clacked straight up the bleachers in my cleats. "Name and number," I said, "and don't be coy. Tempus fidgets." I could feel Carmichael boring holes in my back.

"Who the hell are you?" she said.

"Ray Dante, and who the hell are you?"

As it turned out, Kendra, the girl on the bleachers, had been sitting next to me the year before in MacKeller's US History. I tended to doze, and I confess I'd never got past the overalls and the smirk. I was too late regardless; she had a sailor boyfriend in San Diego and wasn't interested in surrogates, faithful girl that she was. She had a sister, however, and Mia was just my type, she promised. How right she was! Mia had never worn overalls in her life, and she had high sharp sophomore breasts which she kept beautifully displayed.

We went to a movie—a double feature, *M*A*S*H* and *Patton*—and began to kiss as though we thought to resuscitate each other. I reached under her blouse but hit iron.

"What is this," I said, "whalebone?"

"Shut up and get back to business," she said and planted her mouth over mine.

"I've heard of lifting and separating," I said, "but this is armor." Her tongue was in my mouth, dueling with my own, and whatever sense I might have made was lost.

We carried on like this for the rest of the fall, locked up for hours with no sense of time's passage. In the back rows of theaters and in the back seat of her mother's car, Mia, all underwire and body suits, yet her tongue was so busy, her mouth so voracious, I believed we were having sex.

She held my hand in the halls and peeled my oranges at lunch time. She came to every game so she could kiss my bruises afterwards. This even though we played in terrible, out-of-the-way places, desert schools with lousy fields and bad locker rooms. You always knew you were in for it the moment you set your gear down. The benches were scarred by fifty years' worth of initials, while the air was steeped in the sour ferment of sweat. There would be the *plip-plop* of water dripping somewhere. The teams we played were terrible as well, Air Force brats and oil worker bastards, migrant riff-raff of the lunar landscape. Tough kids who did not know how to play the game except to step on your hand and then knee your crotch in pileups. But there was Mia, in a position learned from her sister—sneering at the cheerleaders from the top row of the bleachers, huddled in a red parka as bright as flame, which matched her cheeks in the wind-whipped desert chill. With her watching, I stopped throwing up in the locker room beforehand, no matter how I forced myself, fingers down my throat: such was the ritual.

One night, though, we were snake bit. We marched down the field and fumbled on the five. We stopped them for no gain, *tweet!*, ten-yard penalty and a first down. The whole night like that, over and over again, a bad dream. In the second quarter, our tailback broke his ankle so badly that his foot was dangling by a thread, sickening to see: when they picked him up off the ground, they did so one part at a time. And with a minute to go in the third our tight end, who was also our punter, took a shot to the head. So, on fourth down, when he should have been ready to take the long snap from center, he was wandering the other team's sidelines and asking for bus fare. Georgie looked back between his legs, stood up, and turned to me. "Where'd he go?" he said. "I'm looking backward and there's nothing but end zone."

"He might have gone home," I said. "If he's smart, that is. This night is a wash."

We called time out, and Coach Carmichael raged on the sidelines, pushing players out of his way. There is nothing like a functional psychotic for a football coach, and there are certain ritual gestures that must be performed: the slamming of the clipboard, the grabbing of an unfortunate third-stringer by the face mask. The usual pathologies. When Anthony Meeker, the nerdy team manager, offered him the rejected clipboard, he scaled it into the grandstand and hit one of the drummers in the band.

"Huddle up," Georgie said. "Huddle up, goddamnit, before he comes after us."

Over Georgie's shoulder I saw Mia with her arms around her knees, the big parka drawn up around her face. It wouldn't be long, I thought, and then real life would begin again.

Our quarterback didn't have much leg, but he was the next best thing. Georgie snapped the ball, the lines pushed forward, we heard the *thock* of shoe on ball, and then we took off downfield. Their return man caught the ball on the left hash mark and began running to our right, cutting across my lane. "Just a little closer, you son of a bitch," I thought. This while I had his number in my sights. Then the lights went out.

I saw the hit a week later and it wasn't pretty. Mind you, the whole team was watching the film, and although we had lost a game we should have won and lost it badly, there was still a certain anticipation in the room. The images flickered on the Super 8 projection, and the take-up reel clattered, making all kinds of racket. One of their skinny little receivers had come streaking from my blind side and arrowed me right in the chest when I turned toward the corner. Coach Carmichael ran the film through, my legs went up into the air, and I landed on my head. "Ooh, Dante," my teammates said. "He nailed you. Nailed you good." Even Anthony Meeker, that malicious little shit, laughed through his swollen nose.

"Hey," I said. "I wasn't the only one." I pointed to our tight end who scrunched down in his seat and our tailback who propped his cast in a second chair. Coach was good enough to stop the film and then reverse it so my legs came down, my head came up, and the receiver ran backwards away from me. Then he ran it through again. Four more times, and each time I landed on my head. "Look at that," Carmichael said. "Upsy-daisy, you puss."

The first words I recall upon waking up. I was on my back, the sky was the color of ink, and the stars were winking their secrets. Coach Carmichael was kneeling above me. "There you go. Up and at 'em, you little puss." I wobbled off the field to tepid applause and sat down on one of the wooden benches. I saw two of everything, and try as I might, nothing would come together.

"If a sparrow falls on the forty-yard line," I said, unable to complete a thought.

"Try this." Anthony Meeker broke open an ammonia capsule, holding it under my nose so the fumes stung the back of my throat. Tears sprang into my eyes.

"Christ," I said, "get away from me."

"You're loopy," he said. "Your bell's been rung."

"What would you know about it?" I said. I swung and caught him flush on the nose; blood went everywhere, and I threw him to the ground. Why? What had he ever done to me? I had never looked at him twice before that night: one of those math geniuses with athletic tape holding his glasses together. Greasy hair, never took a shower. The caricature of a stereotype, Tony Baloney. He lay on the ground curled up around himself while two of my teammates kept me from stomping him. Coach Carmichael turned around and took one look at us. "Nice going, Dante. You finally hit something."

One of the assistant coaches escorted me to the bus. "Go all the way to the back, and don't even think about getting off. We'll get your clothes."

The driver sat in his seat at the front and stared at me until I couldn't take it any longer.

"What?" I said. "What do you want?"

"Nothing." He was wearing one of our red high school windbreakers, and even in the shadows inside the bus, I could see that his jaw muscles were working overtime. "What would I want with you?"

As I walked off the field, I had passed directly under the grandstand, and I had hoped for one little glance of understanding from Mia. She was standing, however, staring in the direction of the field, and *her* jaw muscles were bulging, as though she were barely able to restrain herself from running onto the field to make all the tackles that we had missed.

"High school punks," the driver was saying. "Why bother?"

Four weeks later we won a section championship, and at the awards ceremony we each received a gold football charm. I knew what was coming, and I had a chain ready. Ball and chain, just like the cliché. They went around Mia's neck immediately, but I was the one who was hooked.

"You see," I said, "I'm not such a bad guy."

She had been cool to me ever since that night in Tehachapi, and I gathered that I was still on probation. I had broken Anthony Meeker's nose when I was not myself, and for her that constituted a warning. But the gold football seemed to help, and we were back to our back-seat wrestling before the winter formal.

Then a week before graduation I found the football in an envelope which had been stuffed inside my locker. Someone had taken a crowbar and broken out the little vents. A note was crumpled around the charm: "I could never love somebody who preys on the weak and looks down on the lowly." Mia was in San Diego. Her sister was marrying her sailor, and her sailor was heading for Vietnam.

It was the best year of my life. And then I opened my locker.

II

O *Mia*, Mia! I blamed Anthony Meeker, that gamey little shit, for my troubles. Him and his ammonia capsule.

Time passed and I heard that Mia had gotten married, and then I heard that she had married Anthony Meeker, Mr. Tony Baloney himself, he of the greasy hair and taped together glasses. It was too strange to be true, but isn't that the way life is? And then I heard that Anthony Meeker was a gazillionaire, one of those computer wizards who build empires in the air. Or in Anthony Meeker's case, his father's garage.

A fundamental lack of fairness, I thought and still think.

Time passed and I became a Christian.

How? you might ask.

Again, too strange to be true. Even more strange was that I was a Christian of a sort I had never known, a fundamentalist of an entirely different stripe. If I could play football to meet girls, could I become a Christian to get laid?

After high school, I left home for college. This for the money that was promised to me. You know the statistics. But after I graduated, I was a thousand miles north of home, I lived in a damp one-room studio where mildew blackened the walls, and the only job I found was in a nursing home. I had a degree in history, I had written an analysis of WPA projects in rural and remote areas, and there I was, with my lousy academic eyesight, giving sponge baths to eighty-year-olds who confused me for Calvin Coolidge.

"Hey, Silent Cal," Mrs. Bainbridge said one day. "If it weren't for you and that scumbag Hoover, my brother might not have killed himself."

She was sitting up in bed and her head was pitched forward so I could run a washcloth along the back of her neck, where she smelled like a round of Gouda.

"How do you sleep at nights, you little prick?"

"I count sheep," I said, "and I sleep like a baby."

"Hah!"

Mrs. Bainbridge was in the habit of disrobing while in her wheelchair. Tying her up did no good; she wiggled out of the knots and used the terry cloth restraints like tassels, so the nurses called her Harry. As in Houdini.

The first time I found her naked, she had wheeled herself and her gray thatch out to the rec room, only to watch two of the male ambulatories playing cribbage. While they ignored her, she diddled her nipples and licked her lips. "Hey, boys," she cooed. "Plenty to go around." She pointed to me. "Don't pay attention to that man over there. He's an imposter and a spoilsport. Aren't you, Cal? You ruined this country, you and your whole crowd."

She was batting her eighty-year-old eyes at me, her false eyelashes, her only apparel, slightly askew but fanning the air a mile a minute.

"Don't do this to me," I said. "Mrs. Thompson shits in her bed whenever she doesn't like the dinner, which is often, and Mr. Williams in 17A pisses in the bottom drawer of his nightstand. God knows why. The rest of you have lost your minds in other ways."

"Go blow," she said, "before I get ugly."

It was through Mrs. Bainbridge that I saw Jesus. Her granddaughter came to visit every Thursday. Amelia Goodheart. I swear it's the truth. How could I make this up? A quiet, unassuming girl in modest clothes, corduroy jumpers, white blouses and wide bows, she brought sherbet and a Bible passage for her grandmother. One Thursday I was mopping underneath her grandmother's bed while she read from Luke: "Where the body is, there the vultures will gather." Her grandmother was spooning rainbow ice from the carton, greedy little bird that she was.

"What in the hell does that mean?" I said.

"Those with ears to hear, let them hear," Amelia Goodheart said. Her eyes were closed and she might as well have been feeling the words rather than speaking them.

"That's the thing with all those apocalyptic visions," I said. "They can mean anything you want them to."

"If you say so," Amelia Goodheart said, speaking from something like a bubble inside herself. She had long brown hair with a center part so straight she might have used a ruler when she brushed it. She sat on her grandmother's bed with the bearing of a nun.

"Silent Cal here doesn't know shit from Shinola," Mrs. Bainbridge said, mumbling around the pink and green spoonfuls. "He needs to stop sulking behind those glasses of his. You need to get out, spread your wings. After my bath, that is," she said with a wink.

"You could come to the farm with me," Amelia said.

"I don't know," I said. "Animals make me sneeze."

"You might learn something," she said.

"I don't convince that easily," I said.

But who was I to say no?

Amelia Goodheart lived on forty acres with two dozen other true believers. A funny sort of farm in that there were no crops, and the only livestock were the few grubby children who ran around, free of any adult supervision as far as I could tell. As I was to find out later, there was no shortage of oddities at New Aurora. It was a cool fall day as I recall, and a light mist was falling, but as we bounced through the ruts of the farm's graveled drive, there were three matrons and three bearded men cavorting naked in the muddy pond next to the main building.

"Okay, I get it," I said, "you believe in the *au natural*."

"Of course. They're the bodies God gave us," Amelia Goodheart said. "There's no call to be ashamed."

"Well, there's a few who might have cause," I said, noticing a rounded paunch here and sagging buttocks there.

"You've heard of glass houses, I suppose," she said, looking at me in a meaningful way.

I hadn't expected that an hour after her grandmother's bath, I would be unveiling my own imperfections to the air, but she had issued a kind of challenge, and I didn't see any way to refuse when she had shucked her clothes along with her modesty by the water's edge.

"Don't be upset," she said when we were standing knee-deep in pond water, our toes buried in sludge. "The cold air does that to everyone the first time. Especially in front of strangers. The shrinkage, I mean."

"I had no idea you were that experienced," I said.

I had not paid much attention to Amelia Goodheart prior to this, but now I couldn't help but notice the small pink-tipped breasts, wide hips, and the light golden tan that bore no evidence whatsoever of strap marks.

What have I gotten into, I thought, *with this contradictory girl?*

And, *The possibilities of life are endless.*

She introduced me to the other nudists, and I suffered the awkwardness of shaking hands, such a formal gesture in such intimate context. I kept hoping for pockets, but all I saw were beards, top and bottom, appendages swinging. No strangers to the cold were they.

"How lovely," one of the women said, "to have a new member."

"Sightseer might be the better word," I said. "Although both have their meanings."

"You are certainly welcome whatever your inclination."

She had a mop of gray hair, and there was mud caked in her various crevices, but she was happy to welcome me into the fold, she and the others. They dove into the muck like beavers, yelping and splashing and throwing mudballs at each other with the good humor of children. The oldest of the women hit me square in the forehead, cackling with delight. "Life is messy," she said to me as she began her windup, "and you need to live."

Then, when we were thoroughly engaged with life, brown and gray with it, we trooped toward a communal shower house, and I thought the moment couldn't get more interesting.

"So, Amelia," I said, "maybe we could see more of each other. Not that we haven't seen a good bit already."

"You're sweet," she said, "but we haven't been interviewed."

"An interrogation? Now? After such an introduction?"

"We have our ways," she said.

I was given a brick of homemade soap and a coarse brown towel and was ushered into a shower stall that was more of a closet than otherwise. And given her behavior at the pond, I wasn't terribly surprised when the door opened then closed behind me, and I felt a loofah scrubbing the space between my shoulders. Another hand circled my waist before drifting lower. There was a kiss of hair against my backside.

"This is full service," I said, "for an interview. And you're like no girl I've ever known."

But the hands and other parts did not belong to Amelia Goodheart, as it turned out, but were attached to one of the mud-bathing matrons.

"Sorry for your disappointment," she said. "Amelia *is* quite a girl, but you have some things to learn. She'll have to wait her turn."

Thus began my instruction in the ways of New Aurora. I was literally in the capable hands of a fifty-year-old vamp named Louise Pennington, whose little seraglio this was. They were diehard descendants of Perfectionists, those oddball Christians who believed that Jesus had already brought them into the Kingdom of God. And since, in His Kingdom, there was no giving and taking in marriage, a little hanky-panky was nothing more than the healthy exercise of faith. A holy kiss and whatever comes next.

"Getting to know you," Sister Pennington said, "is to love you. We are sister and brother, after all."

"For one big happy family," I said, "that seems a little incestuous."

"You're quite a literalist," she said, "even for an outsider."

We got to know each other rather quickly in the shower. Too quickly, as it turned out, because that was the beginning of my second lesson in the social intercourse at New Aurora.

"We take our time here," Sister Pennington said. "That's part of the etiquette. We enjoy the experience rather than the memory."

"I was a little revved up," I said, "what with all the soap and water. Can you blame me?"

And that was when I learned my third lesson.

"I don't what?" I said. "Jesus is one thing, just as I am and so on, but I guess I'm a little deaf to the details. You'll have to repeat that."

"No e-jac-u-la-tion," she said. "Read my lips. You don't get to come. None of the men at New Aurora come."

"What fun is that?"

"Excuse me?"

"I mean if this is a birth control issue, you know that we have pills now and a whole catalogue of other means."

A hundred years before, the original leader of the Perfectionists at Oneida, New York, had instituted the sacrament of complex marriage, which, in that pre-contraceptive age, was complicated indeed. Hence, the rider of male continence. But in addition to the idea that a woman's body belonged to herself, John Humphrey Noyes held some other progressive notions, such as the prolongation of both partners' enjoyment. So, although there were other means of preventing birth, the practice had been maintained as an article of faith.

"You'll learn to hold yourself back," she said, "like a lemming stopping at the edge of the cliff."

"I don't suppose anyone has exploded," I joked. "From the frustration, I mean."

"Not a single woman has been harmed," she said.

"That's not quite what I had in mind," I said, which was when she turned serious.

"You will control yourself if you want to badly enough, and the sooner you learn that, the sooner you'll get to know Missy Goodheart intimately, luscious little morsel that she is."

"Ah," I said, "so that's the way it is."

"And in the meantime," she said, not without a smile, "you'll have to be satisfied with me."

• • •

You may think me foolish, or at least the captive of my own desires, but I cast my lot with the denizens of New Aurora that night. The muddy pond was my baptism and the shower house my confirmation. What was keeping me in my former life? Mrs. Bainbridge and the other eighty-year-olds at Glendoveer Manor? Each day I went to work I felt myself growing older by decades. I had told Amelia Goodheart that she would have a tough time trying to convert me, but then it turned out she didn't even have to try. I converted myself. Any God who placed such a premium on enjoyment was all right by me. And they were a welcoming bunch.

I was given a room in the main building, a toothbrush, a brick of soap, and my own set of towels. I called the nursing home and told them to take a flying leap. What did I need with minimum wage when I would be employed by the family of God? The family of God at New Aurora, as it turned out, had several lucrative product lines: in addition to premium leather goods, which they produced for a wholesaler in Portland, they also sold herbal folk remedies and essential oils by catalogue. They had quite a reputation among the granola-eaters, and the community was as flush as a blue-chip stock.

What could have been better? Those with leather-working skills cut and stitched, and the rest of us took phone calls, applied labels to bottles, and packaged orders. We wrote catalogue copy, took photographs, and operated the press. During the lunch hour, we were free to interview one another as to the glory of God, and after the work day was over there was the muddy pond or the shower house or any other nooks and crannies of the community's forty acres. Although the average interview lasted an hour or more, one couple had spent nearly three hours conjoined, and George Hawkins, New Aurora's most expert swordsman, had emerged with a beatific smile and his control intact if not his quota of handbags. The best I ever managed by comparison was twenty-four minutes, and even that

ended with a whimper as I shuddered and spent myself inside Louise Pennington. And then I blacked out. Her dismay was palpable, and she had to restrain herself from yelling at me. "You seem sweet and you say that you mean well, but
you're weak-willed and selfish, and how will you ever know Jesus?"

"I can't help it," I groaned. "You're too much woman for me. I would have to
be dead inside and Jesus a Peeping Tom."

You see, there was more to know about the New Aurorans than my first sup-
position of them as nudists. They were serious believers, and except for their approach to sex, they might have been confused for Presbyterians. They met nightly
for prayer and Bible study, they sang before dinner and they raised their hands.
On more than one occasion one of the members would begin to babble in a language that sounded like a parody of Chinese. Once a week, they held a criticism
session, one of the practices retained from the original Perfectionists. Several
members of the community were singled out for discussion by the others, and
their flaws were reviewed and dissected and analyzed, various suggestions for im-
provement being offered. I was a favorite for these sessions because I had so
much to work on. My spiritual life was suspect and my difficulties acquiring the
proper sexual technique were common knowledge, and for the members of New
Aurora, the two problems were one and the same.

Following one such evening, Brother Wistrom, one of the bearded men from
my first day in the mud, pulled me aside and asked, "How can you know Jesus if
you're living for your own gratification?"

"I don't know, Morris," I said. "I try. I really do. But the moment comes, and
it's already too late."

"The next time you get to that point," he said, "relax your abdominal muscles and slow down your breathing. That's all there is to it. You're riding a wave,
and you can't let it crash."

"Easier said than done," I said.

"You need to think of something other than your own desires."

"Like what, for instance?"

"Puppies," he admitted, "or cats lying in the sun. That seems to do the trick.
Something from a greeting card."

Really good teaching is wasted on the young and the stupid, and I wasn't that
young, mind you, but the teaching seemed lost on me regardless. About Jesus or
sex, I seemed to be clueless. I couldn't understand why, if *Jesus loves me, this I know*,
He didn't raise everyone from the dead and be done with it. And although it is embarrassing to admit it, my sexual performance never rose above woeful. I understood that Jesus was the resurrection of love and orgasm was a little death, but I

couldn't seem to make the distinction between resisting the latter and welcoming the former.

Despite my shortcomings, Sister Pennington was not my only female mentor. Diverse pairings were a staple at New Aurora as a means of combating jealousy and exclusivity, so I was free to experience all that the post-menopausal women of New Aurora could offer. Although very much in demand as a partner, Roberta Goodheart, Amelia's mother, welcomed me once in the hope that she might supply whatever was lacking. She was, in her fifties, no bigger than her daughter, but she still displayed the muscular shoulders and thighs and abdomen of the gymnast she had been in her youth. With George Hawkins, she had experienced eighteen orgasms during the course of their marathon, and frankly, the prospect of coupling with such a dervish frightened me. She had visions during intercourse that the community treated as prophetic. But such was my desire for her daughter that I was willing to try anything.

"You will take it easy on me," I said with as much hopefulness as I could muster.

We dropped our clothes and then began a stretching regimen because Roberta, who was very matter-of-fact, believed in the benefit of exercise and sweat and overall lubrication as much as she believed in love, and she knew how much a pulled muscle could impair performance.

"You're stiff," she said. "You never learned how to breathe."

"I thought I was supposed to be," I said. "Stiff, that is."

And I said, "What's to know? I've been breathing all my life."

"As though to breathe were life," she said. "We'll take you to life. Even if it's kicking and screaming."

But I was no more successful in my session with Roberta Goodheart than I had been with Louise Pennington or any of the other matrons. This despite her instructions on breathing, her flexibility, or her insistence that we use the original Perfectionist position: she lay on her side, right leg drawn up, and left me to figure out the mechanics of a rear entry.

"Maybe if you don't have a face to look at," she said.

"I'm not so sure," I said, "that Tab A was meant for Slot B, not from this direction."

"The missionary position is the tool of the patriarchs," she said. "Love can occur, but it's not the only way. Come here." And she reached back between her legs to pull me into her, but by that time the deed was done while I was yet between her fingers.

"I'm beginning to think that it's hopeless, then," she said, wiping her hands of me. "In all my years."

"It's the novelty," I said. "Don't you think?"

"No," she said sadly. "I don't think that's the case here."

"But I'm trying," I said. "I just need a little more time. I mean it's been what, ten minutes? Give me a little while, I'm sure I'll bounce back."

"The problem," Amelia said the next afternoon when my latest failure had become universally known, "is that you don't really love us."

"I do," I said. "I really do. You don't know how much I do."

"I'm sorry."

She turned to face me in the front seat of her car. We were parked in front of her grandmother's nursing home. She was dressed in her modest town clothes, and I could hardly believe that this was the same girl who could recite the preferences of a dozen men and not a few women as well. She leaned forward to hug me, as chaste an embrace as a sister might bestow. This was farewell. I had been asked to leave by Louise Pennington herself, a decision by the community elders unprecedented in the history of New Aurora.

"I don't understand it," Sister P. had said. And I have to admit that she did look perplexed. "We've never been unsuccessful before. You're a special case."

"That's very comforting," I said.

"You're eager, you try, but every time you try to love me, you're the only one who's pleased."

"What will you do?" Amanda touched me on one knee.

"I don't know," I said. "I had no life before, and I have no life now. I don't suppose much has changed."

"There you are," Amelia said. "That's a healthy way to look at it."

III

So my experience at New Aurora ended, but my life took an increasingly sour turn, all my brave talk to the contrary. I went back to Glendoveer Manor for my old job, but no one was interested except Mrs. Bainbridge, who blew raspberries at me for all my crimes. After six months at New Aurora, I didn't have a nickel to my name; I suppose I was lucky to have had the pockets to put one in.

But I was as low as I could get. I dug ditches and picked berries. I worked cleaning up construction sites. I took a job selling cutlery door-to-door, but when I failed at that, I began to wonder if I might not be suited for anything. Fate intervened in the form of a catalogue sales position at Datakom Enterprises, Anthony Meeker's digital empire. The personnel director saw the name of my high school and grew interested immediately.

"You're about the same age as Mr. Meeker," he said.

"It was a big place, and I doubt that he'd remember me," I said. "I was pretty forgettable, and he ran with the fast crowd. We all knew he was destined for great things."

"That Tony," I said during another juncture of the interview. "He was slick before he had a license to drive."

God help me, I thought. But it was my experience at New Aurora that finally tipped the scale. "I did a little bit of everything. Orders, packaging, catalogue copy. You name it." And when he offered me the job, I thought that in terms of what I had learned as opposed to what I hadn't, there was no shortage of irony.

I kept to myself; I rarely went out. I lived as cheaply as possible in a bedroom I rented from a mean old harpy in Beaverton, and I let them pay me in stock options. I worked overtime like a mother and rose through the ranks. In seven years, the stock split three times, and I was a paper millionaire invited to corporate muckety-muck Christmas parties. Which is where I saw Mia again. I was drinking the company Scotch and wolfing down the company salmon when she waddled in, pregnant with her sixth or seventh, I don't know which. Tony Baloney was no Perfectionist, that's for sure, but he had his own research and development team in the making.

"You," she said. "I don't believe it. Don't we have our Nazi guards at these things? Where's the rent-a-cop? This seems like a security breach."

"Look, it's Mamma Mia," I said. "Mamma Mia Meeker."

"I guess I haven't heard that more than a hundred times tonight," she said, massaging her belly. "God save me from originality. So, what are you doing here?"

"I work here," I said. "And you?"

"The same, obviously," she said pointing to her front, ship of state that she was.

"So, where's hubby?"

"Buying a congressman. Or three." She lowered her voice and herself into a chair. "Protecting the Internet from undue regulation. Dear God," she said, "I'm huge."

Her belly was huge, and her face was puffy as though it had been filled with air, but I could tell it was Mia inside, and I was jealous, I admit it.

"I guess Mr. Meeker figured out the hooks on the corsets. That was more than I could do."

"Mr. Meeker had help. Just like he had help acquiring his rugged profile. He's so proud of his nose. It makes him look tough. Like he's seen a little action. Listen," she said suddenly. "I have a favor to ask."

Mia had a friend she wanted me to meet. Wendy. Divorced two years before and treated badly by every man since. I couldn't be any worse. Wendy was the head of Marketing, so it was a wonder we hadn't already met. Mia pushed me toward the dance floor where a disco ball was bouncing pinpricks of light around the room. The strobe light made the dancing look like a seizure disorder. "She's just your type," she said, "completely clueless. She's my best friend, so I don't say that lightly. When it comes to ad campaigns and presentation concepts, she's a genius, but about men she's a moron."

"That should help," I said.

"No kidding."

Wendy was sitting at the bar, wearing a spangled dress so reflective that, when the lights hit her, she was painful to the eye.

"Mia!" She was drunk and nearly fell from her perch on the bar stool.

"I brought you a present," she said. "Don't scare him away."

"You're so nice to me. What did I do to deserve this one?" Wendy squinted at me. She had sleepy eyes that suggested fireplaces and down comforters. "Well, okay," she sighed, "what the hell."

"Try him on," Mia said. "You can always return him if the fit's no good. You don't even have to be nice."

"Excuse me?" I said. "I prefer nice."

"Okay, Mr. Nice," she said. "You can drive me home."

"I'm so pleased with myself," Mia said. "A stroke of inspiration, it was." She waggled her fingers at us. "Call me."

In her apartment, Wendy shrugged out of the glitter and shimmer of her dress with a speed and motion so practiced I couldn't help but think of Amelia Goodheart, and my heart sank. "Okay, Big Bopper," she said, in a voice that was drunker than she was. She stepped toward me in her party heels and a red thong that could have fit in a thimble. But in bed she lay still, her eyes focused on the ceiling, unresponsive to any and all suggestion.

The irony was not lost on me. I had spent the better part of six months hoping to fit into a family of modestly dressed, Bible-thumping eroticists and failing miserably in the process, but get into bed with a liberal tart who treated sex like a punishment, and I turn into Johnny Tall Tale himself. Sister Pennington would have been so proud of me! I rode wave after wave with this disinterested woman.

"Aren't you done yet?" she said, the edge of irritation creeping into her voice. "How much longer do you think you'll be?"

I turned her onto her side and propped her right leg onto my shoulder.

"What are you doing now?"

"Trying to love you," I said. "And hoping to be loved."

"Oh, please. It's a little early for that, don't you think?"

We were married three weeks later with Mia and Anthony Meeker as our witnesses. She was on the rebound, and I was seven years lonely. Her sleepy eyes had seemed bedroom-inclined, and her red thong underwear had led me to believe that our union could be a happy and inventive one. I suppose it was. We never thought of having children; we were happy as a couple, although we hardly knew what to say to each other, we were such strangers. We were so rich, though, it hardly mattered. We could always hire someone or buy something. She took to wearing flannel nightgowns and wool socks because she was always cold and her usual response to my overtures was "That again?" but she never refused me. Then again, she never really participated despite my best Perfectionist efforts. She stayed on the sidelines, as it were. Many years later, she became deathly afraid of pregnancy; it was an obsession for her, that fear. She had no faith in the skills I had learned at New Aurora, and although I used a rubber and she was on the pill, she demanded I get a vasectomy. I loved my wife and I wanted to love her all the more, so I did as she requested.

A day later, my balls were swollen to the size of grapefruit.

"Throbbing," I told my doctor over the phone. "And bruised in ways I wouldn't have thought possible. Like walking around with an udder. God help me."

My urologist said that was nothing, he had known cases much worse. He hinted of explosions and gore. But then he had an odd sense of humor, that guy. When I called again, his nurse offered little sympathy and fewer details. "Try giving birth," she said, "then tell me how much it hurts."

"It always comes to that, doesn't it?" I said. "Bitch and moan, and then when it's over you lord it over us as though we're deficient. Every mother is a tyrant."

"You got it," she said. "And you can't stand blood either."

I was in my office, dressed in sweats and an ice bag, limping from one filing cabinet to another and cursing the pain. Cursing my wife as well? I suppose. Dr. Shaw had recommended that I stay home for a few days, but what would that have accomplished? Wendy was working at home—Datakom was going through a rocky time, and the new product line was critical—and she would have seen my discomfort as pandering for sympathy. Who needed it? I tossed and turned on the couch in the coffee room, pitied myself, and went home at five the next morning. Only to find Wendy and her suitcase gone. And then I called Mia, who told me to come right over to the Meeker palace. Tony was testifying before a Senate subcommittee on antitrust legislation, and she and the kids would love the company.

"Look," she said, meeting me at the door, "I heard from her. She's unhappy, but it's temporary. She'll be back."

"But I don't understand," I said. "I did everything she wanted. I have an ice pack between my legs for her."

"Yes, you do."

"It hurts," I said. "It really hurts."

"Oh, brother. You men are perfect babies."

She took me to a den in the rear of their massive house, shushed her legion of curious children, and turned on a floor-to-ceiling television. "You look funny," she said. "Your eyes are dark and your hair's all smashed. Like you just woke up but haven't slept."

"Maybe I'm still asleep and I'm just dreaming," I said. "Dreaming that I'm awake and dead on my feet."

"You need some rest."

"And more ice?" I said.

"More ice. Coming up."

On the wall opposite the television, there was an oil portrait of the empire builder himself, Anthony Meeker, dressed in a suit and tie, painted when he was about thirty years old and worth a mere ten or twenty mil. His hair had been cut by artists who charged two hundred bucks a trim, but his glasses, cheap black frames, sat crooked on the bridge of his crooked nose. And it seemed to suggest that, no matter our net worth, we never stray very far from our point of origin.

"Pretty awful, isn't it?" she said.

"Nice suit," I said.

"His mother loves that picture."

"It's a mother's picture. Her boy the success, dressed in his Sunday best. It's understandable. What I can't understand," I said, "is why she left. You can tell me that. I'm not a bad guy."

"She's neurotic and you're needy," she said. "She can't believe that anyone who loves her could be very smart. It's a tough combination. I guess it had to happen, and I'm sorry. I feel responsible."

"It's all your fault, then," I said. "But she could have told me before I went to the doctor."

I never did lie down that morning. Instead, I sat with Mia and drank coffee while we watched for news bulletins about Tony Baloney's testimony before congress. The hearings were not going well. One senator after another scolded Tony for playing too rough, for creating a playing field that sloped in his favor and other such strained metaphors, and we could see our paper fortunes teetering. Tony sat alone at a long table, taking it and taking it. But then the news from Washington was preempted by another report: a private jet, miles off course and flying on autopilot. The jet belonged to a golfer whose recent successes had catapulted him to the top of the money list, but now all on board were believed to be dead, victims of depressurization and oxygen loss, and the plane was flying itself. There was talk of the Air Force shooting it down if it threatened population on the ground. The jet tore through the sky for four hours, ran out of fuel, and crashed in South Dakota. If the passengers weren't dead before, they were now.

"That's a terrible, terrible story," Mia said. "Even worse than watching Tony getting kicked in the head. It reminds me of you."

"Thanks a lot."

"No, really. Everyone's dead or unconscious inside the plane, but it keeps flying. And no one can do a thing to help. Nothing except watch and hope against hope."

"I'm feeling a lot better," I said. "Thanks again."

"You've been flying for years."

"No more," I said. "Don't say another word. Please."

Mia left, then returned with more coffee and pastries on a tray.

"So, this may be the wrong time to ask, but what is this I hear about an hour, two hours at a time?" Mia said. "Wendy says she's had enough. You're too insistent, and when it's over she feels like she's supposed to applaud."

"I'm trying to love her," I said. "Is that a crime?"

"But two hours. That's a joke, right? Otherwise I'm jealous with children."

"Maybe it is," I said, "now that I think about it. Just a joke. Maybe it just seemed like a long time to her."

A Tale Told by Rube Goldberg Begins and Ends with Dogs

THE DOG WAS not the dog of her dreams. The contented golden retriever asleep in front of the fireplace. A yellow Lab puppy bounding through the grass of a lush backyard.

No, this one was a mutt, fully grown or nearly so, a collection of mismatched parts with feet the size of dessert plates. Jamie always stopped herself from saying *dinner* plates, because she wouldn't allow the hyperbole to stretch so far.

She had named the dog Ma-mut-do, an abbreviation of Mammoth Mutt Dog, a name she had hoped would sound exotic and meaningful but only confused anyone who heard it. Her eighty-year-old next-door neighbor, for example, was convinced that she had named the dog for the Hunchback of Notre Dame. So she called her Betty instead.

No one was confused by Betty.

After he came to pick up his box of essential oils and his pots of wheatgrass, not to mention his pots of pot, along with his guitars, amps, speakers and all the related electrical paraphernalia, Betty was the last reminder that Spencer had ever lived in her house. That Spencer had ever lived with her. Spencer with his dreadlocks and the earthy aroma of "natural" hygiene. Wasn't it interesting that "earthy" and "natural" could be synonyms for "dirty" and "unclean"? How, she wondered, had she not noticed that before?

Things had started to go badly between them a month after he moved in, when Spencer began staying out later and later after his gigs and she could not keep herself from commenting on the fact, and then Spencer called at four-thirty one morning, locked up on a DUI two hours after his last set at Club Fred. They had partied a little after the doors were locked and the chairs put on the pool tables.

Partied? she had asked. And, With whom? She made sure to say "whom" because it upped the bitchiness in her tone and matched the bitchiness she felt.

Look, Spencer said, it was no big deal. The band and the club staff. A group.

A group, she said.

That's what I said.

I'll see what I can do, she said.

But she went back to bed instead and let him wait. She arranged his release that afternoon, saying only that there had been problems with the bail, even though she had merely handed the desk sergeant a cashier's check for five hundred dollars. She had five hundred dollars but more than a few qualms. The whole process had taken thirty minutes, tops, but Spencer didn't question her explanation or the twelve-hour wait, and Jamie had wondered whether or not she might have overreacted. She felt guilty when they made love that night; he seemed genuinely interested in giving her something rather than merely getting something for himself. And then the next morning, he had slipped out of bed before she knew he was gone, and then there he was: sitting on the front porch, holding Betty on a leash that didn't look up to the task while the dog pulled and tugged and whined.

What's this? she said.

A dog.

I know it's a dog.

You said you wanted one.

Yes, but she's—

She wanted to say "enormous" or "deformed," "funny looking" or "frightening," but she didn't have the heart, not after Spencer said I looked into her eyes and knew she was the one for you.

Betty. Ma-mut-do. A gift. A peace offering. Betty.

And then Spencer was gone not long afterwards, and Betty seemed like one more unwanted leftover, a bad debt, a hole in a bathroom wall, the fester of a remembered insult, another remnant of a relationship turned sour.

You and me, Betty, she said in the evenings. Just you and me.

Since Spencer's departure, the dog had turned sullen, and now in late spring, the days were longer, and Betty became resistant to calls to come into the house. She stared at Jamie with animal eyes while the darkness descended.

You and me?

Jamie was on her own.

• • •

According to the veterinarian, Betty weighed 84.6 pounds, a figure that might increase if Jamie wasn't careful with her diet. She was twenty-four inches tall at the shoulder. Her coat was taupe with silver undertones. Her tongue was dark purple, her legs were short, her chest dominated her body, and her tail was a tightly curved brush. Her ears were as soft as the felt blanket Jamie had had as a toddler.

The veterinarian's assistant said, yes, Betty was clearly some part Labrador, but only a small part, which was a good thing, given her color, since chocolate Labs were notoriously stupid. The tongue, she said, indicated some chow and the tail suggested that a husky might have been involved at some point.

On the other hand, Mrs. Blevins, the eighty-year-old neighbor who lived in the other half of the duplex, saw Betty's chest and her bowlegged stance and muttered something about pit bulls.

I won't be threatened in my own home, she said. And then she made a point of telling Jamie about the pistol she kept on the top shelf of her front hall closet.

Oh, no, Jamie said, she's very sweet. Really. Spencer brought her home.

Oh, Spencer, Mrs. Blevins said. Spencer did that, did he?

Mrs. Blevins liked Spencer. She liked him much more than she had ever liked Jamie.

She won't bark?

No, no. We'll make sure of that. She *can't* bark, Jamie said. This is where I work, you know.

Because I won't have it, Mrs. Blevins said. I can't abide a dog who barks incessantly.

So of course, a day later, Betty began to bark. And bark and bark and bark, and Jamie had to bring her inside the house, aware of the opened curtains in Mrs. Blevins's kitchen window that closed the moment she and the dog went inside. This went on for a week, Jamie letting the dog out into the yard in the morning, the dog barking and barking, and then Jamie bringing her back in again to roam the house, sniffing the kitchen counters, pawing the wastebaskets, drinking from the toilets, and putting her nose in Spencer's crotch, who seemed to like it more than he should and who then laughed when she said she couldn't concentrate with all this new and unexpected commotion. How was she supposed to get anything done?

But then, Spencer moved out and took all of his crap with him. Except for Betty. And just like that, Betty shut up. She went into the yard first thing in the morning and lay down by the back gate, and not even Jamie calling to her from the back door at night or children playing on the commons in the morning or the meter reader three feet away in the afternoon could disturb her.

• • •

Work. She had said she worked at home. *Work, really?* Work, if she were honest, was something of a euphemism. Her life was something of a euphemism. A fraud. An accident, more like. She had no business working at home, and she had no business having a fifteen-hundred square foot, three-bedroom, two-and-a-half-bath townhouse with a fenced yard. Hers alone and paid for, but there you have it. She had no business having business.

This is how accidental life could be: during the last quarter of her senior year, she decided to be nice to herself. She had more than enough units to graduate with a dual degree in history and economics. Her applications to law schools had been submitted; her GPA and LSAT scores were reasonable if not spectacular, and she had some choices to make. For the first time in four years she felt as though she were on vacation. As though she were responding to a dare, she signed up for a life drawing class and film appreciation, and then when she couldn't get into the class on multicultural cuisines (*a new restaurant every week!*), she signed up for a self-defense class.

Mistake.

The drawing class employed live models, who disrobed with a speed she found shocking, especially given the models' various shapes and sizes, with all of their surprising lumps and angles and deviations from the airbrushed norm. Not one of the films came without subtitles, and the self-defense class seemed calculated to show Jamie just how uncoordinated and ill-equipped she was to confront an attacker. She would have found a class in the Chinese stock market more comprehensible.

Midway through the quarter, she nearly withdrew from her entire course load. Her self-defense instructor, while using her to demonstrate a blocking technique, accidentally punched her in the face. Jamie was supposed to move left, but she moved to her other left instead, and then all she saw was her instructor's fist. Her eye was swollen in minutes; her nose dripped bright red blood on her bare feet.

Oof, Jamie said, her cheekbones and teeth feeling displaced.

Goddammit, her instructor shouted. Whadidya do that for?

Her instructor was a former Marine, whose trust in her abilities to follow directions was only slightly less than his belief that college students in general were a waste of his time.

Half of her face was purple inside of three hours.

The next night she watched a Swedish movie in which a woman, abused by an older man and transformed into a heroin-addicted prostitute, takes her revenge through martial arts.

Jamie started laughing at the first roundhouse kick and couldn't stop. She finally left the classroom, aware of the sidelong glances from her fellow students and the professor, who turned out to have a serious, academic interest in films portraying violence against women. Not to mention personal reasons. An hour after class ended, her professor called, hoping Jamie would report the son of a bitch who had done this to her. Remaining passive would only make matters worse, she said. She could tell Jamie stories.

What other sense could she have made of her bruises or her reaction to the movie?

But the pièce de résistance came the next night, when the model for her drawing class turned out to be a three-hundred-pound unemployed construction worker her father's age and sporting her father's gray crew cut; his arms and neck were the color of bricks, while his torso and legs were as white as a bevy of swans. He sat on a stool and dropped his robe. His belly covered his genitals, just the tip of his cock visible on one enormous thigh. A flower seeking the light.

Oh, Jamie said.

What?

Most nights she worked at an easel in the back row, but tonight she had unaccountably chosen an easel nearest the stool and the model, and she had nowhere to hide.

What? he said again. What's with you?

Nothing, she said. I just remembered something.

The instructor, a thirty-something goth with cleavered hair and angry tattoos, moved from easel to easel, demonstrating lines, lecturing about shading, dimensionality. Inhabiting the mass of the figure.

I don't do this because I enjoy it, you know. "Mass of the figure" my ass. I'm fat. Obese. You think this isn't humiliating?

I almost forgot, she said, hoping to think of something, anything, credible to say. My mother is coming to town tomorrow, and I have to pick her up at the airport.

Her mother left during her junior year of high school and divorced her father because, in her mother's words, *Your father is a sad little man who won't spend a nickel to make himself a dollar. He doesn't like people, and he doesn't like the disorder of life. Effort, outside of his routine, is not a strong part of his vocabulary.* She moved to Rhode Island, where her family was from, practically the other side of the world, and while they spoke on the phone once or twice a week, not once in four years had she ever visited Jamie at school. How much could she believe her mother's version of events?

She doesn't live here, Jamie said to the naked man sitting six feet away.

He shifted slightly from one cheek to the other, but other than that he remained motionless. His lips were still. He might as well have been a ventriloquist for himself.

You think I do this by choice? I got bills. Tomorrow's the plasma center. I mow lawns on Friday. Sixty-two years old and I'm competing with zitheads for jobs.

I'm sorry. With a charcoal pencil, Jamie swept the curves of his shoulders, his head, the mass of his massive gut.

You're sorry. What do you need to be sorry about, college girl?

Under the lights, his face grew perceptibly redder, his crew cut and forehead dotted with perspiration.

She's sorry.

I'm sorry, Jamie said again. I didn't mean anything by it.

Hunh, he said.

They finished the rest of the class period in silence; when the hour drew to a close, he stood and drew the robe about him with deliberate care. He stared at the voyeurs in front of him in dismissal.

After class she saw him in the parking lot, now clothed in a sweatshirt and blue jeans, as he opened the door of a rusted Ford pick-up. When their eyes met, his mouth flattened, and he saluted her with a raised middle finger.

She went back to her apartment and stared at what she had done, resisting the temptation to modify her work to the point of incompetence. She poured a glass of wine instead.

She was not particularly talented and her preparation for drawing the human form inadequate. She would have been better served by viewing a fruit basket, and yet anxiety had produced a competence she had not hitherto possessed. The charcoal had created the slabs of his flesh of its own volition, his bitterness emanating like gas from the heavy paper.

By the time her roommate came home, she had drunk three-quarters of a bottle, and she was singing nonsense to and through her sketch.

What is this, girl?

Donetta had told Jamie for a year or more that she needed to explore her wild, and now here she was, spinning around the living room in front of a black-and-white drawing of a naked Hermann Göring. Lordy, lordy.

Jamie woke up on the floor underneath the Pier 1 coffee table, one foot on the couch, her head throbbing inside and out. Donetta's snores were audible from her room at the other end of the apartment. Four empty wine bottles stood in a rank on the kitchen counter.

At some point during the night she had apparently written down the words to her spontaneous song, and even more apparently, she had written them down on the right-hand margin of the drawing to which she had been singing. In bold charcoal letters she saw:

Im old Im fat Im white
You think my ass too tight;
Im fat Im white Im old
Yer brass Yer lead Im gold
Im white Im old Im fat
That's that
Get over it.

There were six more verses, each more absurd and meaningless and stupid than the next. They were poorly scanned and the rhymes were either so exact as to be childish or so slanted as to remind one of Babel. There was even an offensive refrain:

Ima mean mutherfucka,
mean mutherfucka,
mean mutherfucka
I don love the world I live in,
don give a damn who listen
piss and moan and pizzen
don give a fuck you be grippen
rippen, bitchen,
Im risen
from the grave.
Fuck you.

What did it mean? She hadn't a clue. Her doggerel was now indelibly a part of her drawing. She had ruined the one sketch on which she had succeeded. She considered not submitting it, taking a zero for the assignment, withdrawing from school and setting her sights on law school and the future. But at the last minute, she thought what the hell, put the heavy paper in its plastic sleeve and set it in her instructor's in-basket with the rest. She'd take her lumps as she'd taken her bruises.

But who would have guessed that her art instructor would have seen her bruises and made the same sympathetic leap that her film professor had, that she would have a boyfriend to whom she'd show her sketch and her fatuous verse, who would think it exactly what his band needed before producing their next album? And who would have guessed that the album would go platinum and that periodically she'd hear her idiocy broadcast for the world to hear—covered, as it was, by the metallic screech and whine of guitars, the crash of drums, her words screamed by thirty-year-olds posing as post-adolescents? Who would have guessed that life is a tale told by Rube Goldberg with a penchant for irony? She was paid a ridiculous sum, which was so large it frightened her into buying the townhouse, and she discovered a shark inside of herself that she hadn't known existed. The sellers were a month away from bankruptcy and foreclosure, and she haggled them to the floor, paid them cash in a ten-day escrow, and got their furniture in the bargain. What was she supposed to feel in the wake of such profit at others' expense? There were nights when she woke up sweating and guilty and afraid that if she blinked it all might disappear.

But then, she was given a contract for first right of refusal for lyrics. *Her job!* Who could have believed it? She had landed in Bizarro World. She bought books on how to write verse, but after two days of reading, she realized she could knock out the kind of crap she needed on half a bottle of wine and a remembrance of irritations past, without any attempt at analysis. She watched people at the mall and churned out six more anger-fueled ditties in three days. The band took four of them, and she cashed the checks immediately. What did it say about her life that she had a talent for something that didn't mean anything or require any real effort? Through a friend of a buddy of an acquaintance, she met Spencer at a bar, where he played some kind of reggae funk fusion, so weed-mellow it induced comas, Spencer who turned out to be a form of penance for her good fortune and as temporary as a relationship could be. He didn't mean anything either, but dogs came when he called, and they seemed happy when they did so.

One night on the telephone, she told her father about her alternative plans—deferring law school, building up her savings and beginning to invest—and his silence confirmed everything that she had feared. He owned a heating and air conditioning company, and he worked long hours in tight, uncomfortable places. He had encouraged her to get a degree in business, so she'd know something practical about how the world worked, or failing that, become a lawyer so she could sue all the bastards who worked the world to their own advantage. He wanted her to have a job where she could have a nice chair, wear nice clothes if she wanted, but now she had gone one step further: she could wear her underwear or nothing at all at three o'clock in the afternoon if the mood was upon her, making money hand over fist in a business that was just an excuse for bad behavior.

• • •

So she ended up with a house, a lover who left, a dog who stayed, and a job she didn't know how to do. She could have gone to law school and into debt to please her father if not herself, but here she was instead, a homeowner with a sparkling credit score, while friends from college made coffee at Starbucks or hustled enchiladas at Chevy's or went to grad school and delayed their entrance into a real life.

An accident, a trick of fate.

Poor little pretend rich girl.

• • •

One night, despite all of her best efforts—the offered biscuits and treats, the murmured blandishments, even scraps of meat from dinner—Betty wouldn't come into the house at bed time. She lay in her position at the back gate, all but hidden in the shadows, even with the porch light on. Jamie called and called from the back door. When she went out into the yard, she heard a low noise, and when she got within three feet of the dog, she realized that the sound was Betty growling, a dark atavistic resonance from the bottom of her throat and the depths of time. Shaken, Jamie went into the house and turned off the lights. Fine. Let her stay outside in the dark.

But an hour later, when she turned the lights back on and stepped onto the apron of the back patio, she heard the growl again. She had assumed that the darkness and solitude would have wrought some kind of change. A chastened dog, one that whimpered and pawed at the door to be allowed inside for the night.

No.

Something had to be wrong.

She called Spencer's number first, but of course her call went straight to voice mail. She called Donetta next, but she was at a party, she couldn't hear anything that Jamie said for the background noise, and the connection was lousy anyway.

So she dialed her father, who lived thirty miles away and hadn't spoken to her ever since she told him that she had deferred her entrance into law school, preferring to write lyrics for some kind of garage band who got lucky. When he answered the phone, she could tell that he had been in bed and asleep.

Dad, I'm sorry, she said. I should have looked at the clock. It's late, but I didn't realize.

It's okay, he mumbled.

He cleared his throat, and she imagined him reassembling himself, one synapse at a time.

What's going on?

It's the dog, Jamie said. She's outside, she won't come in, and whenever I get close to her, she starts growling.

You have a dog?

I have a dog.

Since when?

Does it matter? I've had a dog for a month or two, I guess. Ever since Spencer left.

Spencer left? Who's Spencer?

My boyfriend who's not my boyfriend any more. It's a long story. What am I supposed to do about the dog?

Let her stay outside. It's plenty warm. She won't melt.

I know, but I don't want her barking in the middle of the night.

If she barks, then you let her in.

What if she still won't come in?

Then, that's a problem.

Her father yawned.

Listen, he said. I'll come over. If you don't mind me sleeping on your couch. I'm too old for midnight drives. Where is this place, again?

So she gave him directions and told him that the couch was all his if he wanted it but that she had a second bedroom with a bed and sheets and a pillow; so much had changed since the arrival of her undeserved good fortune and there was a lot he didn't know.

His fifteen-year-old Toyota rocked to a stop in her driveway an hour later and the headlights dimmed. Her father opened the driver's side door, then stepped out and looked around, blinking.

Dad. Thanks for coming. I don't know what to do with her.

Nice place, he said.

Yeah, it's good.

Neighbors?

She looked in the direction of Mrs. Blevins's side.

Quiet, she said.

Good. So, he said, pinching the bridge of his nose, where's this dog of yours?

Backyard.

She led him through the house and onto the patio.

Where is she?

There. She pointed to the hulking outline of the dog, just visible in the darkness.

Oh, he said. Good-sized. She was growling?

Yes.

I don't hear her now. Maybe she's sick, not feeling good, he said. Dogs are like some people. When they feel lousy, they act worse. You can touch them and get your hand bitten for your troubles.

I don't know, Dad.

We may need to take her to a vet in the morning.

That would be like Spencer. To rescue a defective dog as a gift.

You have a chair I can use out here?

What? Sure, I guess.

She had remembered seeing a stack of four lawn chairs hanging on pegs on the wall in the garage, testimony to the former owners' organization, if not their financial abilities. In six months of home ownership, she had never found reason to sit in the backyard under Mrs. Blevins's watchful eye. Ignoring her witness would have required more energy than it was worth. She handed one chair to her father, saying she had no idea whether the straps were any good or not.

This'll do. Go to bed. I'll sit out here for a while. Sometimes, they just need a little company.

You don't have to stay out here by yourself.

It's fine, he said. It might be easier this way.

Dad, she said. Why didn't we ever have one when I was little?

A dog?

She nodded, and her father seemed to flinch.

Your mother wanted one, but I didn't. They're messy, they smell, and if you want to go anywhere, you either have to take them with you or spend a fortune on a kennel. They're just one more thing. Who needs it? Who needs the complication? Your mother thought it would be good for you. You know, the lonely only child. If we'd gotten a dog, would your mother and I still be together? Would you have been happier?

Who needs it? Really, he said. Who needs it?

Apparently, he said, answering his own question, you did. You do.

It wasn't my choice, she said. Maybe my wish. So, this is what I get.

• • •

Her father opened up the chair, sat down, and told her to buzz off. There were some things that didn't require an audience, and this was one of them. From her bedroom window, she could see the half-moon to the south and, below her window, her father stretched out in the lawn chair. He already appeared to be dozing.

She didn't think she was that tired, but she fell asleep almost immediately, sleeping heavily without dreams, without tossing or turning, without consciousness of being asleep, the way she remembered waking from anesthesia when she was fourteen and had had her wisdom teeth removed, all four of which had been impacted. She had wakened then by bolting upright on the gurney, wondering when the surgery would start, only to realize that her face was swollen, her jaw was tight, and her tongue, that thick and unwieldy muscle, tasted like cotton. Now, she woke with a start, looking immediately out the window. The moon had traveled halfway across the sky to the west. Her father was still in the lawn chair, only now there was a dark shape next to him, and Betty's muzzle lay in her father's lap.

When she opened the back door, they both turned toward her, and she nearly laughed, their expressions were so sleepy, so nearly identical.

Hey, sweetheart, her father said. She's fine. What did I tell you? She just needed someone to be with.

Fire

THE FIRE STARTS in the back bedroom upstairs. The bedroom no one ever uses because it is stacked floor to ceiling with forty years of her grandmother's hair magazines. Not to mention the boxes of her grandmother's wigs and falls and extensions. Ancient synthetics, ripe for an explosion. So, while Cheryl Kendell stands on the sidewalk across the street with a blanket around her shoulders in the cool night air, she watches the firemen at their work and thinks of beehive hairdos fighting for their lives. Synthetics contracting in the heat. Slick pages with their fading colors curling at the edges.

Flames lick against the upstairs windows, and Tina, Cheryl's mother, sobs furiously. "Goddamn it, Mom. All your fucking junk." She snuffles into the blanket she dragged from her bed. "Here I swore I'd never swear again, and now look. Jesus, forgive me."

Nana has been dead for two years, but Tina still talks to her on a daily basis, usually in argument. Old grudges, old scores. The undeclared war of family life. Not even salvation can touch the anger she feels, not on this Friday after Thanksgiving when she is already sensitive to irony.

When the fire breaks through the roof, sparks shoot upward into the black early morning sky like the birth of new stars, like the intimation of danger, and despite themselves, they ooh and ah with the rest of the onlookers.

"Our life is going to be different now, Cherry-Pooh." Tina sniffs. "No doubt about it."

Her mother has used the nickname she was awarded as a toddler, not long after Cheryl's father departed for Canada and the judicial refuge from which he never returned. To be called Cherry-Pooh was to be aware of her mother's bravery, her spunk in the face of long odds. Tina has no idea where they are going or what they might do, but she has made up her mind that they will survive.

Cheryl snugs her blanket more tightly around her shoulders. Fog is forming around the street lights, but their house is still a beacon, a warning in the night. "Now what?"

"We'll find a motel somewhere, I guess." She looks brightly into the black sky made blacker by the bonfire of their home. "Whatever the good Lord decides!"

If her mother begins singing "How Firm a Foundation," Cheryl will not be surprised.

Firemen come streaming out of the house, then watch like the rest of the spectators as the roof caves in. They turn their attention and the hoses to the houses on either side. Streams of water arc gaily through the searchlights. They might be standing at the entrance to an amusement park. It might look that cheerful to someone passing by.

"About time," Cheryl hears Mr. Glendenning say. "Who'd want to save that rat trap, anyhow?"

Maggie Anderson, who is a Catholic and therefore not a pure follower of Jesus, what with the Pope and Mary and all that, puts her arm around Tina's shoulder. "You're welcome to stay with me."

Cheryl's mother sniffs again, a prelude to the gush of tears sure to follow. "That is so kind," she says. "So kind. I guess there's goodness in the world after all. And in the most unexpected places."

• • •

I do not invite confidences from students. Not anymore. In this case it was inevitable, however, since Cherry-Pooh was explaining to me why she had missed the last week of class and why she couldn't submit her last paper on time. All of her notes had burned in the fire. Her rough draft. Her books. *Library* books. Goodness gracious, she was in trouble. She didn't even have the luxury of deciding what waterlogged, charred thing could be saved. It was all gone—*poof*—up in smoke, as the saying goes. She had been writing a paper about *Mariette in Ecstasy*, and she would have to start over. Her notes, her mother's out-of-date computer, her backup floppy disks, the book itself—all gone. She should have saved the paper to her webmail, but she hadn't thought of it, and she should have hidden the book from her mother, but she hadn't thought it would be necessary. She should have known. The young woman, a nun practically having an orgasm on the cover—all of that blood and Catholicism. The confusion of sex and spirituality. A book like that could have made the house explode. Her mother had called me twice that semester as it was. They'd read Greene, they'd read Buechner. Now this. Wasn't the stigmata a sign of Satan? All the students were troubled, she said. They'd signed up for the class thinking it would feature real Christian writers such as C. S. Lewis and Tolkien. Peretti, of course, and the Left Behind series. Instead they were getting Catholics and other perversions of the gospel. Buechner was a Presbyterian, I murmured. Peretti was a hack, *Left Behind* was a comic book with suspect theology, and Tolkien was a Catholic, did she know that? I wanted the students to read writers who respected the mysteries of life and possibilities of transcendence. But she was no longer listening. Instead, she said that no daughter of hers should be required to read filth, not at a good Christian school, not when good, decent people such as herself were paying my salary.

Had she read the book? I asked. What precisely was she referring to?

She hadn't read it; she didn't need to read it to know trouble when she saw it. Wasn't I the college chaplain as well as a teacher? Didn't I have some responsibility to protect the souls of my students? What did I think about that?

I didn't think much about much.

Not anymore.

I didn't tell her that, but I probably should have. I wouldn't miss such exchanges with the parents of students, that much was true. And I wouldn't miss knowing what my students and their parents had to tell me.

How much of Cheryl's story about the fire was true, I couldn't tell. Her complexion was fair and dusted with freckles and when she was nervous or anxious, which was often, blood rushed to her throat and along her jaw as though she were bruised, and she was bruised now. She twisted her fingers as though an illustration of the phrase "wringing one's hands."

"Look, Cheryl, I'll give you an Incomplete for the semester. It's no big deal on my end. You take your time, you finish off this last paper before the end of the spring, I'll read it, and then you'll get your grade. I'll still be here. For one more semester, anyway."

She was shaking her head. "Thanks, Taylor," she said, "but I really can't do that."

A creature of the sixties, I had encouraged students to call me by my first name, the propriety of which was just one more thing for me to question.

"There's nothing on your transcript," I said. And then I couldn't help myself: "There's no stigma attached." She looked at me, a blank look on her already troubled face. "Stigma, stigmata. Po-tay-to, po-tah-to," I finished. Lame.

"I'm graduating this month."

"Same difference," I said. "You graduate, you just don't get all the official seals until the paper is done."

"Isn't there something else I can do?" The mottling along her throat had grown like lace, like the filigree of a chain. I thought she was going to start pulling her hair. "I don't want an 'A' or even a 'B'; I don't care about the grade, only the units. I just want it to be done. I don't want it hanging over my head. I try and I try and no matter what I do, there's always something hanging over my head. My mother is crazy. You know that. I can't deal with anything else."

On and on she went. Those who have taught will recognize the signs: the student who just wants class to be over: the bell has rung, vacation beckons, life is waiting to begin.

If this were a piece of fiction, we would end up together, Cheryl and I, two poor sad sacks with our various problems. We would suddenly discover each other, and our physical union would embody the emotional complicity we imagined in each other. But this is not that kind of story.

At least I don't think that it is.

No. Not exactly.

Help me, Jesus.

• • •

Since Tina's ancient Volkswagen burned along with everything else, Cheryl and her mother take the bus when they return to their house. Maggie Anderson watches from her porch as they stand in the middle of what was once their living room. Two days have passed, so the ground has cooled. With the toes of their shoes, they poke at the lumps of char, their life reduced to its essence. There are no more offers of free neighborly shelter. Not since the fire investigator determined the cause to be wiring thirty years out of code. *It was their own fault. Too cheap to get it fixed.* They are now just a mother and daughter without a home of their own. The night of the fire, a woman from the city's social service liaison gave them a coupon for one night at a decent hotel. Still, by the time the fire crews were gone and they had filled out all the paperwork, it was four in the morning. Cheryl and Tina fell into bed by five and by eight o'clock there were vacuum cleaners roaring outside their door. The next night they rented a room for the month at the Lazy 8 on Motel Drive in the sleaziest part of our town, two double beds and a bathroom, a dysfunctional television, and a Gideon's Bible, cheek by jowl with the railroad tracks. At six every morning, they hear the Southern Pacific rumble through the twilight of their dreams. Her mother keeps talking about graduation, what they will do once Cheryl has her credential and her degree. Look for jobs, both of them. A first real job for Cheryl, substitute teaching at the least during the spring. A better job for Tina. She can get out of the hair business for good, leave behind her mother's legacy, maybe train at a travel agency. All these years while Cheryl has been in school—nothing but scrimping and saving and getting by. They've filled out God's own number of scholarship applications. But now, they'll finally have some options. They'll see the value of higher education. They'll get some *return* for all that sacrifice. His will be done. Amen. So, despite the fire and their loss of the house her mother was born in, Tina is as happy as Cheryl has ever seen her. She sees good times around every corner, and she wakes up singing

"Amazing Grace." Even that first night when the police kicked in the door of the drug dealer's place on the second floor.

So how is she to tell her mother that there is still this one last paper to write?

For the burned-out apostate, no less. The chaplain with the murky reputation.

Me.

• • •

Confirmation of what I suspected came a month before the beginning of the fall semester. My family was gone. Molly and Clark and Hannah left at Easter—*how ironic was that?*—and except for a few desultory phone calls with the children, we had little contact. Molly already had taken up with her yoga instructor. Nothing could be worse, and I took some comfort in that. I was working in my office, filling in blanks for the schedule of services—themes, guest speakers, and so on for the fall and spring semesters—when Gloria Albright opened the door and brought the furnace of August inside. As dean of students, Dr. Albright had hired me seven years earlier, in rosier times. Now, the upwardly mobile Dr. Albright was the college president, in charge of a sizable deficit. According to the campus scuttlebutt, the trustees, all of whom were conservative, reactionary men, had appointed her unwillingly. She had only one mandate: bring the college to fiscal respectability or lose her job in the bargain. If she was successful, she made the board look like progressive, forward-thinking men; if she failed, they fired her, and it was just one more proof of the inadequacy of the female. So she had no reason to visit me unless she was making the rounds in search of allies or firing people in person, and somehow, I didn't think that a cabal was on her mind.

She didn't waste time on the niceties.

"Pink slips are going out tomorrow," she said. "The Board approved the list. I thought you should know."

I felt sorry for her. I have felt sorry enough for myself between then and now, but at the time I felt sorry for Gloria Albright as she touched and retouched her helmet of hair and delivered the bad news as though she were a judge announcing a sentence.

"You'll have," she said, "until the end of the spring. You'll have a chance to find other employment."

"A Baptist college without a minister," I said. "Isn't that some kind of error? Something on the order of a college run by a woman?"

She ignored the taunt.

"You can't turn around in this place without running into ministers." She folded her arms across her breasts, picked a piece of lint off the lapel of her blue suit jacket. "Even the biologists have ministers in their midst. You know that. We'll make do for a time."

"Ah. Spiritual life on a rotating basis."

"Something like that. You made the decision easier for them."

"The divorce wasn't my idea," I said, "and let's face it, I'm not the only one who's had marital difficulties."

Her face darkened; Gloria Albright had experienced her own problems in this regard. She and her husband had nearly come to a parting of the ways. Who knows why? Time passes, passions cool, desires change. Her husband was no academic, he was a plumber, or a pipe-fitter, I believe, so they were an interesting match right from the start, and it was no wonder that there was some tension. There were rumors of one of those almost-affairs between herself and a younger temporary instructor in foreign languages. That Gloria Albright and her husband had patched things up at the same time as the end of the instructor's appointment was purely coincidental, I'm sure. There was a time, just after Molly's departure, when I thought she might be casting her eye in my direction. That's probably just male ego talking, however, of the wounded variety, no less.

"It wasn't just the divorce."

"No?"

"No." She looked at me as though she were a coroner, and I was a corpse on the slab. "I never wanted to mention this."

Just before the end of the spring semester, I had taken a week of vacation time. Big mistake. Molly and Clark and Hannah were long gone, I was holed up in my little rathole apartment, and I was bored and restless, but the idea of leaving town never entered my mind. I suppose I thought that if I left, I might miss my family's return. They might come to their senses only to find me gone. I felt so sorry for myself that I drank a pint of bourbon and six airline bottles of gin, and then spent the better part of four hours in the bathroom losing my miseries. *This is fun,* I told myself while leaning over the toilet. *We're on vacation now!* Two hours later, spent and exhausted, while lying curled around the cool stem of the commode, I had my vision: Jesus loved me! The whole cliché in technicolor with the white of the bathroom porcelain as a bonus. You might be surprised to learn that Jesus wasn't wearing the traditional white robe and beard. No, in my vision he was clean-shaven and his head was closely cropped, and for clothes he sported jeans and a T-shirt. Instead of thunder and lightning, we talked about everything and nothing: his preferences in movies, pitchers of the National League, and the dating scene. His particular favorites were *The Princess Bride,* Sandy Koufax, and dinner followed by a walk around the duck pond. I was impressed. So down to earth! Why hadn't we heard this before? Oh, He said, you can tell people and tell people until you're blue in the face, but who listens? That is so right, I said. Just try it sometime, He said. So I did. I hoisted my carcass from the tiled floor, rinsed my face, brushed my teeth, and then stood on the corner of Blackstone and Shaw in front of that group of right-wing fanatics who every Friday night shout their support for war against the rest of the world. Iraq! Syria! North Korea! Iran! Bomb the axis of evil to smithereens. Make the world safe by destroying a third of it. *Father forgive them, for they know not.* Damn fascists. Even in a whisper my voice was as damaged as Louis Armstrong's, and my sermon on love and the consequences of its opposite was seriously compromised, I'm sure. I wanted to tell them that Jesus and his T-shirt asked for better behavior. Respect what you don't know for sure. My eyes were burning with my own convictions while tongues of fire danced above my head. Pentecost had nothing on me! But then a long black car slid to a stop against the curb and Dr. Albright and her French instructor boyfriend got out. What in God's name are you doing? she asked. Her hands were on her hips. Have you completely lost your mind? She held out her cell phone. I'm already receiving calls. I think I said, The price of telling the truth is ever so high, *n'est-ce pas?* And then I winked at the boyfriend, and I may have waggled my finger in front of his nose. *Bad boy,* I might have said. I may have used some other phrases appropriate to the two of them as well. Get in, she said, and together she and Pierre bundled me into the backseat of her Town Car. You can't keep a minister of the gospel from preaching the one true faith, I said. You can, she said, speaking over her shoulder, if said minister wants to keep his job. This is tyranny, I said, and religious persecution. I have First Amendment rights. I have academic freedom. Shut up, she said. *Shutupshutupshutup.* They took me home, pulled me up the creaking stairs, and poured me into bed. And when I woke the next morning, my headache told me that the drinking and the bathroom of the night before were real enough, but I hoped that subsequent events were merely the chaos of dream and alcoholic nightmare. And when Gloria Albright said nothing in the days and weeks afterward, I consoled myself with the thought that it was only that, a dream, nothing more, and for dreams, of course, we are not held responsible.

However, when Dr. Albright faced me in my office that August morning, I knew that such hope was nothing more than an illusion. "Oh," I said, holding my head, for it had begun to ache, much as it had two months earlier. "Good Lord, I'm mortified. Did I really call you the whore of Babylon? I seem to recall that h ppening."

"I hate to do this, Taylor. I like you, but you were out of control for a while. Preaching to the multitudes. It's understandable, the way you were acting, but you can't say you didn't see it coming."

It was a freight train, and I'd been lying on the tracks, waiting and waiting for the blow yet to come.

"No, you're right," I said. "The writing was on the wall, even if I couldn't make out the words exactly. A Baptist minister giving a sermon on the street corner—what was I thinking? I mean Baptist ministers preach on street corners all the time, but they usually don't do so with Jack Daniels on their breath."

"I think you'll be happier doing something else," she said. "Don't you?"

As though there was something else for a failed minister, slash teacher. "I managed to screw up two jobs in one," I said. "What's left?"

"You could always try your hand at insurance," she said, "or real estate. It's a boom market. Look at the interest rates. You're not so old you couldn't switch gears. Maybe you should go back to school."

So now here I was, at the end of the fall semester, with my one class filled with bitter students and sour, suspicious parents and an administration only too willing to see me go. Was it any wonder that when I opened my newspaper, I turned first to the classifieds to read about my future?

• • •

Two weeks after the fire, Cheryl wakes late. Her mother is gone. Amid the falls and permanents and gossip, Tina is about her mother's business. Unwilling though she may be. There are customers whose grooming needs must be met; there are bills that must be paid. Fire or no fire. Cheryl rolls over and looks at the arthritic alarm clock on the end table. Eight-fifteen. By the time she showers and dresses, and then catches the bus to campus it will be nine-thirty at least. Just enough time to reach her ten o'clock seminar. But why? She has no paper to turn in, in all likelihood she never will have a paper to turn in, and Reverend Tyler—Taylor—is a pain in the ass. The Reverend Taylor Tyler. "A pain in the ass." She shouldn't say it, but there it is. The words make her giggle. To hear them from her own mouth. She lies back against her pillow, listening for those noises on the other side of the door. The *glug-glug, cough!* of a motorcycle trying, but unable to turn over. The hoarse expletive of its rider, and the too-bright, too-brassy laughter of a woman too many years past her prime. Why are they up so early? Or are they just now leaving a party that has lasted all night? Their voices are a doorway to a life not recognized by her mother. What must it be like to straddle the seat of a motorcycle, to ride with her face pressed against someone's back, her arms around his waist? To wear leather, to taste the wind and her own mortality? She hates her own timidity. What else has she never known, protected as she has been by her fearful, unhappy mother? What else has she yet to discover?

Her father, unlike the draft resisters of a decade earlier, left her mother and her two-year-old self for criminal rather than ideological reasons. He used the wilds of Canada as a fresh start against drug charges and his own demons, and he found salvation among a community of New Agers and the language of addiction therapy. He has written Cheryl and her mother on numerous occasions, urging them to join him in the new world of British Columbia, but they never have, not even in the context of a vacation. And this is what she thinks: ever since her father's departure, her mother has retreated farther and farther into her own brand of fundamental Christianity as a charm against fresh misfortune. Her vicarious brush with the illegal has left her shaken, fearful of risk and afraid of the body with its appetites and cravings, its ability to overwhelm reason and good sense. This is her legacy for Cheryl. And from Tina's standpoint, it has worked, hasn't it? Until the night of the fire, they have known a relatively peaceful life, although that peace has been somewhat hand-to-mouth in the financial sense. But even in that regard, their poverty, there is an affirmation of God's plan and His blessing of the poor. She clings to her beliefs with the tenacity of a Huguenot.

So, when Cheryl can hear the sounds of a shower and a man singing "I Could Have Danced All Night" in a voice so off-key as to defy song, she listens as though she's hearing another language. She knows that the man next door is a divorced liquor salesman in his sixties. Why should he be singing one of Audrey Hepburn's songs from My Fair Lady? And the drug dealer in the room upstairs, out on bail and no more chastened than the day before his latest bust, must have a guest, because the two of them have just commenced a vigorous session of morning lovemaking, and the rhythm of their exertions, the vibration of windows and walls and ceiling, is as fascinating as it is repulsive. In another hour she will no doubt smell the smoke of burning cannabis as it drifts through the opened windows.

Is there anyone more mystified by the ways of the world—and of her own body—than she?

"Mom," she says to the air above her head, "you are a pain in the ass."

• • •

Let me tell you about the place where I used to live. It was nothing fancy, a tract house, one of five repeating models. If you drove down the street where I used to live, you'd swear it was Stepford. I could have told you where every bathroom was located, and in the winter when the trees were bare, every roof ridge was identical. But I loved it there. We had a patio, and on summer nights, when the heat lingered past sunset, I barbecued, sending up my own column of smoke to join with the rest of my fire-loving tribe. My children had their own rooms, and my wife had her way with the house as a whole, but the room above the garage was mine. The windows looked east, toward the purple razor of the Sierra, and before the houses were built on the other side of the street, before the trees grew up and obstructed the remainder of the view, I could watch the sun free itself from the mountains every morning. Then the neighborhood changed, and our family changed, and none of us lived there anymore.

In the divorce, Molly took the house, thinking to keep it, but then out of the blue, she sold it, and she and Hannah and Clark moved to New Mexico, and I suppose they're happy enough in the land of enchantment with Molly's pottery classes and Sufi dancing and her displaced yoga trainer from the Bronx, and although the schools are nothing special, the kids are happy and soon enough they'll be on their own.

And this is where I landed: a one-bedroom efficiency on the third-floor of an older building. My room was jammed under the eaves and the ceiling was filled with the odd corners and cutouts of its dormer windows. Duct work had been wedged between the ceiling and the walls, late efforts at air conditioning. At least once a week, I stood up or turned around only to whack myself in the head. I'm not tall, but the ceiling with its many impediments was that short, and although I am hardly old, I was beginning to walk with a permanent stoop.

But the college was across the street, and while I drank my morning coffee, I could watch the parking lot as it swelled with more cars than slots, one of the many frustrations of a sheltered private education on a budget.

I wasn't going to be there much longer, and I suppose I was savoring that sense of belonging while I still had it. Seven years—hard to believe that I had lasted that long. Molly had seen the writing on the wall even if I couldn't, and she and the kids had taken off before the end had come. Lucky them. Ten years ago, I was doing church work and listening for the voice of God in those dreamy moments before sleep. I was happy enough even though the collection plate was never full, and Sunday after Sunday I listened to complaints about whose husband was cheating with whose wife, why Mr. X didn't appreciate the music the previous Sunday and why Mrs. Y didn't approve of Molly's dress or the way we were raising our children. The money in the collection plate was never enough in those days when Clark needed braces or when Hannah wanted clarinet lessons. The money in the collection plate was never enough when our twelve-year-old Toyota needed to be replaced. Did I mention that the money in the collection plate was never enough? So when the chaplain's position became available at the college and when

Dr. Albright offered me the job, I grabbed it as I would have a life preserver, and we settled into the academic life and our tract house. I taught one class each semester and listened to the children of the middle class complain about their parents. I conducted services every Sunday for an entire campus of believers, but the chairs in the chapel were rarely filled. The paychecks were better and more regular than those offered by a small congregation, and I thought our troubles were over, that Jesus had heard our prayers. Maybe He had. And maybe I just didn't like the answers. And maybe I needed to be prepared to listen—to Jesus with his buzz cut and T-shirt and His talk of inconsequential things.

I know what you're thinking: as epiphanies go, mine was pretty weak, the product of midlife and alcohol poisoning, and you'd be right.

Still, we cling to what we have.

• • •

She has only the vaguest notion of what she might do, what she might say, but if she thinks too specifically about what she's planning, she will know her stupidity for what it is. There's every rational reason why it's the wrong thing. But if she doesn't think, if she lets nature take its course, then what is meant to happen will happen. *Stay loose*, she thinks. Be in the moment. Don't become your mother, don't worry everything to death. She selects the sheer cranberry blouse that her mother won't let her wear and her tightest jeans, so often washed they are more white than blue. Bone white. In all of the turmoil of the past weeks, she has lost five pounds, and her clothes feel *good*, as though they have been made specifically for her, so there is something to be said for the positive effects of catastrophe. Her blouse with its spark of color gladdens her, even as the gauzy, see-through material annoys her mother. Her hair, well, her hair is another story; it's a mess, it needs to be trimmed and layered, some highlights wouldn't hurt, but there's nothing to be done at this very moment except pin it back and hope for the best. Her mother may be a hair stylist, but her mother's daughter's hair is a disaster, her worst feature. Isn't that just the way life is?

She closes the door to their motel room with the sense that something big, something momentous, is on the verge of happening, but at the bus stop she only regrets not wearing her coat. The December sky is clear, the morning fog has burned off, but the sun is all light and no heat. And even after she steps aboard the bus, she continues shivering. This is what vanity will do, she thinks, and the words echo her mother's voice. Vanity and superstition. She is hardly vain, she has never had money enough for clothes to be truly vain, since she has always had to make do with discount store discoveries: last year's tops and skirts, secondhand jeans, resoled and serviceable shoes. In her mother's mind, their poverty is a guard against the larger sins. Still, her coat *is* terrible, a threadbare canvas thing with cuffs that are frayed and dark from use; wearing it would give away her disguise. The sophisticated college student would be revealed for what she truly is: a penniless drab just this side of welfare.

Across the aisle in the seat opposite hers, is a man fallen asleep with his head against the window. His mouth is open, but for some reason she has the uncomfortable sensation that he is only pretending to be asleep, and that as soon as she turns away, his eyes will open to slits, so he might watch her every move. Such self-induced panic nearly threatens to dislodge that sense of imminence that rests near her stomach, and she lurches off the bus one stop earlier than she intended. Why does she do this to herself?

A cold wind has begun to blow, and so accustomed is she to hauling twenty or thirty pounds of books in a backpack that she tries to duck under it. Since the fire, though, she has neither books nor backpack, and bending over makes her feel as though she's someone's bad idea of Marcel Marceau. Look who's pretending to be a student! Whatever good feeling she had located below her heart has burned away and has left only a knot inside her stomach. Queasy and yet not quite entirely sick.

She's ten minutes late for class, but when she arrives there's no one in the room, and when she looks again at the door, she finds, in the middle of other announcements, a note that Reverend Tyler is not holding class today. The last class of the semester, and he's gone fishing. Another note is likewise tacked to his office door in the chapel. Now what? She can slide a message under his door, or she can call or e-mail. But that's not the reason why she came. Earlier in the morning she thought that if she could just face him, make him understand the singularity of her predicament, her unique problem, if he would just *look* at her in her best set of clothes, he might make an exception in her case, let her pass the class without that final paper. But now it seems as though her confrontation is not to take place after all.

Shit.

In the chapel office, Victoria, a student aide that Cheryl knows, is typing the program for this Sunday's service. Hymns, readings. The sermon topic. She's wearing a headset and typing from habit and the chaplain's dictation.

"So, what's up with Taylor?"

Victoria looks up, her eyes a blank from listening to the voice in her ears. She stops the cassette player and pulls the headset away

"What?"

"Have you seen Taylor? I need to talk to him."

"He's probably at home."

She inclines her head toward the other side of the road facing campus, then writes down an address.

"His apartment?"

"He won't care. He's lonely. Just knock on the door."

Cheryl thanks the girl, then walks past the administration building and across the street. All this walking. She's still cold, and now there's a heaviness deep in her guts as well. A hint that she might be getting sick. A cup of tomato soup sounds heavenly.

Taylor's building is one of those grand old houses that has been diced up into cubbyholes, terrible little apartments, and of course, with her luck, his apartment is on the top floor, and with every step she takes, she can feel a pull in her lower abdomen as though extra weight has been attached to her abdominal wall with thumbtacks.

At the top of the third-floor landing, she knocks on the chaplain's door. No answer. She knocks again, but now the pain in her abdomen is announcing itself much more insistently: *this is the body*. The thumbtacks have become nails and knives, and whatever pleasure she took in herself earlier this morning is most definitely gone.

"Taylor," she calls. "Taylor. Are you in there?" She knocks one last time. "I need to talk to you about my paper. Are you at home?"

The only sound on the other side of the door is the silence of a held breath. She is no longer able to stand upright, and even her body has begun to form a question mark.

She imagines the chaplain sitting in his apartment, waiting for her to leave. V hy is he hiding from her? she wonders. What does he have against her? Is this what Jesus does to those who take too much pleasure from their own bodies? And why is a school chaplain named for two dead and mediocre presidents?

And that's when she passes out.

• • •

I canceled the last class of the semester. I hadn't planned on it, but when I arrived on campus, there was an envelope in my mailbox with the briefest of notes. From Molly. She was getting remarried in January. I shouldn't have been surprised. Our divorce had gone through without a hitch, as though even bureaucracy agreed that we were no longer meant to be a match. But opening her letter knocked me to my knees, and I said "Oh, shit. Oh, God," loud enough to alert the angels, and it was my good fortune that none of my self-righteous colleagues was in the mail room just then to witness my discomfort.

So, without a word of warning or explanation, I posted an announcement on my classroom door ("No class today; turn in your final papers to my office by Monday at 9:00 am") and then a companion note on my office door before I lurched off campus to the coffee house two doors from my building.

"Molly," I kept muttering. "Molly, Molly, Molly. You have done me wrong, and someday you'll realize the depth of your mistakes." Our marriage was over, and I was stunned, but I wonder if I was as tormented as I might have appeared.

So why did Molly leave? No marriage is without complication, and ours was no exception. The easy answer is that we just ran out of gas. We woke up one morning, looked at each other in the full light of day, and realized that enough was enough. You know how you can look at something—a picture, a word, your lover's eyes—and if you look too hard it no longer makes sense? After sixteen years, two children, and four debt reconsolidations we knew each other so well that we didn't know each other at all.

The more complicated answer is that we both lost our faith, but we lost it in different ways. Molly lost her faith in Jesus and she lost her faith in me. She was jaded, all right, and she knew too much. *I am so goddamned tired*, she said. *I am sick to death of all these pious, goody two-shoes Baptists whose eyes are like knives and hearts are like flint.* She was sick of it, and on Sunday mornings when I stepped down from the pulpit fresh from the delivery of my sermon, I could tell that she was sick of me. *Superstition and make-believe*, she said, *fairy tales for fearful adults. And I suppose all the Buddhists and Muslims, Hindus and Jews are dead wrong?*

Who was I to argue? *Pay no attention to that man behind the curtain.* For by that time, I had traded my spot at the church house door for my office on the sunny side of the college chapel. I felt fraudulent either way, but what was I supposed to do—become a travel agent in the middle of my life? *Use whatever name you want*, I said to Molly, *we're all just trying to make our way through the complexities of life.*

No, she said, *no more phony-baloney. I'm burning my bridges, buddy boy. It's time to be honest with ourselves.*

She could no longer tolerate the rigor of our conventional life and faith while I couldn't conceive of any alternatives.

So I left the house, and then she sold it so she and the kids could discover the Land of Enchantment. Life is what it is, but I had followed all the rules! I can't say I thought very highly of the divine at that moment. Which made it all the more surprising when Jesus paid me a visit while I languished in the bathroom that night of my binge. Did I mention that I called Molly before I took my position on the street corner? Although the hour was late and an hour later for her, she answered the phone on one ring.

"Molly," I said, "we're two lost souls, you and I. Why should we be so unhappy?"

There was a pause on the other end of the line. "Oh, Taylor," she said, "speak for yourself," and then she hung up, so quietly I didn't know right away that she was gone. So, I spoke for myself and Jesus in his T-shirt; is it any wonder I spoke with such passion that night? She had a life, while I only had a headache, and now she had her yoga instructor besides.

Since that night, I had spoken with Molly only once, and that was over something innocuous: the new owners of our house had called with some question about the manufacturer of the living room carpet, a question I couldn't hope to answer. And then her letter came. *Dear Taylor*, it read. *I just thought you should know before you hear it from the kids* . . .

In the coffee house, I ordered two large cups to go, thinking that caffeine might be the spark I needed to get myself back on track. No more Mr. Booze for the minister, I decided. The last thing I needed was an additional headache.

I walked home, a cup in each hand with steam rising from the lids, like twin smokestacks of grief. So, this was the end. Of so many things. The end of my marriage, which until that moment I hadn't believed would finally occur. And then there was my job: although I had one more semester left, I had to take stock of what I might do once the month of June arrived, but at the moment I couldn't think of a thing.

And yet . . .

And yet . . .

Our sky, which during the summer is brown with dust and the heat of trapped exhaust, was deeply blue, scoured by the cold wind gusting from the ocean one hundred miles away. It may have been the first time in months that I had looked at that brilliant blue dome, seen it for what it was, and appreciated it as the threshold of the divine.

I was such an ass.

So, Molly had found a new life, a new love. A new way of looking at the mysteries of our life. The tone of her letter was happy and optimistic, and if there were any darker moments they only came when she worried about how I would take the news.

I was such an ass.

I would have to quit running in place, hoping that the axe would not fall. It had already fallen, and I would have to make some decisions, take some steps. *The first day of the rest of my* . . . etc., etc. What was the worst that could happen?

I walked upstairs with my coffees, and that's when I saw her. In a heap on the landing in front of my door, with her jeans, the inside and backs of her legs, streaked red.

"Cheryl?" I said. I set my coffees down on the floor and shook her by the shoulder. "Can you hear me?"

She blinked her eyes and groaned.

"Come on," I said, "I'll make you some tea. Or coffee. I bought extra. I thought I needed two, but I guess I was buying it for you and just didn't know it."

"You weren't in class," she said finally. "I looked for you."

"I'm playing hooky today," I said. "Call it an early vacation."

"You teachers. My mother thinks you're all lazy as sin."

"It's a wonderful life," I said, "if you can get it." And I was reminded all over again that it wouldn't be mine much longer.

"Oh, god," she said, sitting up. "I feel awful." She looked down at herself, and her face and throat began their familiar flush. "And totally stupid."

"I have some sweatpants you can borrow," I said. "They're too big, of course, but you're welcome to them. I thought I was going to start working out, but you know how it goes. They've never left the drawer. So much for good intentions."

"Oh, god." She grimaced and rolled into a ball on the floor. And then she began to laugh and hiccough and cry. One right after the other. "Can you believe it?" she said. "My mother believes the stigmata is the mark of Satan. What would she think of me?"

• • •

This is not the story I had intended to write. I thought I would tell you about how I left the ministry—parish as well as educational—about how I tried my hand at several things in the aftermath. Real estate for a time, until it became clear that I was completely unsuited for the work, even if it was a boom market—every house seemed perfect to me, and I couldn't help feeling hurt when buyers didn't see the same potential as I did. I made more money than I was used to, but it seemed like a bitter way to live. And then landscaping, but I couldn't stand to cut things as short as most customers wanted. Grass must be sculpted into putting greens, bushes must be tidy, and hedges must be boxed. What's the point of Nature in your front yard if you're only going to chop it down, trim it into unnatural shapes, clip it so it's near death? That seems like an unnecessary need for control, if you ask me. I sold my equipment the day that Dr. Albright called me. It was the end of that next academic year. Finances at the college had been restored—an alum had died, and he had been most generous in his will; who says the deus ex machina ending is dead?—and Dr. Albright was generally hailed as the school's savior since her powers of persuasion were responsible for such beneficence. She was calling, she said, to offer me a job.

"It's nothing great," she said, "but I need a coordinator for Student Activities. You'll have to put up with ping-pong tournaments and movie nights, car shows and fashion shows and software exhibits. Not to mention the annual mission boards fair."

"When do I start?" I said, for the past year had been like a year of waiting in the desert. "Normally I don't take charity, but this time I'll make an exception."

There was a moment of silence between us before she said, "I don't know what you did for the Kendell girl, but her mother has been calling all year, demanding you be rehired. This after wanting you fired. What are the odds?"

"Go figure," I said. "I don't have a clue."

"Well, whatever it is, can I tell her you're back in the fold?"

"Be my guest."

The morning that I found Cheryl in a heap on my floor, I tried to help her to her feet, but the moment I let go, she slumped back down.

"Whoa," she said. "A little too soon."

"Maybe you should sit here."

"Yes, maybe I should sit here."

"And maybe I should call a doctor."

"Don't be ridiculous." She shook her head. "Look, I think if I could just lie down for a while. I'll be fine."

"I don't know about that," I said, but I put her arm across my shoulders and picked her up; Cheryl wasn't very heavy, but I wasn't too steady either, I have to admit, and I nearly dropped her when I opened the door.

"You can lie down for a little while," I said, "but after you wake up, I'm driving you home."

"Fine," she mumbled against my shoulder, and then I spread her across my unmade bed because I'd left my place in something of a shambles that morning. Newspapers on the floor, dishes in the sink, sheets and blankets in a jumble. I picked up as best I could while she snored. I found my sweatpants and laid them next to her feet. She was a mess. Molly was getting married, and my kids were a thousand miles away. And I was soon to be unemployed. But then I have mentioned all of that previously, haven't I? I didn't know then that Cheryl wouldn't wake up until three hours later—a little groggy, but feeling some better, only a little light-headed—and she would change into my sweatpants and a sweatshirt while my back was turned. I didn't know then the reception her mother would give me when I delivered her daughter back to the parking lot in front of their motel room, for she was at least semi-crazy if not a full-blown lunatic.

"Oh, my god," Tina cried. She had been looking out their window when we pulled up, and she came charging out, looking back and forth from me to her daughter as though we were a mystery that needed to be solved. "My baby, where have you been?"

"Oh, Mom," Cheryl said, "don't go ballistic. You knew I'd be at school."

"But—"

Cheryl stopped her mother before she could get going again: "I had the worst cramps of my life, and Pastor Tyler brought me home. Look at me," she said, "I'm a wreck." And she held out her jeans which looked like evidence in a criminal proceeding. Which was when I tried to excuse myself, but her mother grabbed my arm and wouldn't let me go, this woman my own age, who was only trying to keep her world in some kind of order.

"I've been so awful," her mother said, beginning to weep. "I've been so awful."

I didn't know then that her mother would believe (and no argument to the contrary would convince her otherwise) that my pink slip was somehow related to her earlier complaints about my class, and that she would see my situation as one particular mission in her life. Getting me rehired might not get her to heaven, but in her mind at least, it would keep the divine scales of justice evenly balanced.

I didn't know all of that then, but this is what I did know while I washed my cereal bowl and watched the blanket covering Cheryl rise and fall: I knew that I'd give Cheryl her "C" and exchange academic integrity for compassion. I mean, what does it really matter in the long run, one paper more or less? We all wanted to be through. Done and done.

Through the dormer window above the sink, I could see the sun beginning its early December descent, a smooth flat disk, a lens into the future. Throughout the morning, while the wind whipped dry leaves along the sidewalks and gutters, it had shined weakly in the pure blue sky without offering much in the way of heat. But, soon enough, summer would come, and with it the one-hundred-degree temperatures our community is known for. We would dash from air-conditioned home to air-conditioned car to air-conditioned office, and still we would sweat. We would bank our blinds against its rays. We would think of reasons to stay indoors. We would curse the fire of its zealous and jealous life.

Next Day

SOME MORNINGS, Zay wakes up to the unblinking sunlight of a California dawn, uncertain as to where she is. The bedclothes, the dust on the dresser, the nightstand with the clock radio, the lamp, and the box of tissues with the next available tissue too precisely held up for view are made strange by virtue of their clarity. Twenty-five, no, nearly thirty years have passed—*is it possible?*—yet her vision is still n easured by their underground apartment in Portland and its narrow sidewalk-level window: rain-streaked, blurred by water and footsteps, as soft-focused as memory. So much time, so little time. How can she be the same person?

How can she not?

Her husband, an oral surgeon who leaves early for his daily regimen of root canals, extractions, and jaw realignments, is gone. He, who has not gained a pound in thirty years, backs his BMW out of their garage promptly each morning at six. Their daughters live in other states with their jobs and their lovers, and their son, who leaves for college in a month, has chosen to sleep until the time of his departure. She faces her dislocation alone. Usually this sense of foreignness lasts a moment only, the time it takes for her to turn on the radio and hear some announcer gabbling the news, but this morning, instead of the constancy of their unchanging weather or the slide in tech stocks, there are too many voices, events that she cannot comprehend, and when, after selecting another station, she hears "Dome epais," the duet from *Lakmé*, her equilibrium is sent reeling: the mattress tips, and the world seems to have turned upside down. But it is not until after she has run the laundry and vacuumed the living room and finds herself standing in front of her son's room, her knuckles to the painted wood of his door, the only waking human creature in a house with six bedrooms, that the mooring of clock and calendar threatens to come undone.

• • •

It was another time, another state, another door, another life:

"Mrs. Perls," Zay called from the hallway, "is everything all right?" She knocked on the older woman's door, softly at first, then more loudly, until she was using the side of her hand rather than the knuckles. As though she were the police, she thought, the goon squad. The pigs, as Richard would call them, in that pugnacious way he had of trying so hard to be up-to-date, a short man, a young man older than his age whose impulses were fiery but five years too late. A quality as endearing as it was embarrassing.

She tried again: "Mrs. Perls, can you hear me?"

No response. Except from down the hall, where she felt—rather than heard—a door open quietly, then just as quietly close again. Mrs. Dolby no doubt, the hallway gossip, blabbermouth, and scold, who could silence any conversation by her mere presence. Once she got going, it was impossible to escape. Zay turned back to the door. "Was it you I heard, Mrs. Perls?" She turned the knob; the door was unlocked and opened easily, too easily, and Zay took one uneasy step inside, shivering, pulling her caftan more tightly around herself as a gust of damp, freezing air spilled into the hallway. "Mrs. Perls? It's me, Zay, your neighbor. You know, number one-oh-six."

For the past three months, she and Richard had lived across the hallway from Mrs. Perls. As manager of the building, she lived in the largest apartment—two full rooms plus a bathroom, with a window overlooking the traffic on Front Avenue. Other than her infrequent forays down the hall to the bathroom, Mrs. Perls kept to herself. Each week when Zay paid their rent, the older woman, opening the door only as wide as the safety chain allowed, took the check with fingers that bore more resemblance to the talons of some sort of exotic bird; Zay would catch a glimpse of long, lacquered nails, hear the sandpaper of the old woman's harsh voice, and then the whiff of a body long unbathed, that odor competing with a gust of some pungent, expensive lotion—Youth Dew, she thought, too strong even for Chanel—before the door was shut in her face, punctuated by the sound of at least three, maybe four, locks latching, bolting, hooking shut again.

Although she had occasionally thought that they might have some things in common, she had never harbored the illusion that she and Mrs. Perls would become great friends. They would, for instance, never drop in on each other for a cup of coffee and a few minutes of gossip. Nothing like her mother and her mother's canasta cronies. The women who traded romance novels with each other, their true currency. Zay had never supposed that she and Richard would have stayed here this long in the first place either, and nothing could have prepared her for her first full look at the interior of Mrs. Perls's apartment. One entire wall of the living room was dominated by a rack of glass shelves which were lined with Styrofoam heads adorned by wigs in various styles and shades of red. The other wall was covered by signed and framed celebrity photographs. Bob Hope. Fred

Astaire. The center of the wall was dominated by six different photographs of Frank Sinatra. A kind of shrine. Unreal. Icons of her parents' generation, each with his arm around a smiling, more youthful, black-and-white incarnation of Mrs. Perls. Something of a compensation. That a woman like Mrs. Perls could have had her moment once upon a time, no matter what she looked like now.

Various stories circulated about the manager, and Mrs. Dolby was happy to share them: Mrs. Perls had been a Vegas showgirl in the forties. She'd been a gun moll in the Chicago mafia. She had run a speakeasy. A brothel. She had entertained President Kennedy. What difference did it make? She was living in the Hill Villa now, along with the rest of the pensioners and ne'er-do-wells.

A record was turning on the box phonograph, the needle scraping against the label. Old Blue Eyes singing Christmas tunes. In February. Jesus. Enough is enough. Zay lifted the arm and set it on the cradle.

"Mrs. Perls?" she called again. "I'm not trying to pry, but I was in the hall-way, and I thought I heard a noise."

Signs of recent habitation were spread like a trail of bread crumbs. A dirty bowl and spoon stood on the drain board while the faucet dripped into an un-washed saucepan. The smell of oatmeal.

"Mrs. Perls?"

She pushed past the batik curtain which hung in the doorway between the liv-ing room and bedroom. The window was wide open, and sleet drummed the bu-reau beneath it upon which several porcelain figurines had been posed. A ballerina en pointe. A hunter and his retriever. A girl staring into a mirror. Precious German kitsch. All coated with a layer of ice. Down on Front Avenue, a bus roared past, nego-tiating the long curve. Steam drifted in its wake. Which was when Zay turned from the window and saw Mrs. Perls, asleep, it seemed, in her bed, except that she was lying on top of the blankets, her housecoat untied, her pillow across her face.

"Oh," Zay said. "Oh, Jesus."

The old woman had flung one arm across her end table, and a ceramic lamp had smashed into pieces on the floor. There was her noise. And next to the white puffy hand, four pill bottles, the lids off and emptied. Codeine, Demerol, mor-phine tablets, Percodan. *Jesus, Jesus.* A smorgasbord of painkillers, a buffet of death. Zay touched the cold hand for a pulse and, after flipping the sides of Mrs. Perls's housecoat across her belly to hide the sagging skin and the patch of grey pubic hair, pulled the pillow away from her face. *The mask of her final moments.* She had not gone easily.

Zay was still holding the pillow when Mrs. Dolby came to the door, a look of silent surprise on her face. A repressed scream.

"She's dead," Zay said. "I took my shower, and I heard a noise, and when I opened the door, there she was."

Mrs. Dolby began to back away. She made a sound in the back of her throat as though she were choking.

"Oh, no, no," Zay said, remembering the pillow still clutched in her hand. "It wasn't like that," she said, her free hand pointing to the night stand as evidence. "It wasn't like that at all. She overdosed. I guess the pillow was . . . I don't know. To keep it dark?"

The older woman stopped her retreat, her curiosity gaining the upper hand, and together they looked at the building manager's body in its last position on the bed: at the mound of her belly beneath the housecoat, at the puckered skin around her jaw, her swollen fingers squeezed by their many rings. The henna-tinted mop of a wig crumpled on the mattress next to her perfectly bald head.

• • •

That fall, when there were gas lines an hour long, and heating oil was at a premium, and the word "Watergate" was just becoming familiar, everything else in her life had fallen apart as well. With Geoffrey deferring to his father's lawyers, Zay and Richard had moved in together, into the apartment house on the edge of downtown. Richard could not stop apologizing about the arrangements—one room on the basement side of the building, a two-burner gas stove behind a stained folding screen, the bathroom down the hall. Until he met Zay, his rented room in the attic of an old house had been suitable for someone so rarely at home.

"It looks like we've hit bottom now," he said. "Literally and figuratively. From the heights to the depths." Doubt had made his baritone unsteady. "I couldn't find anything else, though, not for what we can afford, not so fast. We can move in right now, if you want. We can always look for something else later." He shook his head in resignation while Zay turned a slow, uneasy circle in the center of the room, taking in the radiator hanging from the ceiling, the plaster crumbling around the pipes. The window with its view of a cement retaining wall. The layers of Congoleum that, in their wildly different colors and patterns and styles, presented themselves like an archeologist's dream.

Remembering her parents, their descriptions of early travails, Zay had endeavored a tone of cheerfulness, good humor; she said that an apartment like this would be a memory in the making, something that in twenty years they would remember with fondness. They were starting out together, after all, and a little slice of poverty wouldn't hurt them, not when they'd been through so much already. It could only bring them closer together. She'd had enough of entitlement.

Richard had exhaled loudly, theatrically relieved, as she dumped her bag on the sagging mattress in its unpainted metal frame. But she really wasn't so sure, was she? No. No. *No.* And if she were honest with herself, not even when she declared it a love nest fit for Juliet. She wondered how much of her certainty had been forced upon her by Richard's doubt, her role as the positive one, the more experienced one. The one who—if she were honest with herself—had forced these changes upon them all. After all, she had to admit this as well, for all his faults and insecurities, Geoffrey had never asked her to live like this.

So how could she have said anything different? There was Richard, still wearing his lab coat, his uniform as a student in dental school, his shoulders already rounded from bending over molds and X-rays, then bending over the mouths of charity patients who, according to Richard, never bathed, much less brushed or flossed. Even in those days when they were first together, guilty and determined and deliberately oblivious to the consequences they had already set in motion, his first act after coming back to his attic in the evening—before a kiss, before a hi-how-was-your-day—was to wash his face and hands with an antibacterial soap, never mind that he had done that before leaving school; he needed to put enough distance between the poverty of his own bad teeth and those whose mouths with their decay and neglect were symbolic of deeper disorders. His stuffiness and rigidity about such matters worried her. So different from what she had first imagined, and how different from their first rush toward one another! At Zay's urging he had grown a beard, but its sparse, erratic growth only made him look younger rather than more tolerant, a yeshiva student, perhaps, or a boy playing with a Halloween disguise. She would have ruffled his hair, if she weren't warned by his look of seriousness. Of purpose. And before she could make any such mistake, there was a knock on the door: *their door,* she had realized with a start.

"So, you kids want the place or not?"

"We'll move in today if that's all right." Richard held up the key. "We can get a second copy, can't we?"

At the entrance of the manager, Zay had turned away as though to inspect the refrigerator with its tiny freezer choked by frost, the pool of brown liquid in the bin labeled "meat"; her first glimpse of Mrs. Perls had been little more than a head of flaming red hair and a cigarette dangling between those elaborate nails.

"Sure. Any hardware store. I got a passkey, but I don't keep duplicates, so if you lose it, you lose it. Don't come to me crying."

Richard put the key in his pocket and ushered Mrs. Perls back into the hallway, offering his assurance of their fitness as tenants. The murmur of their voices reached Zay from far away, as waves heard from a cottage of childhood. It had been her mother's precept that life was lived in the main by people who slept through most of it, and it suddenly struck her that this was indeed a waking moment: I live here, she had thought, in this place, with my lover. I have thrown away my marriage for a basement apartment. And our landlady is an old harridan with a call girl's nails and the smeared lipstick of a floozy.

Her mother was right. One day you wake up and think, how in the world did I get here?

"Harridan," she had said, savoring the word. She sat down at the table underneath the narrow set of ground-level windows, examining in the half-light her own nails which, during periods of turmoil, she had never been able to refrain from biting. Footsteps echoed just above her head. A pair of jeans and work boots, someone wrestling the garbage cans out of the alley. A waterfall of bottles cascaded into the city truck idling in the street in front of the building. Footsteps again, the cymbals' crash of empty cans. The roar of the truck backing up, retreating from the end of their dead-end street. Richard opening their door sheepishly. Like a husband.

"Honey," he had said, "I'm home."

• • •

The police stayed in Mrs. Perls's apartment for two hours or more, taking pictures and measurements, even after the ambulance arrived, sliding on the steep, icy streets. Mrs. Perls left the building in a body bag, her exit aided by two city employees who guided the gurney up the stairs to the entrance of the building, after which two police officers—a uniformed woman and an older man in plainclothes—sealed off the doorway with yellow tape. Withdrawing a spiral notepad from his overcoat, the older detective, gray-haired and gray-faced, signaled Mrs. Dolby to follow him down the hall, while the woman turned to face Zay.

"You live here?" She was one of those women who carries her weight above narrow hips and long, thin legs; a barrel chest and enormous bosom were further inflated by the bulky police jacket, putting Zay in mind of the Michelin tire advertisements. The policewoman, the recipient of a badly timed permanent, signs of which were still evident in the burn mark just below her hairline, folded her arms across her ample chest. "Across the hallway, I mean, from the deceased?"

"Yes."

"Officer Perry." The woman held out her badge, a gesture undermined by the small, square hand behind the badge, a hand surprisingly small and shapely. A recent manicure. "Mind if I come in, ask a few questions?"

"I have to go to work. I'm already an hour late."

"I'll just be a sec. I'll give you my card. Your boss can call me if need be."

Zay let the policewoman precede her into the apartment.

"I'll need your name," the policewoman said. "You know, as a witness."

So then she had to go through the whole story, that in a moment of whimsy, her mother had named her for a breeze. But Zephyr was not a name that anyone was liable to say and Z. sounded too cold, too much like unconsciousness or sleep. So Zay it was. At different points in her life, she had nearly changed her name just as she had recently changed her life. If the right impulse were to present itself she might yet become Linda, perhaps, or Gale—*another breeze!*—or Charlotte or Della or Yvonne. Heavens. But she had to admit that she felt more like Zay than any of these others, and Zay she was likely to stay.

"Interesting," the policewoman said, although it was clear she wasn't. "Are you married?"

So then she had to explain her separation. The divorce that was imminent. One more personal question and she would be inviting Officer Perry to dinner.

"You were the first one to find the body."

"She was lying in bed. I didn't touch her, though. I just moved the pillow. It was on top of her face." Zay stepped behind the folding screen with the clothes she had laid out on the bed what seemed like an eternity before. "I'm making some tea. Would you like some?"

"No, I'm fine, thanks. So, how did you happen to be in Mrs. Perls's apartment?"

"I was coming down the hall from the shower, and I heard this noise, so I went in." Zay filled the teapot then lit one of the burners. She shrugged into her bra and panties, skirt and blouse while waiting for the water to boil. "I can't even tell you what the noise was for sure. The lamp, I guess. When I tried the door, it was open, which was strange, because it was always locked. There must be half a dozen locks on the door, in case you haven't noticed. So, then I found her on the bed, Mrs. Dolby must have heard me, and that's when we called. I called. End of story."

"About that cup of tea. Maybe I'll change my mind. If that's okay with you."

"Sure." Zay pushed the screen together and set it to one side. "Will you call my boss?"

"I'll call your boss. Give me the name and number, I'll call your boss from the squad car. I'll turn the siren on if she doesn't believe me."

Officer Perry scratched her head with the top of her pen. "Let me tell you, never let your sister-in-law experiment with your hair. But then, you don't look like the type. Go back a bit, will you? What happened during the hour or so before you found Mrs. Perls?"

"No, nothing. I took my shower. The power went off once, right in the middle of washing my hair, and I thought to myself, 'Great, I'll be finishing up in the dark.' The window in the bathroom's been painted over, you see, so it's like a tomb in there when the lights go off, which only happens when it rains, meaning it only goes off like twice a day. But they came back on almost immediately, I got out, went down the hall, and that's when I heard something from Mrs. Perls's apartment."

"That's it?" Officer Perry sounded somewhat disappointed, as though she had expected some previously undisclosed revelation.

"That's it. Sorry."

If the detective really cared to know, she and Richard had been arguing. About stupid stuff. Laundry, breakfast, you name it. Not dish-breaking, insult-hurling argument, but the quiet, snarling, morning-after variety: "So, do you think we might have *underwear* by tonight?" Richard left while Zay was pulling her caftan over her head. One moment he was there, the next moment she was in the darkness of fabric, surrounded by the odor of her own body, when she heard the door close, and she was alone. Younger than she by three years and less experienced in the skirmishes of domestic life, he had discovered escape to be his most effective weapon. She had turned on their garage-sale Philco to the public radio station and listened while the high, unearthly tones of "Dome epais" rose toward her ceiling. A braid of twin spirits. Then, after padding down the dark hallway in her socks and that filthy caftan, she had taken her shower at the end of the hall, in the chipped, claw-foot tub with its patched-together hose and nozzle, the ripped plastic curtain, all the while thinking about the passive-aggressive aspects of Richard's character and how infuriating it was—that his absence could pose as much turmoil as his presence. Especially since she knew the argument was really about her meeting Geoffrey for lunch the day before. He could be so tiresome, so petulant. Over nothing, a lunch. A lunch that had nothing to do with the *marriage* but everything to do with the *divorce*. Which she and Richard had prompted in the first place.

• • •

Three months after their breakup, Zay could not entirely understand that Geoffrey was no longer her husband in anything but the technical sense. When she saw him in the booth at Lubek's, hunched over, smoking a cigarette, his eyes underlined by shadow, she barely resisted the old impulse to put one hand on his cheek, bring his head down to her breast, the old habits pulled so strongly, to mother this boy who was five years her senior, the pattern of their marriage. He had called

Dr. Browning's office, where she worked as receptionist and general factotum, full of his usual woe and remorse. At 11:30, just in time for lunch.

"I wasn't going to call you, but then I called you," was his explanation.

"And here I am, just like always."

"Not quite," he said bringing the shadows under his eyes to bear fully upon her, "not quite like always."

"Why? Are you buying?"

When they had been married, Geoffrey had rarely been awake for lunch or ready with the money to purchase it. A member of an experimental theatrical troop, Geoffrey was rarely home before three in the morning. He insisted that the group—although without a stage, a script, or financial backing and unlikely ever to have any one of the three—was on the verge of a major artistic breakthrough, but Zay believed any breakthrough was likely to be more cathartic for the actors— so self-involved were they—than for any potential audience. There were Lisa's revelations regarding her father's abuse of herself and her two sisters. Or Virgil's confession of his attraction to other men, a confession more shocking to Virgil than it had been to anyone else. On such revelatory occasions, Geoffrey had come home, waking Zay to news that could have waited for a later hour of the morning. Geoffrey's own moments of self-laceration involved his father, that overbearing, over-indulgent patriarch, from whose hand flowed fifty-dollar bills, the source of their marriage's last month's rent. The month before as well, come to think of it. In the wake of the separation, if there was any one person whom Zay was most sorry about disappointing, it was Geoffrey's father, whose reference and connections were responsible for Zay's position as Dr. Browning's receptionist and whose irony at Geoffrey's expense had always come to Zay's credit. She had once written a thank-you note and from that time forward she could do no wrong. The last Zay had heard, the theater group had disbanded—there was, finally, a point after which one could know too much about others—and Geoffrey's father was demanding his thirty-three-year-old son get a job. To be about his father's business.

Richard was another story altogether. The ambitious son of working-class parents without Geoffrey's sense of entitlement. A dental school student in his last year and one of Dr. Browning's patients, he had come to the office with a fever of one hundred and five, sweating and delirious. A staph infection picked up from the clinic and left untreated. She had told him that it was irresponsible, waiting so long to come in. "Who are you, to be talking about irresponsible?" he had said, looking at the red silk blouse she had debated about wearing that morning. A Christmas present from Geoffrey's parents. "I don't have the time to be sick. Much less the *money*."

Dark-haired, dark-eyed, nervously thin, burning with fever and plans. How different he was from Geoffrey's blond, well-fed, indistinct good looks! Even his teeth were wild, snagged and crooked, a walking advertisement for the need of his own services. He leaned into her window and stared down her blouse without bothering to disguise his desire. She imagined his body a kind of humming transmitter, set to a frequency she might receive.

She had looked up his phone number the next morning and, without telling him she was married, invited him for coffee the first day he was feeling better. "I'm feeling better now," he said. "How about this afternoon?"

They both had known why she had called, and they made love that first day in Richard's attic room in Richard's bed with its squealing springs and loose-limbed metal frame. Buttons scattered onto his floor when he tore at her blouse. She bit his shoulder; he pinned her wrists. He was still sweating from fever, his eyes were red-rimmed and bloodshot, and his lovemaking was as furious and angry as it was quickly finished.

"What kind of game is this?" he had said afterwards, grabbing her finger with its wedding band, twisting it so she whimpered. "I don't know why you're here."

And her only response was to be angry as well: "How should I know? Maybe I just wanted a poor boy. Someone to exploit. Someone with lousy teeth."

She had hoped to hurt him while hurting Geoffrey at the same time, but to be truthful to herself, she had known—the moment she had entered Richard's attic—that her life with Geoffrey was over. Geoffrey had stretched her loyalty too far. No matter how Richard responded. She had intended only the momentary encounter, she hadn't counted on anything beyond an afternoon, she hadn't expected Richard's sense of *responsibility*, so novel in her experience with men, his underclass quest for a middle-class life and all its values. Her life thus far had consisted of a series of impulses: she had studied art in college because she had liked the cover of the art history text; she had married Geoffrey because when they first met, the sun had been behind him and the tips of his hair had glowed; and now there was Richard, whose temper and energy and ambition seemed an answer to the lethargy and aimlessness that had grown over her like moss over a rock during the previous three years.

Now, Geoffrey shifted forward in his seat. "I know what you're thinking. You're thinking, 'Here it comes, Geoffrey's going to start begging. *Come back, Zay, oh please, oh please, oh.*' I'm not going to do that. I have a little more pride than that."

"I never thought any such thing," Zay said, though frankly the dread of such a scene had nearly kept her away. Even as it had been the source of some fascination. But, now that it was not to occur, she couldn't help but feel a twinge of disappointment. "Give me a little credit. Give yourself some credit."

"I just wanted to let you know that I'm seeing someone, so as far as a divorce is concerned, I'd just as soon make it a quick one."

What was this?

"Look, right before the group busted up, Anne and I got together. If you want to know the truth, we had a little thing going even before you left. I didn't tell you about it because I was a little embarrassed, and I didn't want you to think I was just trying to one-up you."

Anne Berquist, that little ferret? Who, along with her shrewd, close-set eyes and tiny, pinched face, had the most enormous breasts for a girl so short and sparing otherwise.

"You're not serious."

"Dad's pissed," Geoffrey said. "He's still mad about you leaving. He hates Anne, by the way, no surprise there. Which doesn't make me unhappy either."

He and Anne were planning to get married once she finished her degree. A June wedding. And Geoffrey was interviewing for positions with various companies, all in sales. It was amazing, he said, how many places thought that an actor was exactly the sort of person they needed to push a product. Insurance, real estate, pharmaceuticals, you name it. He had even interviewed with a yacht dealership. *Yachts!* He was excited, there was no getting around it, but he refused to look her in the eye.

"So, I can't be bitter anymore," Geoffrey said. "I don't have it in me. How's your dentist?"

Zay spent the remainder of her lunch hour fighting the sense of being blinded, as if she were sitting by a window in full view of an afternoon sun, so bright that sight was blotted out. What had she done? To all appearances, Geoffrey was happy and no longer in need of her help. He had Anne for that now. He didn't need Zay any longer. That's what he had called to tell her. That this was the outcome of her grand, impulsive passion: to free him for his own. To free him for his life. To give her back a legitimacy she had never wanted. And this was what Richard was so put out about, storming off this morning? This was the worst she could do?

Men could be such idiots.

• • •

Not long after Richard graduated, they moved to the homely heart of California, to the constant light and heat and dust of farmland, leaving the rain and the gloom and their underground apartment for good. Richard had a connection—a friend of a friend of a friend; even among the working class there are such inbred associations—and an established practice was waiting for him. After years of scholarships, he was that rarest of creatures: a dentist without debt. He did not even have to buy his own equipment. Money poured in after their months of thrift. During those first years—despite all her best intentions and Richard's newfound means—she was still homesick for the dark winter of the northwest, but then Mount St. Helens erupted, and it seemed to be a kind of signal to Zay that whatever life she knew in Oregon was over. She was already a mother by then of two girls, but not until the curtain of ash began to rain down on the forests and rivers, not until she watched those televised moments, did she know that something irrevocable had occurred. And not just for those in the immediate vicinity. Even now, so many years later, she asks herself this: if the ice-cream cone of St. Helens were still intact, would she still be here in this artificial land of bird-of-paradise and palm tree, guava and perennial roses? Is this the only life she might have lived; is this the only life she has inhabited? Every time she looks in the mirror, she sees someone she might have known once upon a time: this middle-aged stranger whose hair belongs to her mother. There is a dowdiness she never would have recognized. When did that happen? The answer is certain even as it is less than conclusive, just as beyond her son's bedroom door there is certain to be the sleeping boy in the form of a man, although there is also the possibility that were she to open this door, she would find nothing more than the signature of the male: his escape—an opened window, its curtain flapping outside, caught like a flag in the morning breeze.

• • •

"Mrs. Beringson. Zay." Officer Perry put a hand on Zay's knee and shook it, a form of threat in that gesture for which Zay was unprepared. "I lost you for a moment. Are you sure there wasn't anything else?"

"No. Absolutely nothing. I can't think of a thing."

"Nothing? Nothing about previous encounters with the deceased?"

"I hardly ever saw her. Today was the first time I ever walked through the door. It's crazy."

"Maybe," Officer Perry said, scratching her scalp again, "but maybe it's not any crazier than believing your sister-in-law knows what to do with a Toni. Listen, call me if you think of anything else. I may be in touch with you later. If we have any other questions."

"Of course. But I don't really know anything other than what I told you."

The older woman stood up, straightening her belt over the bulges of her polyester trousers. "Thanks for the tea."

"Don't forget to call my boss, okay?"

Zay moved through the rest of that morning as though paralyzed; her mind was working while her extremities remained numb. After standing in the freezing rain for twenty minutes, she caught the bus for work, and two stops later an enormous woman with three large shopping bags sat next to her. She sat down with a grunt, her shopping bags and a very wet umbrella wedged against Zay's legs. Zay turned her face to the window and listened to the woman breathe until it was time to get off. When she stood to move out into the aisle, the woman barely moved, and Zay was forced to climb over a pair of massive knees and thighs, as though she were scaling a series of damp ledges. At the office, after a stern lecture from Dr. Browning—he had been forced to field his own phone calls, not one of which was from Officer Perry after all—she sat at her receptionist's window, taking names and making appointments with the absent-minded attention of a driver on a stretch of too-familiar highway. By the end of the day, she could not have said what it was that she had done during the day; not one caller's description of pain or symptom, behavior, or reaction could replace the picture she retained of Mrs. Perls's body and her accompanying wig.

That evening, when Richard came home, he carried a paper cone of flowers. Apology for the morning's argument. She cleaned out a jar and cut the stems while he struggled out of his overcoat and lab coat and sorted out the books and assignments jumbled together in his backpack.

"What's with the tape across the hall? It almost looks like a crime scene or something."

She told him the story, going over it again as she had for Officer Perry, about coming out of the shower, her long thick hair wet and turbaned in a towel on top of her head, and then as she came down the hall, hearing something, that thump or bump, a phantom sound. Maybe the headboard against the plaster wall? Then a crash. Then the sight of Mrs. Perls on her bed. The wig next to her. The opened pill bottles. The ceramic shards of the lamp on the floor. Mrs. Dolby accusing her silently of murder.

"Poor Zay, poor baby," Richard said, holding her. "What a lousy, mean-spirited thing. The old biddy."

I'm so sorry. *So sorry.*

She would remember that moment as the sweetest they would ever have. A melting into each other when Richard's insistence during sex was matched by her own energy and resolve. Her own claims. Two equal combatants. Nothing after would ever quite live up to its promise, although she wouldn't notice this for years to come.

In the days to come, Zay *would* notice other changes: the yellow tape across Mrs. Perls's door would slowly droop from the door frame like a badly tied hair ribbon, until one day it simply disappeared and the manager's apartment was occupied by an elderly couple whose energy with paint brushes and cleaning rags, hammer and nails, pipe wrenches and pliers was impossible to ignore.

The cold of that icy, unheated winter would likewise give way to the warm rain of an early spring, and then one day Officer Perry showed up at the door of their apartment. Raindrops were jeweled in the frizz of her still-damaged hair.

"Listen," she said, "I've been meaning to stop by. And it looks like I came in the nick of time."

Zay was standing in the middle of their apartment, surrounded by empty and half-filled boxes. Soon enough, she and Richard would be climbing the stairs to the front door with those same boxes and shoving them inside a small rental van, but now, although their door was open, the police officer blocked the threshold.

"You're moving."

"Yes. To California. My husband—my fiancé, actually—has a job there."

"How nice for you."

"I suppose it is. I've never lived anywhere but here. In Oregon, that is. Not this building."

The police officer laughed. "I meant a husband with a job. That's nice."

Zay, too, was laughing. She couldn't help it; suddenly, it was all so funny. "It is nice, isn't it?"

"I hope he makes a ton of money. And you can lie around all day, eating bonbons and drinking Scotch."

"That does sound like fun," she said, but as though down a long hallway of years, she had a glimpse of herself, waking late to a morning of alien expectation, and fun was not an accurate description. No, not quite. "Well, it would be a change."

Their boxes lay around her, waiting for her attention. Richard's textbooks, her clothes. Objects of optimism and fate.

"I should probably get busy," she said.

"And I won't keep you," the officer said. "I just wanted to let you know that the final ruling was suicide, after all. The old lady had more junk in her system than Hendrix."

What else could it have been?

"Your neighbor didn't do you any favors, you know."

"Mrs. Dolby," Zay said.

"She said she saw you suffocating Mrs. Perls. She said she caught you in the act. You were holding a pillow over her face. She said she saw Mrs. Perls's legs kicking."

"But I told her," Zay said. "The only thing I did with that pillow was to move it. She saw the pill bottles."

"She left a note, you know. That was the clincher."

"I never saw it."

"She was dying anyway, and she knew it. Cancer of something-or-other. There was no point in fighting it, she said. All those pictures on the walls? She wasn't just a fan. She'd had a thing for Sinatra for years, she went to Vegas every chance she got, but he wasn't interested. Like there was a chance. There was one line from the note I remember: 'I'm an old, tired, unhappy woman, and there are others to take my place.' How about that?"

Zay shook her head. Amazing. How could she have missed it? So cold and wet with the window open and the rain blowing in, and she must have been in shock. She couldn't be sure that anything she remembered was the truth. Mrs. Perls's death might have been a story she was telling to herself.

"I can't believe I never saw it," she said finally.

"You remember how she must have pushed the lamp off her end table? The note was in her *other* hand. She was holding it in her fist. The coroner had to pry it from her fingers."

Wasn't that always the way? You look in one direction, but the answer always lies in another.

"But I can't believe Mrs. Dolby would do that. Lie like that."

"People see what they want to see. Anyway, it's over now, and you're in the clear. You and your boyfriend can move to California, and you can put this behind you."

• • •

She has done just that, she has put it behind her, and for nearly thirty years she has been caught in the stew of an ordinary life. Her decisions have never been deliberate, never calculated or weighed in any rational sense, but she has been satisfied with the outcome nonetheless. Everything has turned out all right. It has. *Really.* She will insist upon that to anyone who asks. Babies and diapers, Richard's practice and their secure place with the others of their kind. Richard introduces her to colleagues as his rock, his reason for being, and maybe it is a kind of truth, but Zay better understands the necessity of the lie. They have no great love for one another, not now; after so many years, their marriage has turned into a kind of settling, and they do not often speak of the turmoil that marked their beginnings, preferring the realism of their years together rather than their first romantic gestures, those moments of passion, accusation, and reconciliation. They have turned her impulse into a life.

Since coming to California, they have made three more moves, one every ten years or so, each time into a progressively larger, more distinguished home. Their latest—six bedrooms, two stories, on five hillside acres overlooking a dry river-bed—is so much larger than necessary, especially now that their daughters are gone and their son is nearly so, but they have no plans for contraction or economy in this next decade of life. They have chosen to move forward and forward only and forestall any chance of regret. Which makes it difficult to know why she is being haunted by Mrs. Perls just now, Mrs. Perls with her wigs and her rings and her photographs.

Zay sometimes thinks of her life as a series of layers and layers. Of nothing profound, mind you, just the detritus of life: of soda pop and toothpaste, file folders and paperweights, the mundane objects of the everyday. If someone were to excavate her memory, he would need to make sense of such trash first. Mrs. Perls, on the other hand, is of a different order. Buried years ago under a mound of minor concerns but resurrected for some reason, still able to beckon.

• • •

One o'clock. Her son, wearing boxers and a T-shirt, wanders into the kitchen where Zay, while eating her lunch, is trying to read an article about the East German dissident Vera Wollenberger. After the opening of secret police files, Wollenberger discovered that her own husband had been her most damaging informer. It may be a revelation for historians, this betrayal, but hardly a newsflash for husbands and wives. Zay wonders why anyone should be surprised. Even in the best of circumstances, a marriage is a kind of betrayal, an exchange of an ideal for a reality. Different only in degree. Her son is so sleep-fuddled that he runs into the refrigerator before opening it to peer inside.

"Oh, man," he says. "There's nothing in here to eat."

"There's ham on the bottom shelf, cheese in the bin," Zay says by rote. "Make yourself a sandwich."

The week after her discovery she divorced the man code-named Donald.

"Boring."

"Too bad."

He looks once more into the refrigerator's clutter before letting the door swing shut. "Ah, fuck it," he yawns. He looks at his mother. He looks *through* his mother. As though she were a window. "I'm going back to bed."

"Fine. You do that."

Has she become invisible now, as well?

Did Vera Wollenberger confront her husband, she wonders, or did she move out one night without a word of either accusation or explanation?

I can't really say how I felt, Vera Wollenberger told reporters. *It was such an extreme situation, rather as if one had died for a moment, and then returned to life. The surprising thing was the reports were written as if about a stranger, not about a wife. To him I was an enemy of the state, and he had done everything to fight me—the enemy.*

Enough, enough. Time to go shopping for dinner. She gets her purse, finds her keys, and passing by the closed door of her son's room, taps her fingers to the wood. *Good-bye.*

Her drive is not long. Two miles of sanitized streets and lookalike strip malls. In the supermarket, she retrieves a cart and wheels it through swept aisles of cat food and laundry detergent, pork chops and eggs and heads of lettuce. She will make enchiladas tonight, so she buys tortillas and cheese and chiles and sauce. Black beans and Spanish rice for the sides. This will be nice, she thinks. A California dinner. Richard will be pleased. But for some reason she cannot rid herself of the picture of Mrs. Perls's face, her body on the bed, the wig next to her head. She feels what it must be like to come to the end of things, and she pays for her groceries while shaking her head so violently that the checker must surely think she has some disagreement about the cost of living.

Leaving the parking lot.

Why is she revisiting all this now?

She is fighting it, that's the way it feels, as though she's holding on by her fingers, this slipping out of one life, one time, and into another. Fighting it. She is leaning to the other side of the seat for the phone in the glove compartment. She needs to call Richard, maybe her son. Why? She doesn't know exactly. Maybe that by speaking to one of them, she'll be able to hang onto the present moment and let the past die from neglect.

Her eyes are on the parking lot the entire time, but while she fumbles for the phone in the midst of clutter—the gas slips and maps and owner's manual—she finds herself slipping from the road to the glove box and she doesn't wake until it is too late: an SUV, one of those lumbering giants, has backed out of its parking space, wallowing across the asphalt, and Zay, distracted, doesn't see it. She reacts an instant too late. The smash of chrome and the tinkling bells of shattered headlight glass echo across the parking lot. She is still ransacking the glove box when her head lurches toward the dashboard. *Oh, where has she gone now?*

• • •

The evening after her lunch with Geoffrey, she had come home, busy with plans. She would do the laundry, change the sheets, make dinner, make amends. She had stepped off the bus three stops before her own in order to shop for their dinner. Something simple and cheap that might also pass for complicated and expensive. A bottle of wine, a lasagna, maybe. She trudged up the hill from the store with two grocery sacks in her arms, holding on tight to the bag with the wine, while a steady drizzle fell. Cars and trucks raced through the rain, sending up rooster tails of spray from the wet pavement while their wipers slapped back and forth. She shivered in the chill and struggled to keep her balance as the sidewalk turned to ice. Ah, but finally the gray clapboard sides of the Hill Villa emerged from the gray mist, and she walked down the stairs to the front door, juggling keys and bags like some sort of circus performer. One of those plate spinners on Ed Sullivan, maybe. Inside the door she set down the groceries and, taking off her scarf, shook out her hair.

"Well, look at you." Mrs. Perls standing in her doorway with cigarette and whiskey glass held in the same hand. "You're so young, aren't you? So pretty. Extraordinary. You and your long, thick hair. I'll bet you have men falling in love with you eight days a week."

"I wouldn't say that," Zay said. "Not exactly."

"Don't be so modest. I've seen your type come and go." A gust of acrid smoke escaped along with the older woman's bitter laugh. "Don't take me seriously. I'm old and envious. I looked like you once upon a time. I had a figure. And hair like yours. Don't laugh, it's true."

"I wasn't laughing."

"I dated Sinatra, you know."

"I didn't," Zay said. "I didn't know that."

"Me and Frank. Swanky Frankie. Three weeks at the Sands. It was fun while it lasted. Then he sends me a nightgown and roses, and I knew my goose was cooked."

Mrs. Perls dropped her cigarette to the wood floor of the hallway, stepping on it with the toe of her carpet slipper. "Now, you," she said. "You smell like sex. In the present tense, I might add. And not with your little Poindexter."

So that's when Zay stumbled, one of her knees must have buckled at just that moment, and down she went like a pile of sticks. In front of her own apartment door, no less.

"Hey, hey. Little Miss Cream Puff," Mrs. Perls said, standing over her. "Maybe you need to eat something, maybe."

How did the old witch know?

How could she have known that lunch with Geoffrey had turned into an afternoon with Geoffrey, a farewell to the marriage for old times' sake? She hadn't meant for it to happen, but they were husband and wife, still, no matter what had happened recently, and old habits never really die. Besides, there's no harm done, not really, not when it's just between herself and Geoffrey and doesn't concern anyone else. No one else needs to know. She got to her feet, a little unsteady in her ridiculous shoes. Her groceries were scattered across the hallway floor. The bottle of wine, miraculously unbroken, had rolled three doors down. Somehow, she unlocked and opened her door, got herself and the elements of dinner inside, piece by piece. And then, there was not even time to sit down at the table and make a cup of tea before making her dinner of atonement before there was a knock on the door, and who could it be but Mrs. Perls again, holding a can of tomatoes that must have escaped her earlier.

Mrs. Perls has her tomatoes and a shoebox under her arm. She's had her Scotch and now she's turned into Chatty Cathy after weeks of silence and indifference. Mrs. Perls believes that Zay is just the person to look at her photographs, the record of her life. Just the person to understand the sort of person Mrs. Perls is. Well, she isn't, she has to cook dinner and maybe start that bottle of wine if she is to keep going, if she is to get through this night, but she can't say no to their landlady, now can she?

Mrs. Perls is nattering on. Sinatra and Dean Martin, Bing Crosby and Hope and Astaire and Danny Kaye and all those old warhorses from the forties and fifties. Who gives a shit? she wants to say. Who gives a shit? Mrs. Perls is full of inside stories and she knows from personal experience which one of the boys had the biggest *shlong* and which one was all talk. Zay can't remember which is which. They're all full of it, she thinks. There's the back of Mrs. Perls's head, her red hair that looks suspiciously like a wig because it's too perfectly coiffed to belong to someone living, and then there's the way she sorts through her collection of photographs as though she would like to dive into the box of her past, disappear into it, she has just the picture she wants to show Zay, a picture of herself thirty years ago. I was about four years old, Mrs. Perls says, then laughs at her own lie. Maybe fourteen. *Ha, ha, ha*. What a joke.

Yes, Mrs. Perls says. Here it is. She brandishes a snapshot and holds it for Zay to inspect. A professional must have taken this, Zay sees. Someone with some craft, albeit a few decades out of date. Mrs. Perls, ever so much younger, naked in some phony pose on a fainting couch, her long hair coiled around her breasts as though playing Godiva. Even so, take away the ferns and the columns and it's impossible for Zay to miss it, how much she herself resembles this younger incarnation of Mrs. Perls

Look, Mrs. Perls is saying. Look, here's another one. Me and Bogart before he met Bacall. Oh, she was a sly one, all right.

Her pasta is sitting on the table. Water must be put to boil; the sauce must be prepared.

Mrs. Perls holds up a snapshot of Gable. I could tell you stories, she says and seems about to start.

What I wouldn't give, Zay thinks. What I wouldn't give to see this old lady dead.

The Volcano Lover

GEORGE DAILEY AND TRUDY LIEBERMAN were in their early forties when they found each other again. Their first meeting took place at a dinner party held by the Hollenbecks a month after the eruption of Mount St. Helens. Bringing George and Trudy together had been the Hollenbecks' intent; dedicated match-makers, they did not even try to disguise it. Abe Hollenbeck, George's employer, declared it time for him quit mooning. George was going to get over Sondra some-time, and it might as well be sooner rather than later. So at dinner he and Trudy were seated across from one another, and topics of interest common to both were introduced with the spontaneity of an agenda. But since smoke still paved the sky the color of cement and threads of ash rippled along the ground like fallen kite tails, all talk eventually centered on the mountain: what each person was doing that Sunday morning when it had blown up.

Abe and Bette Hollenbeck had been eating croissants and early strawberries on the back deck when they heard the first radio reports; they had looked but had seen no change, only a rare day of sun in May. Dick and Harriet Dereiko had been grocery shopping, and the produce manager informed them while he sprayed the lettuce. The irony, Harriet said, was that just a week before she had spoken with Harry Truman, the owner of Spirit Lake Lodge, about his plans to reopen when the volcano scare was over.

"It was so pretty there," Harriet sighed, "and now everything is gone. Gone. We lived in Los Angeles for so long being told that we were going to fall into the ocean that I never really thought anything would happen. Now the lake is full of mud, the lodge is buried in ash, and poor Harry was probably blown to bits."

"Who could've expected it," Lindy Allen said, "when every night on television we're given the latest update? It's like the second coming. Everybody talks about it, but it never happens."

"Listen, though," Bette said in her peremptory way as hostess, "listen to this, you guys. Trudy has the real story."

"Go on, Trude," Abe said. "This is not to be believed."

Trudy seemed reluctant, but the other guests around the table insisted.

"I was camping," she shrugged, "and our campsite was pretty close."

"Pretty close," Abe said. "She says pretty close, but what she means is that she was camping on the south slope of the mountain, and it's only God's luck that the eruption blew out the *north* face."

She and her companion had hiked out when their car would not start. They had forded swollen creeks, they had clambered over giant trees leveled by the earthquake, and always at their back was the ominous cloud of dust and ash to the north. They had taken the pictures to prove it, enormous billows of gray boiling against the lid of the sky.

"As horrifying as the pictures make it, they really do not do that cloud justice," Trudy said. "It could have been World War III. I wouldn't have been surprised."

"Wasn't it illegal?" Harriet said. "I mean, to be there?"

"Well, I wanted to see it. We both did."

"And can you imagine," Bette said, taking over, "in the end she and Simon had to be rescued by a National Guard helicopter. Simon broke his ankle when his foot got caught in some rocks and tree limbs. Trudy had to carry him for a mile and a half over her shoulders before they saw the helicopter. Just like a movie, only the woman rescues the guy. I saw her that night on the news, being interviewed, and they had a caption underneath her name: 'Local Woman Cheats Death, Saves Boyfriend from Volcanic Eruption.' So I yelled at Abe to come here, come quick, our little Trudy made the news!"

It was an amazing experience, George thought, the sort of experience that was as foreign to him as snake charming or hang gliding the pyramids. George tried to picture this small, compactly built woman desperately signaling to a helicopter hovering overhead while apocalypse threatened; the image, however, refused to form. During dinner George had admired the dust of freckles on Trudy's shoulders, the remnant of last summer's tan; he had watched as a vein in her neck faintly beat its pulse against the short necklace at her throat. She seemed level-headed enough, even for a woman who made her bed on the side of an active volcano. Abe had hinted that Trudy had recently broken off a long-term relationship herself—to the aforementioned Simon? George wondered—that she too was the victim of bitterness and regret. If that were true, he could detect no signs of lingering trauma. Her eyes were green, flecked with gold, and clearly engaged in the present moment. The bigger question was whether he could possibly hope to capture her attention, she who had so recently experienced the end of the world—what could he offer in the face of that?

The morning of the eruption, he had raced to Sondra's apartment, responding over the phone to something unspoken in her voice. She met him at the door in a housecoat, her face creased with sleeplessness. She wanted out. While a cloud the size of a nuclear explosion rose over the southwestern corner of Washington, he was getting dumped.

There was no spark, she had decided. He wasn't dangerous enough. He was nice, he was considerate, he was good enough in bed—that wasn't the problem, she assured him—but some women needed an element of risk or threat, a sense of desperate helplessness that he was not able to supply. He could plot his finances to the last penny, but now and then she wanted a drunken sailor in port. That might not be a very liberated sentiment, she said, but not every woman could counter a thousand years of conditioning. She still wanted somebody who might take a mind to grab her by the hair, tear her clothes to rags. Include her within the scope of his rage. She was so very sorry. Did he think she was too weird?

He was too polite to say yes, of course. Absolutely. Too weird for his taste.

But he didn't say it because he couldn't.

• • •

After dinner, Bette Hollenbeck directed everyone in rearranging the den furniture so they could dance to Abe's collection of swing and jazz recordings. Since George and Trudy were the only singles, they were naturally thrown together at first, and although they expected to dance with others after the first couple of tunes, they soon realized that only the married couples were changing partners. No one broke in on them as if by contract.

Eventually, he led Trudy out onto the Hollenbecks' back balcony, where Abe kept the party liquor and made brandy and sodas for both of them. Even with the sliding door closed and the drapes pulled, the noise from Abe's stereo was brassy and emphatic; it echoed against the dark line of trees at the rear edge of the property. A light mist had begun to fall.

"Mmm," Trudy said, "it's hot in there."

"That's the spotlight. We're the center of attention. They're doing their best to set us up, even if they're as subtle as a cannon."

"Bette means well. She's probably my oldest and dearest friend. We shared cigarettes in the bathroom at St. Cecelia's. We wore each other's clothes."

"Abe signs my paycheck," George said, "so he's mine."

"Do you think," she said, cocking her ear toward the sliding door, "they're talking about us right now?"

"It's possible."

"We could give them something to talk about." She stepped behind a dark jumble of abandoned patio furniture and, after a few deft movements, returned with her bra and panties.

"Your turn, Georgie Porgie," she said.

It seemed to be a dare that could not be refused. His essence, if not his manhood, would be threatened. He took his place at the far edge of the deck where she had been all quickness, and nearly fell over when he could not get his pants past his shoes.

"Don't hurt yourself," she laughed.

"I'll try not to."

While his pants hung around his ankles, it hardly seemed the time or place for such concern, and he wondered further to what use a pair of his cotton briefs might be put by this relative stranger.

"We leave 'em," she said, answering his question. "Right here in the middle of their goddamn deck. We dance one more dance, then get the hell out. Just let me know if you feel the wind come up. I don't need my bum dancing in the breeze."

Her eyes were too-bright with the wine from dinner and the drinks after, and plotting seemed to give their green shine extra voltage.

They opened the sliding glass door and ducked around the curtain just as "Moonlight Serenade" began to play. They danced, aware of the weight of scrutiny, then—as Glenn Miller left off and Bix Beiderbecke began—said their goodnights to the Hollenbecks.

"Night, kids," Bette said.

"Be good," Abe winked.

"Goodnight, goodnight," George and Trudy said, an amiable pair of co-conspirators.

The front door closed behind them, and Trudy dashed to her car with George hurrying behind her.

"Can I drive you home?" he asked. "Or we could go for coffee."

"I can manage, thanks. Maybe another time."

"I'll call you then," he said.

Trudy huddled in her overcoat. Suspended in her short dark hair, drops of mist reflected diamonds from the street light overhead.

"Fine," she said, opening her door, "I'd like that. I'm listed. I'm just not good company."

"You're terrific," George said, "terrific company. And we've already had our clothes off."

"There's that," she smiled. "Call, then."

But she was not, in fact, listed. And he took that to mean that her answer Yes was in fact the answer No, and that her trick with their underwear, rather than a shared experience, was merely a ruse designed for her quick exit. Once again, he did not have a clue as to the nature of women.

Three weeks after the Hollenbecks' party, Abe cornered him in Fitzgerald's, where George was entertaining Buddy Wentworth, one of Alpha Systems' best clients.

"Bette's mad at you," Abe announced. "Mad as hell." He sat down on the bench seat next to George, forcing him to slide over. He had been diagramming Alpha's latest network package, but Abe would not see that as a deterrent. They were his products, after all.

"Have a beer, Abe," Wentworth said. He was already pouring a glass from the pitcher. A millionaire at thirty, he could afford a taste of gossip and intrigue in his vendors.

"You haven't called Trudy. She thinks you're conceited as hell, not calling her after that stunt you pulled with the underwear. I thought you'd be at her place half an hour after you left ours."

"Who's Trudy?" Wentworth said. "What underwear?"

"That was her idea. Completely."

"I'll bet." Abe dropped a slip of paper with a number onto the table. "What's the matter with you? You don't like her looks? She's fabulous, she won't keep forever. God knows why that last one gave her the kiss off."

"Maybe she unlisted him."

"You call her. Tonight. This afternoon."

"Yes, boss."

Abe stood, drinking the last two-thirds of his glass in a long swallow. "Buddy, I'm sorry I interrupted, but my friend here is a moron. He's a helluva salesman, I can't live without the guy, but he's an ass and a moron. Stupid, stupid, stupid. A fabulous woman—this woman is a one-in-a-million opportunity, I swear it—and he can't even pick up the goddamn phone."

"What underwear?" Buddy said. "What about the underwear?"

• • •

George did as he was told. He dialed the number that Abe had given him. The phone rang four times and then he heard the sound of an answering machine switching on and Trudy's recorded voice, *At the tone, please leave your etc.*, etc., etc. He put the edgiest voice on it that he could. He curled his lip like Bogart, squinted like an old sea dog, but it was still the voice of that nice George Dailey in his ears.

This is George Dailey, met you at, tried to call, Abe gave me, call me, blah, blah, blah. He did what he could do, and now it was up to her. Which as it turned out was nothing. How could he be surprised when he had his own prior disappointments as precedent? He in whom the capacity for danger had been found wanting? Even so, every evening after work, he looked at his answering machine as a traitor.

Time passed. Things happened. George heard through the Hollenbeck grapevine that he had missed his chance after all. Trudy was married. To Simon. Her partner in near-death. They had taken the trip to the mountain as a last-ditch attempt to revive a fading relationship, but something in the wake of their experience had caused first a break-up, then a reconciliation. Meeting George had been the briefest of interludes. She was pregnant within the year and, according to Bette, deliriously happy. A year later, George was likewise married. Sondra had come back, repentant and bruised, emotionally and physically. After a torrid romance and an equally stormy breakup with a shipfitter from Swan Island, she no longer wished for a husband with dangerous tendencies. She promised devotion and fidelity. She admired his conscientiousness and balanced their checkbook with a zeal exceeding his own. Over the next five years, two more Daileys were added to the population, as well as a mortgage, three cars, two dogs, and half a dozen stray cats. George was satisfied that all was in place. Then came the unraveling. Abe Hollenbeck fled to the Caymans three weeks before a federal grand jury could indict him on embezzlement and tax evasion charges. He took only a toiletry bag, his passport, and Alice Bevington, his secretary. Bette bore her sorrows with as much dignity as she could muster, but a few months later she was back in Ohio, living with her family—her aged parents and an incontinent beagle named Bill. Alpha Systems, it turned out, was a card house built in a wind tunnel. There was nothing left. Left to his own resources, George moved from one sales position to another as companies merged, folded, downsized, and restructured. With enough to drink at lunch and dinner, he found it difficult to remember whether he worked for Alpha Systems, Beta Products, GammaNet, or Delta Design. What did it matter anyway? Sondra went back to nursing, her profession before marriage and motherhood. She took pride in the crisp starch of her whites and the meticulous precision of her records. Who could have predicted that danger would once again sing its siren song? She left one spring night with a dermatologist who owned a red sports car and a five-bedroom pied-à-terre in Reno.

In the wake of her departure, he consulted lawyers and therapists. His lawyer filed motions on behalf of his rights to custody. His therapist confronted him with the need to express his anger. He fired his lawyer when his custody petition was denied on a technicality; he fired his therapist when he broke his bathroom door into splinters. A second therapist suggested that he should find a hobby—woodworking or fly tying, for instance. A book group, perhaps. He took up bowling instead, finding solace in repetition—in the geometry and grace of shots that rolled true. Bungee jumping it was not. But it was an alternative to drinking alone at night, and there was something fundamental, Zen-like, in the variables of speed and weight, angle and rotation, that appealed to a mind desperate for physical constants. He bowled only after midnight, uninterested in league or tournament play, the point of the exercise neither camaraderie or prize money, but the ritual movement of his own body sending an object sixty feet away to do his bidding. He only threw a first ball, he never shot spares if pins were left, he never kept score.

• • •

"Now that's a helluva nice line. You could be somebody, you know that?"

He looked up from the ball return on lane sixteen. A man in his sixties, the shape of Tweedledee and Tweedledum—tiny feet, a pear-shaped body, a small head with a thinning crest of dyed black hair. He wore a bowling shirt with *Morty* embroidered above the left pocket.

"I was just telling my niece over there that here's somebody who knows, not one of these young punks who thinks you gotta fire the ball like a goddamned cannon. It's not enough to knock the pins down, you gotta break them besides?"

George shifted from foot to foot, waiting for the older man to finish. About once a month on average someone would intrude on his session, no matter how late or early—someone old or drunk or both, a lonely heart in a dark time, taking advantage of someone without a defense. The only remedy he had found was to call it a night; there was no getting rid of them. The desperation that impelled someone to speak to a total stranger in a bowling alley at two in the morning also seemed to provide a superhuman persistence that no response—courtesy, anger, or indifference—could discourage.

"Morty Singer," the older man said, extending his hand. "I don't mean to interrupt, but my niece and I was wondering if you would like to join us in a little pot game. Nothing big, you understand. Five bucks maybe. Or less, whatever you prefer. She's my sister's kid, a little unlucky in love; otherwise, she's not here bowling with her old uncle. Unlucky? I don't know, bad judgment maybe. Some women seem to have a knack for falling head over heels for morons. She loses her head, not that I think any the less of her. What I'm saying, I think it's something genetic. My sister was the same way, and it just rips your heart out to see them unhappy, because they're always going to be unhappy, sooner or later, given the schmucks they choose."

His ball was already in his bag, but then he thought, What the hell, why not? One game couldn't hurt. One game with Morty Singer and his hard-luck niece. With any luck he might win enough to cover his games. His niece was sitting at the scorer's table on lane thirty-two, and though she was a study of boredom, her head propped up on one hand while she shaded strikes and spares with the other, there was no mistaking the athletic shoulders, the forceful hands of Trudy Lieberman.

"You," she said, her green eyes tilting up into his own. "I know you. Don't I?"

"Briefly. We met at the Hollenbecks' before Abe went on the lam."

"Oh," she said, looking down again. "George."

"You remember."

"Sure. We must have danced for two hours, and no one would cut in on us."

Morty hovered behind his niece's shoulder. "You two kids know each other? I shoulda known. It's the sorta thing you see on TV."

"Morton," Trudy said, "give it a rest already."

"What? I can't be happy? Mr. George here seems like a nice enough sort. Too nice for you, sweetcakes. I forgot you like them nasty, don't you?"

"Morton, I'm warning you."

"Awright, awright, let's bowl, okay?"

"Fine. Let's bowl." She picked up her ball from the return. "Straight score, no handicaps. Ten-dollar ante. That okay, Georgie Porgie?"

"I thought you said five, Morty."

The older man shrugged. "Beats me, this girl."

"Five or ten," Trudy said, "it's your call, Mr. George."

"Ten. Ten's fine."

She stepped forward with the ball. Her delivery, beginning with a conservative four-step approach, was fluid and well-practiced. Her ball rolled smoothly down the lane, hooking into the pocket at the last possible instant, all ten pins erupting around it. She posed at the line in her follow-through, admiring her handiwork, then, while touching the gold post in her right ear, turned and said, "Next," with a smirk directed exclusively at him.

They bowled for four hours, he lost a couple hundred dollars, all to Trudy, who had a knack for encouraging double or nothing bets and bowling just well enough to beat his best efforts. Sandbagged by a pro. The sun was cresting Mount Hood when they pushed through the double doors.

"I'll buy you both breakfast," she said. "It's on me."

"No, honey, you're just spending our money to make us feel better. This old poop better head home." Morty enveloped his niece in a hug, then shook George's hand. "She's a pain in the ass, isn't she?"

They watched Morty guide his stomach behind the wheel of an ancient Honda. He did not so much get in as strap it on. George caught a glimpse of ripped seats, a drooping headliner, a sea of paper cups and sandwich wrappers rippling along the floor.

"You have to like him," Trudy said, "even if he drives a recycling project. Come on, let's get some chow. I know a place where the coffee's so hot you can't taste the lousy food."

He followed as she drove to a storefront cafe in Sellwood. Everyone seemed to know her, and coffee came immediately.

"So, what happened?" She held his left hand flat against the table and traced the white circle still visible from his wedding band. "You got married."

"And divorced." He told her the story, which in the past year had turned stale in his own ears. He no longer had the capacity—or the energy—to play the role of aggrieved husband. "So, Sondra's in Reno along with the kids, and I'm here. It surprised me—it still surprises me—but I guess it happens all the time."

"Oh, sure. You can't hardly step outside without tripping over a millionaire dermatologist."

"You know what I mean."

"Yes," she said, "I know. Boy do I know."

Simon had taken off five years ago. "He told me I was killing him. Little old me. I was expecting too much of him. Setting too high a standard. Poor Simon, he's in Florida now, living among the oranges. I heard he's married to some bar floozy with a leaky boat, and they're running day trips for the tourists who don't know any better. He's like the poster child of irresponsibility. We didn't have any kids, so I don't have to feel guilty about that."

"But—"

"I know. Bette told you I was pregnant. Bette told everybody I was pregnant. I was pregnant a lot. Miscarried five times that I know of. It seems I don't have a body that can keep a kid inside without gushing. We tried doctors and faith healers. I even went to see this old woman named Miz Lydia, who claimed that I could have a baby if I swallowed olive pits and drank a solution of turpentine and spirit gum. Which, to my mind, wasn't so much worse than the fertility specialist who said for forty thousand dollars we had a fifty-fifty chance. Simon liked Miz Lydia. He even offered to mix my drinks."

"I'm sorry."

"No, listen. I'm sorry. I should have called you after Abe and Bette's party, explained how things were with Simon and me. After we had our little scare on the mountain, Simon blamed me for everything. It may have been my idea to go up there, and I probably pressured him into driving around the barricades. But he acted like such a baby when things started to go badly that I thought if we made it out alive, I better call it quits. I told him we were through while we were in the air. The guardsman in the helicopter tried to pretend he wasn't listening, but after they unloaded Simon's stretcher, he tried to ask me out. So, I thought, Jesus, men are buttheads, aren't they? You probably got lumped into the same category. A couple of days after the party, Simon called, and I started to feel sorry for him. He seemed so lost, and I thought it might be at least partly my fault, but I don't think he forgave me even after we were married."

She held his hand. "You would have forgiven me, wouldn't you?"

He felt the earth tilt on its axis as he answered: "Of course. Of course I would have."

• • •

After several dinners and movies, after shopping together for the wedding presents of others, even after the steady humiliation of bowling with Trudy and her uncle, he marveled at his good fortune: that she should be available for him. She was beautiful and smart, full of good humor and alert to the world's absurdities. When she laughed it was full and rich, concluding with an unabashed snort. Nothing like the laughter of the few unattached women to whom he'd been introduced recently, women whose amusement was martyred by the panic of fleeting time. He was not blind to her defects, but he did not wish to be accusatory, to be another butthead man. There was a streak of temper—entirely arbitrary as far as he could tell—that he found difficult to ignore but impossible to hold against her, for it seemed to emanate from the same wellspring from which her vivacity and spirit came. The first time they made love, for instance, followed one dinner in Chinatown when she had called him Buttlips and Fathead and Shit-for-Brains and a host of other obscenities. He had failed to grasp a particular nuance of Simon's failure of romantic character: after they were married, he had refused to throw out pictures of a high school girlfriend.

The pictures were twenty years old, the girl was married and the mother of four children, so what was the harm? he had wondered. The harm, she said, was that he refused to throw them away. She had thrown her napkin in his face, her silver to her plate with a clang that had alerted their waiter. She had called him names that stung with greater impact than if she had cursed his family tree. She fled to the bathroom, and although he waited for an hour in the red-flocked lounge and sent the hostess in to check on her, she would not come out. Finally, he sent the hostess in to the restroom with his car keys, paid their tab, and took the bus home, thinking that he would in all likelihood not see her again. His car would just have to take its chances.

But at midnight, after falling asleep on his couch, he was awakened by a pounding on his door, and there she was—sobbing, falling into his arms and cursing her irrational behavior. Demanding his love. She tore at his buttons, she yelled when she came, she pummeled his chest with her hard little fists and scratched his back with her nails until he bled. How could he not be touched by this display of contrition? In the morning, he might have thought it merely a dream, if not for Trudy's sleeping form beside him in his bed. Not to mention his aches and pains upon awakening. He checked himself delicately. He might have pulled a muscle, he thought, he might have ruptured an organ in the middle of that tempestuous night.

• • •

On another night they were supposed to see *La Bohème* in celebration of its centennial, but Trudy was at home sick in bed. The flu. Fever of 102 degrees, alternately sweating and shivering. Her nose was red and her cheeks flushed. She had thrown up half a dozen times. Like a geyser, she said. She wouldn't want a dog to see her. Over the phone, her voice rattled and rasped.

She insisted that he go without her; tickets were expensive and impossible to get. Or he could scalp their seats, and it wouldn't be a total loss. He refused to go anywhere but her apartment; he put the tickets on her nightstand along with the wads of used Kleenex and pill bottles of expired antibiotics.

"You think these will help?" he said, looking at a label two years out of date. "You have the flu."

"That's right, and making me look at a pair of sixty-dollar tickets will make me even better."

"I bought the CDs this afternoon. I thought we could listen to it. Domingo and Caballé."

"Christ, are you out of your mind? My head's splitting." She groaned and covered her eyes. "Don't look at me."

"You're beautiful."

"Ha. I feel like shit and I look worse. When I get sick, I turn into a witch woman. You're taking a huge risk here, bud. You should go away before I bite off your head and suck out your eyes."

"I'll take my chances."

Fifteen minutes later she rolled over. "God, are you still here? Don't you have any sense?"

"No. I don't."

"You're impossible. Listen, if you're going to stay here, go watch television or something. Call Morty and go bowling. Go to a movie. Do something. Let me get some rest."

He retreated to the living room, stretched out on her sofa, and fell asleep to Letterman. She woke him at four in the morning with the sound of her shower, the chugging of hot water through the pipes. Her night clothes lay in a wet, sweat-drenched heap in the middle of her bedroom floor.

"You okay?" he called.

She pulled open the shower curtain. "Jesus, how about a girl's privacy?" Her complexion was pasty, but her eyes were bright. "If you're still here, you might as well join me," she said, pulling him under the water by his tie.

Later, in bathrobes, they listened to the RCA recording of the opera, Trudy crying silently during the whole of the third act though she declared Mimi's death at the end of Act Four anticlimactic and unnecessary.

"Tell me the truth," she said, "am I Mimi or Musetta?"

"You're as sweet as Mimi," he said, aiming to strike a diplomatic middle, "and as fiery as Musetta."

"And you," she said, yawning, "are full of crap."

Later still, while the mid-morning sun streamed through Trudy's bedroom window, they cuddled in bed and played Revelation:

"My parents were in their forties when I was born," George said. "They had assumed they would never have children, so when I came along, they didn't know what to do with me. They treated me like any of their other old friends, and I learned how to play bridge and mah-jongg and shuffleboard when I was seven. When it rained my mother made me wear plastic bags over my tennis shoes so my feet wouldn't get wet, and I would have to wait until she couldn't see me to take them off. I didn't want other kids to see them, although sometimes I got caught by my friends, who would laugh at me, or by my mother, who would be gravely disappointed."

"I buy napkins and napkin rings when I need to cheer myself up," Trudy said, "and I have drawers and drawers full of them at home. When I overeat, I drink vinegar as punishment, which I think has more to do with the way that my mother teased me when I was eight, poked her finger in my tummy, and said, 'If you don't watch out, you're going to be as fat as your Aunt Irene.' She hurt my feelings terribly because Aunt Irene—Morty's wife—ran a good 275 even after a full night's sleep without snacks."

The recollection made her shoulders quiver, and he touched them as though touching some ancient Ming porcelain. Her opera tears had mottled her face once again, and the fever, which had broken during the night, had filmed her green eyes in pink; he could have called attention to these details no more than he could have slashed her into pieces with a cleaver.

"Every year before Christmas my father would tell me that Santa couldn't come this time, that there were cutbacks, and he'd decided that the Daileys had more than their share anyway. He didn't mean any harm by it; it was just a joke, like wrapping some tiny, insignificant present in a series of larger and larger boxes that each have to be unwrapped, and then the present itself is rather a let-down. Every year on Christmas Day, after telling me that Santa wasn't coming, there would be piles of presents; my father would tell me that Santa had changed his mind after all, that we were extraordinarily lucky. But rather than feeling lucky, I simply felt guilty. I thought that I'd probably gotten gifts that should have gone to someone else."

"Like what?" she said. "What could they have given you that you didn't deserve?"

"Like you," he said. "Like you."

• • •

Because they were older and they had been alone for some time, they had assumed that they would never be with anyone again. As a result, their conversation possessed the quality of a confession spoken only to the mirror, intimacy that seldom occurs with another, and then only after the first bankruptcy or brush with infidelity. They spoke of first loves and first lovers. Peak experiences. Most embarrassing moments and most shameful secrets.

As it turned out, the trip to the mountain had been her idea all along. Simon had been extremely reluctant, and when the mountain erupted, their tent collapsed. The ground rocked beneath their sleeping bags. The wind howled. Simon's eyes glazed over, brown agates. He shook his head in fear and disbelief. Because of her, they were going to die. She was responsible, she was the pigheaded one, he hoped she was happy.

When he broke his ankle, he was a good quarter-mile ahead of her in his sprint to safety, and she had half a mind to leave his sorry ass to the ash. And when she hoisted him over her shoulders in a fireman's carry, he moaned—from pain or humiliation, she couldn't be sure. Her knees buckled underneath his weight, but she tottered off as best she could, trying not to jostle him too much.

She heard the helicopter before she spotted the green tadpole shape. She set Simon on the ground and tore off her blue slicker, then her flannel, which was red, and began waving the shirt over her head, hoping the color—if not her boobs— would attract the pilot's attention. The pilot hovered fifty feet above them, the rotor sending up whirlpools of ash and grit, while another guardsman dropped a harness to them from a winch. She helped Simon flop through the yoke. He gripped the cable so hard his knuckles turned into walnuts. He did not look back at her once. As he ascended, rising toward the helicopter and safety, his body and feet turned in the swirling air. Like someone hanging from a rope in a bedroom closet, she thought. Like a dead man.

"Goddamn you," she yelled, though she doubted he could hear anything for the roar of the rotors. "Goddamn you to hell."

She stood on this newly created moonscape, looking up while the dust and ash rose around her. If they flew away now, she thought, she would be the loneliest woman on the face of the earth.

The Nothing between Us

I: Happiness

Laugh, if you will: my memories of that time begin and end with salad bars. Angelique had moved in during an April rain. She brought with her three cardboard boxes of books and knitting supplies and a cardboard suitcase that contained a week's worth of dirty underwear, some overalls and sweatshirts, and a stuffed rabbit named Jonathan, whose right ear was missing, the victim of the dog at Angelique's last place of residence. Everything was wet since the boxes leaked and the suitcase hadn't closed in years. Neither of us had any money whatsoever. Angelique had two crafts fairs coming up in June—she had arranged to share a booth with a girl named Simplicity—and Mr. Benton had hinted he might have the money to pay me at the end of May for articles I had written for *The Lamplight*, his neighborhood paper, in February, but that is what he had said in March and April. I had written features and columns in March and April as well, and I continued to churn out material dutifully in May, hoping that if I produced something every week, he would finally feel compelled to pay me. And yes, the name Simplicity is real. I met her. She was the daughter of reformed capitalists, who had renounced their business but not their annuities. Even so, they did not want their daughter to be corrupted so they kept her away from their money. Consequently, Simplicity did not go to college. I'm not even sure that she finished high school. She lived very simply by what she earned from crafts fairs, selling leather goods—wallets and key cases and small purses—that she made herself. Her parents went skiing twice a month, declared their desperate unhappiness in contrast to their admiration for their daughter, whose life was a model of a pure work ethic and the exchange of a genuine service, product, and value. I met them once at Simplicity's booth. They were open and gregarious, happy Republicans, well-suited to each other and completely full of shit. On the other hand, Angelique and I were not a good match. We had little in common except our poverty. Our lovemaking was clumsy and a little disheartened, and we had a difficult time maintaining a conversation. Do you know that there are some people with whom you can talk about anything for hours on end? We were the opposite. Angelique could answer the most nuanced question with a word or two, and I had a difficult time thinking of anything I wanted to ask her. We had nothing to tell. How did we ever find each other attractive, much less discuss living together? I have no idea. We were both sophomores in college, but neither one of us had a thought to share. For the two weeks after our finals were over, we had no money at all; our attempts at dumpster diving produced little that we could stomach, so we scrounged bottles and cans and used the change for meal money. At that time every lousy pizza joint in America had an all-you-can-eat salad bar. Ninety-nine cents bought vegetables, dressings, processed cheese, and synthetic bacon bits. If we didn't have enough change, one of us bought the salad while the other sipped water and sneaked bites when the pimply-faced manager wasn't looking. (There was always a pimply-faced manager, who ten years into the future owned a software company and could buy small countries.) We learned to rotate our spots, although after walking two or three miles for a salad and then walking home again, we were ready for our next meal almost immediately. One evening we walked from our apartment in Sellwood to the Slice of Heaven pizzeria in Oak Grove. Our luck that day had been up and down. Mr. Benton had told me flat out: he was never going to pay me, he couldn't possibly afford it; if he needed to fill space, he could always take pictures of flowers. The senior citizens who read *The Lamplight* liked flowers more than they liked prose. That week alone, I had written three neighborhood columns, two features on parties in the park, and a spotlight piece on Maybelle Woodley, the eighty-year-old dowager from Eastmoreland who was single-handedly funding an opera in the schools program; my payment was a byline and the glory that is print. I would have been more valuable with crayons, Mr. Benton said, and a sketch pad. But he had a friend in the sports department at the *Oregonian*; if I didn't mind writing about trout, there might be some work, since I seemed to know where the periods needed to go. And, in a tarp-covered barrel behind the transmission shop on 17th, we found a month's worth of Coke bottles. We took half, replaced the tarp, and left the rest. Even so, we had nearly three dollars, so we were assured of a decent meal. With two or three return trips through the salad bar line, and if we stayed away from the kidney beans, we might even be full without needing to break wind while walking home. We could sneak bread sticks and raisins home in our pockets. Angelique wore her corky hair in a French braid, and we held hands on our walk. In the restaurant, the manager who took our order was someone we hadn't seen before, so he was courteous enough. At a long table by the front windows, a party of twelve was celebrating a child's birthday. A banner with "Happy

Ninth Birthday, Sammy" had been taped to the inside of the window. The table was awash in plates and napkins, spilled sodas and half-eaten slices of pepperoni pizza. Torn wrapping paper littered the floor. A sheet cake had been demolished. Five mothers sat at one end of the table, drinking beer from a pitcher while their offspring threw pepperoni slices and frosting at each other. The woman at the end of the table—Sammy's mother, perhaps—brought us two paper plates, each of which held a slice of pizza and a wedge of cake. She wore a caftan and had dark circles under her eyes. "You look like you could use an entrée and a dessert," she said. "I know what it's like that first year. You're happy but poor, and then the years go by and you end up in a war zone." She waved her hand at her table. "It comes soon enough. Be happy. Enjoy," she said. At the age of nineteen I was full of self-righteousness, among other flaws: "I don't know whether to be insulted or grateful," I said. "She was nice," Angelique said. "I want to remember this." She closed her eyes, and tears drifted down each cheek. "Oh, come on," I said. "Olive you." I had put pitted black olives on my fingers in memory of my childhood and Thanksgiving dinners, such was my attempt at wit back then. I should have been seated at the other table. "Don't ruin it," she said. "Please? Leave it alone." I put my hand over hers. "We could get married," I said. "Seriously." Angelique shrugged, said, "Don't be ridiculous," but I knew she had made a decision.

II: The Worm in the Apple

Shopping online, Angelique is uncertain which Icelandic sweater to buy, and in the end, she buys all three. She cannot try them on, of course, and she will, no doubt, look like a Christmas carpet in all of them, but that's what return envelopes are for; she has the money, and there's no reason to be stingy. Good grief, not at this late date.

She has a rationalization, after all: her whole life has been a process of overcoming a woe-begotten childhood.

Her parents, shiftless and unthinking and unprepared, had six other children, all of whom were younger than she was. She needed to get away to be less of a burden on the rest; she needed to get away to make a life of her own; she needed to get away because she needed to get away.

So she went to college on a scholarship, but when her roommate began engaging in group sex in the bed four feet away from her, she left the dorm and moved into a succession of sketchier and sketchier living arrangements, social dynamics that felt all too familiar, a repetition of her familial history.

Her last apartment was with the wannabe writer, who had taken her to dinner one night, she suspected, so that he would have an audience for his opinions and pronouncements. She had kissed him because she knew that by doing so, he would ask her out again, which he did. And she moved in with him because sleeping with him was not the worst thing that could happen; sex occurred only sporadically and didn't take all that long when it did. At least she had an address. And then they got married, which was impulsive and unnecessary and made everything more complicated in the end. What had she been thinking? She was making a bad decision, she knew it at the time, but on the other hand, she knew it was a safe thing to do: he was not poor by circumstance, only by choice. His parents weren't rich, but they had plenty of money, which he didn't want, and they didn't understand why he lived the way he did. She didn't understand it either. Unless you were a nun or something, poverty by choice was just stupid.

He was a bad writer, too, which was maybe the saddest part. Because he wanted so badly to be good, and he worked so hard without becoming so. And while that wasn't the primary reason for their divorce, it certainly hadn't helped. That was clear. On the other hand, he was pompous and opinionated and judgmental. He went slumming, romanticized the experience, and then found fault with those who didn't have to struggle week to week or month to month. As though to be poor granted one membership in an exclusive club. He thought that visiting the winos on Burnside qualified him to write stories about the down and out when, unlike those parts of town inhabited by those disenfranchised by ethnicity or economy, Portland's Skid Row was probably no more dangerous for the able of body and mind than a Saturday morning pancake breakfast. That's when he wasn't writing mediocre, pedestrian journalism about gentrification in Sellwood and church bazaars in Westmoreland. When he wasn't sitting in a classroom discussing Orwell or Huxley or Malraux. After all, that's what they were—students—children who bought textbooks and discussed ideas, as though such things mattered more than rent or groceries or the back molar that needed to be filled. This is what happened when there was too much literature, too much art. Too much vicarious poverty, as though adopting the political causes of underclass anxiety was more honest than making one's way through a real career, a real marriage, and the real life of family. He showed her his stories and his articles, and there was no doubt he expected her to read everything; what was more, she was supposed to be impressed, but her usual response was irritation since he invariably had gotten it all wrong anyway. All the romance without any of the reality, no matter how long she waited for him to wake up to the facts.

There were others after him and before her recently-deceased husband. A political activist, a jazz trombonist, a vegan yoga instructor. On the other hand, Max had been a tax attorney in a suit and tie, and she thought she had finally dodged the bullet and her own bad judgment. She met him, a fellow college classmate, the year after graduation. Solid, secure, stable. They engaged in gleeful, energetic sex, married when it made sense to do so, and moved to the oblivion of the Midwest for him to attend law school; they made babies, a career, a life. But then, Max quit his practice at the age of fifty-two and turned to mysticism and esoteric spirituality, reading everything from the Kabbalah to Edgar Cayce. His bald head shone when he spoke, and his voice shook with the force of his own enthusiasms. Why has she always gotten involved with such extremists? Why? Even when they began with conventional aspirations they turned into Saint Francis or Gandhi or Tolstoy.

At least Max made money before he indulged his whims, thank god for that, and he never felt guilty about either the money or the whims, so after his death, she became a grateful widow, one who was and is willing to bless each day and the material goods that affluence can buy. Her children have not exactly discouraged her either. Her son recently purchased and installed her new computer; her daughter sends her links to shopping sites every other day. As though thirty-three years of marriage can be set aside, if not forgotten, by the anodyne of spending. Not possible, of course, but it does fill the hours. Since Max's death, her life has seemed like a held breath. Waiting for what's next.

Lately, in addition to shopping, she has been puzzling over the Facebook pages of family and friends. They seem so busy and engaged. Their status updates are alternately witty or profane or banal. She gets friend requests from names that are like recovered memories; there's no telling if she ever actually knew the people to whom those names belong. They write breathless notes, longing to reconnect. Reconnect? Why would they want to do that? She ignores each request, believing that maintaining one's reserve is a sign of a healthy self-regard, but then in a spasm, she accepts them all, unwilling to differentiate between her best friend of the seventh grade and the contractor from the second house that she and Max built. However, she does have to confess to looking up some of the names from her past as well. The political activist, for example, is now a real estate developer in Santa Fe, and the trombonist a math teacher at a middle school in Glendale. All grown up, she thinks. After years and years of denial. They have put away their fantasies and toys. When the name of her ex-husband brings no results, she feels first relief and then curiosity, followed by the irritation she remembers from his high-minded posturing of thirty-five years earlier. Did he think he was too good for such things?

Maybe he became so morose, in the wake of their divorce and his own literary failure, that he turned to the streets about which he tried so often to write, becoming one of those crazies pushing a shopping cart, carrying an ancient boom box, and fighting for discarded cigarette butts. Maybe he joined one of those cults that advocated a separation from the world. Maybe an isolationist who lives off the grid without electricity, who keeps chickens and goats and a garden, barters with others, and has a yearly income of four hundred twenty-seven dollars and sixty-seven cents.

Maybe he is merely dead.

Doesn't she feel better now?

III: The Mirror of Condolences

The news of her husband's death comes in the alumni magazine, so it seems you are not so out of touch after all.

Her grief was unspoken yet easily inferred. Fantasies—of a gracious letter, a meeting, a dinner, a date, a remarriage—come unbidden, and you know once again, beyond a shadow of a doubt, that, age notwithstanding, you are still possessed of the emotional life of a fourteen-year-old.

Be a hero, you think. *Leave her alone.*

She doesn't want to see you. Or hear from you. Not then, not now, not ever.

But Directory Assistance for the 513 area code gives you a listing for Angelique Aronstein in Indian Hill, Ohio, wherever that is, and your fingers hover above the phone until the receiver falls into the cradle.

Thirty-five years after the fact, the last days of your marriage, each day a fresh accusation, can still make you cringe.

Pompous, she hissed.

Self-absorbed.

Cheap.

Intolerant of others.

You think you know what's right, you're certain you're right, but you don't have a clue.

You and your hair shirts.

Third-rate.

You can't decide if she made this last accusation or not, but you know in your heart of hearts that it's true. True—even more now than then.

All you want to do is convey your sympathy upon her loss.

No, that's not true. Max was a name and a face, proof that Angelique made her way in the world without you. And, except for the confirmation of the passage of time, you couldn't care less.

All you want to do is apologize. Another lie, as unconvincing as the first.

It would be easy enough to say that your life has been frozen for thirty-five years in a perpetual state of grief, but that wouldn't be true either. You put aside your intentions of young adulthood, those impossible ideals. There have been two other marriages, a child, but now there is only the dolor of a one-bedroom apartment; there have been bad jobs (the usual litany: tyrannical employers, lousy pay, and nonexistent benefits) and one decent one (albeit soul-sucking and spiritually demoralizing). You moved one state south to California, hoping for restoration and rebirth, but got recession instead. Retirement looms chronologically, and you tell yourself that then you'll write once more, you'll pour out your soul in ways that have been formerly closed, but given your late start and the state of economy, the practicality of retirement recedes to a small point on the horizon. None of it matters. You thought you were making a life when, really, you were hiding from, *fleeing from*, the one you were amidst.

Wanting to apologize to Angelique is another way of saying you'd like to apologize to your twenty-year-old self. For how little you knew, for how immature you were, are, and continue to be, for how little you have learned since.

IV: A Meeting in Some Future Time

This is how it may go: she will sit in the restaurant in the hotel atrium, aware that a mistake has been made. She is also aware of the passive voice construction and all that it implies. But she can't quite believe that she is herself responsible for making it. The mistake, that is. Forces beyond her control. A complex of circumstances. Can one be responsible for choices prompted by one's unconscious? Or fate? She will never know what prompted her to answer his letter.

There will not be many guests staying in this downtown hotel in the city where her ex-husband now lives. Business is bad, storefronts are empty, and there are dazed men standing on street corners. Some are wearing suits in the harsh glare and heat of late spring, as though they will give up their briefcases in exchange for the right to bale hay. After a late evening flight, she took a Third World–worthy taxi, then spent the night listening uncomfortably to the great silence of a hotel with five floors of empty rooms arranged around this open atrium. Who knew that comfort could be derived from the muffled sounds of drunken laughter, the strident box springs of sex, or the unforgiving clash of domestic unhappiness?

From her seat in the restaurant, she can see the door to her room on the fourth floor. Twinkle lights, meant to provide atmosphere and festivity, serve only to accentuate the twilight gloom and the jungle of potted ferns so artificially healthy as to invite inspection and disbelief.

Her waiter comes and goes in a great show of activity although only two other tables are occupied.

As he pours her water, she will say, "My friend should be here soon." She can't help thinking that "friend" is often used as a euphemism for "date" or "lover" but one would have to make a long stretch for it to replace "ex-husband."

By her watch it is already 12:15, and she thinks, fifteen minutes more, but no more than that, and then she will feel no guilt in leaving. After thirty-five years, after she has traveled twenty-five hundred miles, how can he be late? That takes some balls, and she will almost allow a wave of admiration to sweep through her. What she doesn't know, however, is that he will have begun his preparations three hours earlier, showering so compulsively that the steam and condensation have coated the windows in each room in his apartment, then changing his clothes three times in a fit of indecision and horror, and pacing, pacing, pacing the hall. He should have gotten a haircut, he should have lost weight, he is already disheveled, the years have not been kind. He is not aging as gracefully as he would like. More Mickey Rourke than Harrison Ford, without any of the pleasures of either. Why, oh why, did he do this? He will leave his apartment forty-five minutes early, drive three blocks to the busiest street in town, only to have his alternator—and battery—die. At times such as these, he curses his own obstinacy, his refusal to carry a cell phone, yes, he is something of a Luddite, albeit a selective one, and it takes an hour for a tow truck to arrive, hook up his car, and take it to a repair shop while he arranges for a rental.

He will call the hotel, ask for Angelique, but she will have already descended to the atrium restaurant and will be unable to hear the phone ring. He doesn't have the number of her cell phone.

He will drive, then, like a maniac, through freeway traffic, through fading downtown streets, to a parking garage next to the hotel. Across the street, through the lobby, in front of the maître d's podium.

And that's when he will see her for the first time in thirty-five years, with the sweat running down his sides, his back, and underneath the elastic waistband of his boxers, and he will think, no, he will *know*, that this is a big mistake, a huge mistake. Although he recognizes her instantly, she looks nothing like the twenty-year-old girl who made macramé hanging planters and woven bamboo centerpieces. She has cut her hair, she's wearing a suit, and it's possible that she's had some work done around her eyes and along her jaw, neck, and chin. Why did he do this, again? Why did he write her a letter, finally, extending his sympathies and his apologies and his grief to her for Max's death and the intersection of his life with hers so long ago? He included his address and phone number. Who did he think would benefit from that? He might as well have begged her to call. He is craven, and his selfishness knows no bounds, and he will be forced to cringe in the present as well as the past. He will have years and years and years and years to be ashamed.

"I am so sorry," he will cry after brushing past the hostess, who seems frightened by the haste of his approach and the disarray of his appearance. The frantic cast to his eyes.

"I am so sorry," he will sob to this woman of his past.

She will grab his hand, wondering to what extent she'll regret this later.

"It's okay," she will say, "really. Shhh, now. Have a seat. I've waited for people before."

· · ·

This may or may not happen. Who knows such things? He might never write. He might write but in a more formal tone. She might not respond. She might respond but without the offer to meet. She might come to town, but he might not be late. You get my drift, there are so many ways for the future to unfold. They are two people with a past with each other, a past so long ago as to be nearly forgotten, histories belonging to two other people, that what happens next is seemingly infinite in possibility. All we know for certain, Dear One, is the nostalgia of memory and the patience to wait upon the switchbacks of time.

Christmas in Jonestown

FORTY YEARS AGO, I was cleaning toilets for a collection agency and dreaming about building a Christian utopia. I was twenty-four, broke, and a little nuts. I worked nights on the fifth floor of a building in southwest Portland. I emptied trash and restocked toilet paper and tried to imagine how twenty people might live together in one of the abandoned campgrounds in Colton or Estacada, which was one of the problems I never solved since the campgrounds were not abandoned and I could not figure out how their already established spaces could be emptied out for our use. That, and how you can make people live together without killing each other either metaphorically or literally given the morning when I removed *The Oregonian* from our mail box and saw the first pictures from Jonestown. Stacks of muddy logs unblurred into bodies and Kool-Aid became a metaphor for poison. So that dream died, but it was a slow death until it wasn't, and then I thought, *graduate school*. Because I couldn't keep going this way, waxing floors and replacing trash can liners, and repeating the footnotes that I had read in the Moody's Study Bible as though I had just thought of them. But that was later, much later. Years and tears later. As if that weren't enough, three days a week, I clocked out at six in the morning and drove across the river to the southeast, where my roommate had an unlicensed roofing company. There, I spent the next six hours using an air hammer to nail down asphalt tile he had obtained from his pirate suppliers. I didn't sleep more than four hours a night, usually, but I didn't believe that the rules of sleep applied to me until I fell off the gable of a second-floor bedroom and somersaulted into the waiting arms of an overgrown boxwood. *Praise Jesus!* My roommate laughed and laughed. I threw a pry bar at him, but he couldn't stop laughing. As a roofer I was shit, he said, but as a stuntman I had potential.

At the time I had a girlfriend who had straight thin hair and flat, nearly opaque blue eyes. When she wasn't wearing a white lab coat for her job as a veterinary assistant and cooing to the Chihuahuas and Siamese in her care, she habitually wore overalls and bulky hand-knit sweaters. Her face was as pale as the moon when it wasn't red and chapped and shiny from Vaseline, but she rarely smiled, even when she claimed that Jesus had come to her in a dream or a vision—she was never clear about this—to tell her that she was His Chosen One, which I took to mean that we would never have sex before or after marriage. That was a bitter blow. My god, I had even pretended to speak in tongues! And since I had spent seven dollars on a black doorstop edition of the old American Standard version and I carried it around like my own personal cross and credential, I felt that I had been cheated. Still, one cannot lose hope, and that is a Biblical truth available for exegesis in any number of places. I believed. Oh, how I believed! I refused to stop imagining a time when her Oshkosh straps would come down, and I'd get past all that wool, and how we'd live communally, one gentle family in a barn with o ners of our like-minded friends. Did I mention that we met at a church retreat for twenty-something singles? I pretended to like dogs and cats, fur and drool, and I let myself believe I had found my way and someone to do it with while speaking a Phoenician dialect of my own making. That's what I mean about unbridled optimism: it can lead you to all kinds of rubbish and make-believe.

Now, in Jonestown they had lost hope and gained all manner of crazy in a much bigger way, believing that their Guyana paradise-compound was about to be invaded by the Feds. Shooting a congressman was probably not the best way to keep a low profile and one's name out of the news, so Jones probably had a point that the end was near. But still . . . cyanide in barrels of Flavor Aid and then lying down in the mud? As my non-believing mother used to say, "Nothing ever gets that bad that a hot shower can't fix." Police your area and tidy the corners. That was her recipe for a trouble-free life. And, "Human beings never fail to meet and exceed the lowest of your low expectations." Which was the sum and substance of her cautionary advice. You might not think so, but my mother had a sunny disposition since she was never surprised or disappointed. She could always imagine something worse. Take me. She had high hopes, but she also had her principles, and when I turned fervent, she closed her eyes, handed me ten dollars, and said a haircut might help. "And that girlfriend of yours," she said. "A dress wouldn't be entirely out of the question."

But to get back to my night job . . . The week before Christmas, my girlfriend had made our situation clear. She was leaving. Packing up. Taking off. She was leaving Portland, so this had nothing to do with me. Or with what I wanted. That's what she said. She liked our church, she liked her job, she liked *me*, she particularly liked my dreams, but she was going back to her parents' house in Tucson regardless, where she would wait in the desert for Jesus to reveal Himself again. Because visions don't happen in a rain forest.

"This has nothing to do with you," she said, and when I pointed out that that was clearly a lie, she offered no rebuttal.

We spent the next hour kissing and fumbling with our clothes, although in her case, she was kissing and holding on to her straps, and every ten minutes re-applying her Vaseline, so that by the time she left, my mouth was as swollen and slippery as bacon fat in a low-temperature oven.

And then, when our hour was up, she pushed her duffel bag into the back seat of a cab bound for the airport, where she would board a flight for Arizona and her encounter with the divine or, at least, lower humidity. She checked her watch. I saw her. *Who does that in the throes of a long goodbye?* "I'll call," she said wiggling her fingers in a wave. No, you won't, I thought. And she didn't. Just a note two weeks later indicating how much better she felt, with or without her expected vision. It wasn't personal. Sweet Jesus and all His apostles. It wasn't personal, like hell. This is the thing that I learned: when someone says that she can't love you because of some principle or other, it simply means that she doesn't love you. Not like that. Something is lacking, some chemical or pheromone or scent, and she was just going through the motions of love and attraction. She just couldn't pretend any longer, and no matter how hard you imagine otherwise, it's impossible not to personalize it or make the deficiency yours. She couldn't love me, but she couldn't say it, and since she couldn't say it, she had to get out of town.

So I took my deficiencies to work that night, feeling bitter and less-than, and I began by throwing around the trash cans while dumping the garbage, and then throwing the cans in a horrible clatter that echoed in the 5,000-square-foot bull-pen. That brought out one of the secretaries who worked in the offices on the perimeter. What she was doing there at eleven-thirty on an almost-Christmas night, I had no idea.

"Hey, hey, hey," she said. "What's all this?" She wore a frosted beehive at least ten years out of date and patted it, like an animal in residence atop her head. "This is a place where people work, you know." Up close, I realized that, hairdo notwith-standing, she was only a few years older than I. She weaved a little, back and forth, and her eyes were red and puffy. Her dress had bell sleeves and was cov-ered in paisleys. In addition to the bloodshot eyes and silvery beehive and the pais-leys that seemed to move like eels, she had the deepest tan I'd ever seen on a Portland resident in December, the consequence of a recent trip to Hawaii, the circumstances of which I'd learn about in due time.

"Sorry," I said. "I didn't know anyone was here."

"You'd be right about that," she said. "No one."

"What?" I said.

"No one. That's me."

"I thought I was alone," I said, "but I wasn't."

"You put in your time, you play all the right cards, and it's still not good enough." She sat down in the nearest desk chair with a graceless thump, her legs apart and her elbows between her knees and the animated print of her dress. Let out a fragrant sigh, a maybe-burp. "I have kids, you know."

I didn't know. She had two. A boy. A girl. Ten and seven. They were precious. They attended a school for exceptional children and overly-invested parents, and her darlings could now read Latin and French and Esperanto, in addition to English. They had learned to snorkel and scuba dive in Hawaii and became creatures of the sea. I took her word for it.

Her motherfucking, slimeball, son-of-a-bitch husband was another story. A doctor two years out of residency who was giving it to one of his nurses, a fact about which he had informed her while they were lounging on beach chairs on Kailua and watching their children act like dolphins from Ovid. He'd been living a double life for more than a year, and this vacation was their swan song, a Dear Jane goodbye with palm trees and coconuts and mythological overtones.

"Can you believe it? It's such a cliché. I worked while he went to medical school. My name is Joy, by the way, speaking of clichés. And irony. Ironic clichés."

Clichés and irony notwithstanding, Dr. Horndog had their darling precious maritime children for Christmas—he had taken them to his other life where he and his nurse were no doubt buying her children whatever they wanted to make her look hard and mean—and she had come to the office to forget her humiliations, real and imagined. Did I realize that she was working on the company's customer satisfaction survey? For a collection agency? Who could possibly be satisfied by a collection agency? At Christmas, no less . . .

Now, you can believe me or not, but this was my first response: "Jesus loves you, Joy," I said, and I wrapped her in a hug, which was usually successful in our Sunday evening Twenty-Something Seekers class but made her go as stiff as her Aqua Net hair. And, as if that weren't sensitive enough, I pulled out my doorstop of a Bible which had been riding shotgun in the janitorial cart and started reading Psalm 1: "Blessed is the man," I read, "or woman. Man or woman. Gender is as gender does, and you need all the blessing you can get," I said.

To which she said, "Amen, brother." And that was all the encouragement I needed, no matter the depth of her irony.

"Blessed is the man that walketh not in the counsel of the wicked
Nor standeth in the way of sinners,

Nor sitteth in the seat of scoffers:
But his delight is in the law of Jehovah;
And on his law doth he meditate day and night.
And he shall be like a tree planted by the streams of water,
That bringeth forth its fruit in its season,
Whose leaf also doth not wither;
And whatsoever he doeth shall prosper.
The wicked are not so,
But are like the chaff which the wind driveth away.
Therefore the wicked shall not stand in the judgment,
Nor sinners in the congregation of the righteous.
For Jehovah knoweth the way of the righteous;
But the way of the wicked shall perish."

Oh, I was on a roll, I tell you, for there was no limit to my pomposity or my certitude, and I could have expounded upon all the benefits of righteousness, which I knew more in theory than in practice, but she wasn't very interested.

"Aren't you sweet," she said, "but I'll have you know that the wicked tend to have all the fun. They prosper just fine. And they make the rest of us feel like shit. Don't you know that? How young are you?"

"I'm old enough," I said, although with no particular assurance.

"Look, when you're done here, let me show you something."

She waited while I finished throwing garbage into the bin on my cart, and she watched while I raced around the hallways with the dust mop. Then she pulled a set of car keys out of her purse and shrugged herself into a peacoat.

"You better drive," she said. She pulled an empty flask from her purse. "I'm in no fit state, I tell you."

She stumbled a little bit and leaned on me, but my guess was that she wasn't nearly as drunk as she wanted to be.

Downstairs in the basement garage, her keys opened a brand-new Mercedes complete with paper dealer plates.

"I can't drive this," I said. "No way."

"What's the matter? It's an automatic."

"I drive stick just fine. It's this—" I waved at the deep metallic red of the Mercedes' body, one of those sweet two-seaters generally driven by women in their sixties—"it's too much. I can't drive this; I'd be a nervous wreck. We can take my car, and I can bring you back later."

"Oh, my god, you little nance." She rolled her eyes. "Fine."

She rolled her eyes again when she saw Frankenstein. The monster slumped in the back corner of the basement, all four colors of primer and three years of mismatched parts, the glory and ingenuity of Speed's Downtown Auto Body and Repair.

"And this is?"

"A gold 1968 Mustang with a yellow '67 front fender and red '66 trunk with enough Bondo to keep a battleship afloat."

"Uh-huh."

"It will get us where you want to go."

Which had not been the case a month earlier when I had spun out on a patch of black ice on the Capitol Highway bridge, sending front and rear into the cement guardrail and backing up traffic for half a mile on the one-lane overpass. In the aftermath, I had called my mother with what I had hoped was tact. "I have good news and bad news," I had said. "The good news is that I'm okay."

"And that's the good news," my mother had said, and even over the phone, I could hear her sigh and the sound of the desk drawer where she kept her checkbook.

Given my usual scraping-the-edge, end-of-the-month bank balance, the good folks at Speed's had taken some delight in patching me back together again in the least expensive way possible: available mismatched parts, no paint, a clown car fit for its driver.

"Just my luck," my friend with the silver beehive said, "that your car would match your pants."

Because, after all, one does not do janitorial work in one's Sunday best, and while I had better, cleaner jeans, these were not those, holed and frayed and unclean as they were.

"Consider the lilies of the field," I said. "They're better dressed without even trying, but a driver's license, much less a new car, won't be necessary in the ever after."

"Fine, fine. It'll do." She opened the door and fell into the passenger seat, emitting a sound that was equal parts laughter and tears. "This is what I get."

And I thought, *Praise Jesus.* A soul crying to the Lord.

And *Score.* But I can't say I didn't feel a bit nauseated by my insincerity.

Because I looked at life then as a game with winners and losers with stories of conversion as the ultimate trophy. Was that the way that God saw it? On the other hand, this woman was already convinced of divine retribution; the sweet gospel of grace had to be child's play after that. Truth be told, though, in all my years as the truest of true believers, with myself as the only exception, I'd never witnessed another, man or woman, take the bait.

She pointed me in the direction of Macadam Avenue and a jazz bar in the Goose Hollow neighborhood. "You'll have no shortage of people to talk to there," she said. "They all need a little salvation."

There was one person in particular, she said, that she'd like me to meet. He had a view of life that was every bit as extreme as mine although much better informed.

"Mr. Magoo," she said. "That's not his name, but that's what everyone calls him." She looked at me sideways. "Bring your Bible."

"Oh, no," I said. "You don't mean Albert Steinmetz, do you? Dr. Steinmetz?" For from the moment that she mentioned Mr. Magoo, my heart had constricted and my fingers had grown numb.

"Yes," she said, "that's his name. Why? What's the matter? He's the sweetest man alive."

• • •

So let me tell you how I knew Dr. Albert "Mr. Magoo" Steinmetz. I hadn't known Jesus but a few weeks, ever since the draft lottery of 1973 left me with the number eight. Did I think an all-expenses-paid trip to Vietnam was imminent? I can't say that I did. Not really. Nixon had more than enough troubles by then. He and the war were so unpopular that sending the sweet white cream of the educated American middle class to the jungles of southeast Asia was the last thing he wanted to do. In truth, I was more oblivious than anxious. Even so, my low-level anxiety had taken me to the chapel on campus, where a student protest was in full flower. Someone handed me a sign (Side A, painted by others for all to see and cheer— "Fuck Nixon!"—with Side B, my own addition, for those in the know: "Number 8 ain't so great!"), and I was marching with the rest.

Dr. Steinmetz stood off to the side, wide as a bullfrog and squinting through his Coke-bottle glasses, along with several other faculty members, all of whom were known to me, even if they couldn't have picked me out of a line-up as one of their own. What I should mention is that, as a student, I was lousy and defensive and nobody's favorite, and that was due to Jesus, too, at least in part, since at the moment of my conversion I had come to believe that my professors were representatives of, at best, an indifferent secular society or, at worst, the Antichrist. So while across the river at Reed College, Steve Jobs was dropping out and making plans to change the world bit by byte, I was marching in a circle while I held a pasteboard sign, one that indicated an alliance with a liberalism I could not t ıst to be anything other than the devil's fifth column. How could I continue this counterfeit life when to remain was to live in the lion's mouth? On the other hand, leaving school meant the possibility of a wardrobe dominated by camo green. My mother would have called that "the horns of a dilemma," but she wouldn't have tried to solve it one way or another. She would have poured a glass of cheap red wine while listening patiently but offering no suggestions because she believed that life was nothing more than a series of unpleasant choices. Truly.

"There are moments of pleasure," she often said, sipping her preferred plonk, "brief, fleeting, and temporary, and then there's everything else. That's what you live with."

She believed this, I'm sure, even if this was rooted in the presence of my father's absence and the fact that his absence was the result of his periodic bombast and violence, along with the restraining order and divorce she obtained after he had threatened her with a ceremonial saber once employed by a member of Roosevelt's Rough Riders. "He didn't mean it," she said. "He was drunk. He was drunk a lot." In her case it meant the choice between life in a fourteen-room house near Forest Park or an apartment among the pawnshops and thrift stores of Sellwood. She could live with poverty, she said, but she sure as hell couldn't live while dead.

My choice had been Jesus and the lure of a larger, extended family, which I thought could be obtained at Dale Galloway's 82nd Avenue drive-in church. He called all God's lambs to meet Jesus at the snack shack, and I answered in the company of a girl, who I thought might be a girlfriend, but whose interests in me were wholly evangelistic. She had me fooled, of that there was no doubt. Did I want to accept Jesus as my Savior and Lord? Apparently, I did. Somehow the conversion stuck, even after my hoped-to-be girlfriend took off for Hollywood and the lure of bright lights, cameras, and mini-skirts with three tiers of fringe. When I told my mother about meeting Jesus amidst the hot dog wrappers and discarded popcorn boxes, she said, "Isn't that nice?" And when I told her about the "girlfriend" who was now among the missing, she said, "And that didn't tell you anything?"

"Like what?" I said.

"Like maybe you should have asked for extra butter," she said, "instead of a side of predestination."

My mother would have liked Dr. Steinmetz. With a tattoo on his forearm courtesy of a childhood spent in Bergen-Belsen, he taught New Testament Greek with a dry humor and a shake of his head. *You Christians!* Why should faith depend upon the translation, an interpretation of a single word here and there? Parsing the particulars and losing sight of the One. Was God not big enough to encompass all things? He smoked cigarillos throughout class, and the ash dusted his glasses and the dark suits he wore regardless of circumstance or weather. What sparked his interest in the gentile portion of the scripture, especially since so many gentiles had not-so-long-ago been in the business of trying to kill him and all his kind, I didn't know.

"Such privileged young people," he often said. "So pampered and well-fed."

So we marched around the chapel and chanted our slogans, and we postured for the local news crews, and then Dr. Steinmetz fell in next to me. "I have a question for you about your work."

"My work?" I said.

"I have noticed," he said, "peculiarities. Peculiarities that I would like you to explain."

"I'm not sure what I could tell you," I said, although I very well knew that I could.

I have said that I wasn't a good student, and ever since my encounter with the divine at the drive-in, I had become even worse, resentful of my professors and suspicious of their motives, since I believed that they were leading us all down the riskiest of garden paths. Critical inquiry was nothing more than a euphemism for heresy. That was my thinking. I couldn't even relax in a class on New Testament Greek. It was taught by a Jew, after all, a nonbeliever, and that was proof enough that something wasn't right, even if all the pre-seminarians loved him and trailed along after him like puppies jumping for treats. I saw it as one more proof that even our churches of the mainline variety were on the take. Could you blame me for dropping out?

But the real reason was that I had copied one of Elizabeth Newman's translation assignments, work that was often cited in class as brilliant and original if not inspired.

"You're sad, and you're stupid," she hissed. "Idiot, why couldn't you have copied from the Revised Standard? You have it sitting on your shelf, don't you?"

That Elizabeth—one more girl whose intelligence seemed to remove her from my own social and romantic sphere. Do you see a pattern emerging? She was fond of Dr. Steinmetz, and she was fond of me for about two minutes. She also was fond of her own particular syntax, and I guess that was what Dr. Steinmetz had noticed: two translations with the same idiosyncrasies, and he knew who had copied whom.

So, here I was: a Christian and a thief, and I had stolen the eighth chapter of Romans, or at least another's reframing of it. I couldn't face my Holocaust-survivor professor, and I couldn't get any lower. I filed my withdrawal papers the next day and relinquished my need-based funding with a signature. I never spoke to Dr. Steinmetz then about my so-called peculiarities, and I had no intention of doing so now five years and seven lousy jobs later.

"You see, Joy," I said, "that's why I can't go in there."

We sat in my Bondo-mobile with the windows down despite the chill; through the open doorway, I could see Dr. Steinmetz at a table with a wineglass in front of him and his customary cigarillo burning in an ashtray to the side, looking for all the world like Mr. Magoo come to life if Mr. Magoo were in the habit of haunting jazz clubs populated by students of the trust funded classes.

"Oh, boy," she said. "He probably doesn't even remember you."

"You're welcome to go in for a while if you want. I'll wait. But I'm not going in there."

"You're one sad sack of shit, aren't you?" she said, and then she opened her door, and the dome light winked in the darkness.

• • •

How does one go so wrong? I wondered. When I dropped out, my mother looked at me hard and said only, "Well, that's that."

"It wasn't for me," I said. "College. Not my thing."

"I don't suppose it was."

"No."

"You need to find your own way," she said. "Blah, blah, blah. You know the drill."

Did I?

I worked in a pizza parlor and a used car lot. I picked strawberries and blackberries with thirteen-year-olds and Guatemalan refugees. And then I started emptying the trash of the exploited white-collar class of the service industry. Boo hoo hoo, poor me. I went to church and dreamed of starting over in ways that were as ideal as they were delusional, dreams I couldn't seem to give up, not even after Jim Jones and the Flavor Aid and the Guyana mud.

Joy went into the bar, and when she entered, Dr. Steinmetz staggered slightly as he got to his feet, and then they embraced, and she pointed back at my car, and I scooted down in my seat to avoid being seen. They were talking and she was drinking from his glass and smoking his cigarillo, and then I must have dozed for a moment because the passenger-side door opened and the dome light came on, and I was left blinking.

"Onward, James. Take me home."

"Wait a minute," I said, trying to remember where I was and where I had been. "Your car. Don't you want your car?"

"Don't worry about it. Rides are easy. Rides are the easiest thing in the world." She lit one of Mr. Magoo's cigarillos, then opened her window to wave out the smoke. "He doesn't remember," she said, "in case you were wondering. He doesn't remember a thing about you."

"Well, that's something," I said. "Small mercies."

She directed me out to the Sunset Highway, past the zoo and through the Sylvan-Highlands before she had me use a tucked-away exit, one I'd never seen before, much less considered. The traffic lights at the top of the off-ramp blinked on and off, on and off in their three-in-the-morning solitude while two mock Tudors faced the highway.

"This is out of the way," I said.

"This is where I live."

"In two houses? His and hers?"

"No, dummy. We have renters."

The houses were an inheritance from her grandparents, so in addition to working at the collection agency so that Doctor Horndog could go to school, she had also provided the roof over their heads and a secondary income on the side. Until she was no longer needed, of course.

We walked up the steps to the front door of the house on the right, the only illumination coming from the stars above and the headlights on the highway below. She unlocked and opened the door and then began switching on lights: porch landing, front hallway, the rooms to the rear. The interior smelled clean: some kind of scented soap and furniture polish. A housekeeper was clearly on the payroll, even if a Christmas tree drooped in front of the front window, a wreath of needles surrounding its base.

"I don't water it," she said, catching my gaze. "After he took the kids, I kept hoping for spontaneous combustion."

She kept flipping on lights until the house was ablaze, upstairs as well as down. A floodlight illuminated the back patio, and the ripples of a pool appeared from lights above and below the surface of the water. Steam rose from the circle of a hot tub into the December air.

"Come on, Mr. Jesus," she said. "What do you think? Ready to live a little?"

With a quick twist, she had extricated her beehive from the paisley dress, standing in front of me in her bra and panties and then only her Hawaiian tan lines. Even the beehive came off, a wig, as it turned out, covering her cropped dark hair.

"Maybe we should introduce ourselves?" I said.

"I thought," she said, "that's what I was doing."

"No," I said, "names, a conversation, you know, getting to know you."

"Me, Joy," she said. "You know that. And you: you're the bullshitter with the Bible. The plagiarist and the coward. I know that. As if names and dates and history matter in a pants-free zone. Don't be a prune."

"Look," I said, shrugging off my jeans, "I think you mean prude, but I'm as horny as the next guy, I'm as horny as your husband, but I have my principles."

"Ex," she said, and she only needed one glance to counter me twice, "ex-husband, and I'm not so sure you do. Have principles, I mean. You're a man, aren't you?"

"Look, Joy," and I moved in for another embrace, although I can't say for sure it was entirely innocent or that I could have recited Psalm 1 from memory if that had been my intention. Not when she was standing in front of me with the remnant of her Hawaiian vacation staring me in the face and not when she kissed me and set off the disturbance that had been building inside my boxers.

"Fucking Christ," she said, pushing me away. "What does it take to get a little romance?"

"Um," I said, as articulate as I could manage.

"Little boys and monsters," She sighed. "Are there no good men?" Mascara ran from her eyes. "You're all dicks."

• • •

But all accounts, Jim Jones was as smart as he was charismatic and as charismatic as he was crazy, the kind of crazy fueled and abetted by various kinds of illicit medication. He was an evangelical who was keenly aware of racism and income inequality, a spiritualist who understood the methods for leveraging political power. What I'm saying is that he was a burning pile of contradictions and he carried along his followers in the holocaust of his own making. He had passion and he had faith, and that passion and faith became theirs and turned into their collective undoing in the sweet punch of death.

Now, I live in the district represented by Jackie Speier who, forty years ago, lay on the airstrip with five bullets in her right side and left for dead, while her boss, Congressman Leo Ryan, whose only hope was the Resurrection at the end of days, was totally dead. They had been attacked at the direction of a man whose paranoia had taken root in those contradictory elements of personality—the good and the crazy, the nasty and the sane—to which we are all liable, even as we pretend otherwise.

We start off with good intentions, and then we find another road and then another until we come to the end of all our branchings, a terra incognita of our own choice. How did we get here?

• • •

I woke up in one of the back bedrooms upstairs, surrounded by posters of Luke Skywalker and Han Solo and a headache that might as well have been a phalanx of the Emperor's stormtroopers. Eleven-thirty in the morning. My roommate would be having a fit, stomping around, threatening to push me off the next job site should I ever deign to show up. There are falls, I thought, and then there are falls.

After my failure, Joy had pulled out a fresh bottle of Old Overholt with an unbroken seal. "At least there's this," she said, and handed me a glass. "So, your girlfriend dumped you?"

"She did," I said, looking at the amber liquid. "Not the first time that's happened. Dumped, discarded, deserted. Take your pick."

"Well, that makes us quite the pair."

"I suppose."

The whiskey went down, burning, and I coughed, but I held out my glass for another pour, and I suppose this continued for some time: she drank and I drank, and she poured and poured, and she poured again. We had eased ourselves into the hot tub. She exited once to turn up the heat, and we let ourselves become parboiled. We talked, I guess, through the steam, and at some point, my doorstop American Standard went into the drink. I think I was trying to exegete Elizabeth's version of Romans 8, the chapter of my shame, despite its many assurances otherwise. Given our mutual abandonment, we might have consoled each other underwater since any number of things were going on below the surface. I said we might have. Did we? I'm not being coy or evasive. I don't know. I don't know when we left the pool or how I ended up in her son's bedroom, my clothes in a cold, damp pile at the foot of the bed. Sometime during the night, I threw up, but I managed to do so in the bathroom, getting most of it in the toilet, which to my mind qualifies as an honest-to-god miracle.

And that's how I woke up: a twenty-four-year-old virgin with a hangover who might or might not have had sex.

My face in the bathroom mirror was colorless except my eyes, the whites of which were the color of Pepto Bismol, one side of my face lower than the other, my nose dominating the center, and that was the moment that I knew that I was—objectively and literally speaking—ugly. I could have said ugly as sin, but making my appearance a metaphor would have diminished the fact of the literal, even as it also represented that deeper truth. Ugly, with no make-up or mask to hide behind.

Joy stood behind me in the bathroom, and we contemplated the me-in-the-mirror together.

She handed me back the Bible, which was now as swollen as a balloon from its time in the hot tub. "You may want this," she said. "I put it in the oven on low, but, well, this is what happened."

"I don't know," I said. "Maybe. Maybe I'll leave it with you."

"A memento," she said. "How sweet. A token to remember the evening by. Like a corsage." She sniffed the stiff, wrinkled pages. "Like a corsage, but not."

"I don't know what happened," I said after another moment. "I don't remember a thing."

"I have faith," she said. "It'll come back to you."

I got dressed in my clammy jeans and sweatshirt while Joy watched. My boxers, which smelled like mushrooms, I stuffed into her son's wastebasket.

"I lied," she said at last. "He remembered everything. I just didn't want you to feel bad. Or worse, I mean. Mr. Magoo said you were bright enough."

"Did he?"

"Yes. You didn't have to leave school. You just didn't believe you were worth very much. You quit. You could have fought, you could have negotiated, *you could have lied*, but you quit."

"You'd get along well with my mother," I said. "You'd understand each other."

"Leave the mothers out of this, shall we?"

It was after noon by the time I left, and the sky, which had been clear and starry in the early morning, was now gray. Mist hung in the air, and frost rimed my windshield. My breath ballooned with the captions of everything I couldn't have said.

She walked me to my car in her bathrobe and hugged me in full view of her tenants: an overweight husband and a pinched-looking wife, who were at that moment carrying Christmas presents from their car inside their rented house while their two small children screamed in their car seats.

"Goodbye, Joy," I said. "Forgive me. Nothing was— I'm not— It was quite a night."

"Jesus loves you, you know," she said.

"No need to mock me now," I said. "I'm too easy a target."

"Call me Hulga," she said, and although I was the one who would get the English degree in the years to come, she had the better grasp of her O'Connor, then and now, even if she had got parts of the story backward.

Retirement Dogs

YOU SEE THE MEN in our neighborhood: big, stoop-shouldered, shuffling men, retired after thirty-five or forty years of hard, physically demanding labor, carpenters and plumbers, police officers and letter carriers, walking the little mops and sausages that their wives have procured in the first flush of their husbands' retirements because it wouldn't do, no it absolutely wouldn't do for them to have nothing with which to occupy their time. Leashes drag the ground or stretch to the point of breaking. Shrill yips and yaps echo between the eaves as one retirement dog passes another. The men shrug their shoulders and avert their eyes, studying the sidewalk. These are the men who once barbecued whole pigs in the middle of our street on the Fourth of July. They drank suitcases of beer, worked the pit with pitchforks, and shouted instructions and imprecations to their teenaged children. Now, tiny poop bags dangle from their unleashed hands.

By dying early, my father was spared such indignities. By dying early, my father was spared the full bloom of my mother's dementia and the possibility that she might have purchased a Pomeranian and a rhinestone-studded collar-and-leash set while calling him by a former lover's name.

So, that's the story: my father died, and I came home because my mother was wandering the neighborhood in her nightgown at three o'clock in the morning looking for Bill, the aforementioned former lover. I came home only to find that the neighborhood of my childhood had become haunted with the husks of men I once knew, now shepherded by their Maltese and Shih Tzu and Havanese attendants.

I came home while my mother still knew me as her daughter.

She had forgotten my father and their thirty-seven years of marriage and remembered instead the two-week fling in Pismo with Bill in the fifth year of her marriage to my father. She and Bill ate fried seafood and drank cheap rosé in a bad hotel while my father changed my diapers and called his sister for back-up childcare.

I came home in the middle of a three-year NEH grant, the purpose of which I no longer knew or cared about. I came home to take care of my mother because my father was dead and my husband had cooked the books on his restaurant and was drinking everything in sight, and I wanted out before getting out was no longer an option. I came home only to find the sidewalks awash in small, yapping fluffballs and despondent, shackled men.

"Mr. DeBennedetto—" I say to our neighbor from down the street and our former postal carrier—"you have a dog." His Jack Russell terrier is beside him, and although the dog is no puppy and his muzzle is more gray than brown or white, he pogoes in the air, barking and yipping, a whoopee cushion in pain. All because I'm a stranger and he's a dog and not barking is not an option.

"*We*," he emphasizes. "*We* have a dog. Marla brought him home from the pound while I was watching Monday Night Football at the Dew Drop. She texted me that there was a surprise waiting. Dinner, I thought. A new recipe. Something with garam masala. Isn't that a thing? Or maybe something to spice up our romantic life, like a new nightgown or unguents. But when I got home, there was this snout poking over the back of the couch, and Marla was cooing about how cute he was. How we were saving him from the gas chamber. Even though I don't think they do that anymore, the gas. They use drugs, don't they? I said, 'Marla, we didn't talk about this. Marla,' I said, 'you have to give him back, you just have to,' which is when Marla began to cry and I began to cave because gas or drugs, it's all the same, isn't it?"

"I'm so sorry," I say. "I can't imagine a dog as a surprise, not unless you're a seven-year-old and this dog is a puppy with a bow. Which he's not. And you're not."

Which is when Mr. DeBennedetto says, "How's your mother?"

And I don't have much to tell him, except for the fact that this morning she tried to put coffee in the toaster and her dirty laundry in the microwave.

"I hear that Jack Russells can live as long as fifteen years," I say.

"I know," he says. "We'll die within days of each other."

Then there was my father, whose death none of us could have foreseen. A motorcycle cop for more than twenty years, he died not from being flattened by a garbage truck going the wrong way on a one-way street or by a grandmother in a Toyota failing to look before making a lane change, but when he fell off the roof of our house. He was replacing some asphalt tiles on the second story when he must have stood up and become light-headed, lost his balance, and fell to the driveway below. At least that's what the medical examiner surmised. His head cracked like Humpty Dumpty on the cement, and blood pooled like an oil stain. My mother blamed his bowed legs from all those years on his police hog. In a moment of lucidity, she had warned him against it and tried to stop him from getting the ladder from the garage. She was pacing inside the house, waiting for tragedy to occur, when she heard his body hit the pavement.

When she called me, she couldn't recall my father's name, blathering about Bill instead.

My father had programmed the phone with my number, and she was in the habit of speed dialing at all hours. I had become conditioned not to expect much from her calls.

"What, Ma," I said, while scrolling through the websites of divorce lawyers.

"Bill's dead," she said. "Bill. He didn't land on his feet."

"You have a cat?" I said. "And he's dead?"

"No!" She shouted, and it was clear that she was frustrated. "*Bill.* He's on the driveway."

By this time, Mr. DeBennedetto and Tommy Haslett, another neighbor from the other end of the street, had spotted my father and alerted 911, and an ambulance was on its way, too late to do any good as it turned out. Also, by this time, a crowd had formed since it was a Saturday morning, and the entire street was marked by yard sale signs and used furniture and not-so-gently-worn clothing, bargain hunters and trash pickers.

"Oh, Bill," my mother said, and the crowd parted for my mother and her madness and her cordless phone, so I heard it all. "He's broken," she said to everyone at large. "*Il s'est cassé la tête*," she said to me on the phone, her high school French emerging unbidden from some dark doorway.

"And who," I asked, genuinely mystified, "is Bill?"

• • •

All was made clear in time. Mrs. DeBennedetto wrestled the phone away from my mother and gently told me that Bill's broken head actually belonged to my father, and after his funeral my Aunt Jane, my father's sister, told me about Bill and my mother's two-week dalliance with him in the wake of my birth.

"She was fragile, even then, and she couldn't cope," Jane said. "Not with her husband on the back of that motorcycle, and not with a brand-new daughter who was crying twenty-three hours a day. You were a handful, you know. Colic. Or just ornery. On the other hand, Bill was an old high school crush who had a car and a hotel room and a collection of plaid sport jackets. She came back to her senses when he started leaving her at night so he could gamble at the Grover Beach casino. She came home to you and your father, that's what you need to remember. Even though the sex was great. So she said."

"Eww," I said and stuck my fingers in my ears, "la-la-la-lah-lah."

"Oh, please. You think you're so liberated, but the thought of your parents wanting some is more than you can take."

"I can't think of *myself* wanting some without throwing up a little bit."

Sex had never been great with Peter. Tolerable mostly. Bordering on pleasurable only once in a great while. But never great. *Never*, more's the pity. Not that he knew or recognized it or even considered the possibility that the experience might be other than golden. He talked about it afterwards like a sportscaster reporting the highlights. I knew that if I told him the truth, he'd sulk, and then I'd feel obligated to charm him out of his mood, a gesture not worth the effort or outcome. *Let him have his illusions*, I thought, and then as a rider, *maybe I'll have some peace of mind*. Which was necessary since I had come to the crossroads of my grant-funded study of Ernest Hemingway's wives. I had promised in my grant proposal a big, provocative book, an expansion of my dissertation, that used Hadley, Pauline, Martha, and Mary as the embodiments of his own clichés of femininity, but of late that ax seemed well-enough honed. What more was there to say, other than to make it worse than it actually was? And, if there wasn't more to say, then it was worth only a big fat yawn. All this while Peter was in hock to the Russians who had muscled their way into all the hipster restaurants in the Hawthorne district. And because he was in hock to the Russians, he was fabricating the daily receipts, and because he was in for a penny, in for a pound, he was also drinking, and because he was drinking, what had once been tolerable was now just ten minutes of distraction before he got out of bed once again and opened the cabinet above the refrigerator and started shuffling bottles. So, after my mother called and Mrs. DeBennedetto intervened, I didn't need another excuse to call for an Uber to the airport.

• • •

I landed in Fresno on an August afternoon, as the temperature was cresting at 108 degrees. An honor flight from D.C. was coming in at the same time, and the tunnel from the gates to the concourse was jammed with eighty- and ninety-year-olds in wheelchairs and walkers and canes, in various stages of infirmity and military dress. Their wives and middle-aged daughters were waiting with signs and flags and little dogs in arms: Chihuahuas, dachshunds, and pugs. Some wiseacre had an air horn with which to celebrate the men's return, and every few seconds the terminal reverberated with the pain and echo of high-pitched barks.

"Wendy," a voice called. "Wendy, yoo-hoo."

Samantha Guidry, who grew up three houses away from me, was waving wildly.

"What are you doing here?" she said.

"I could ask you the same."

She had an oversized bag looped over one shoulder and across her chest, and the head of a silky Pekingese played peek-a-boo behind her arm.

"The Grand's on this plane," she said. "He went back with two other army buddies to see the monuments one last time before they die. They've become morbid old fucks. And I ended up watching Coco for a week. Fucking little fuck-turd. I can't wait to hand her back." She paused, and I could see light come and go from her eyes. "I'm sorry about your dad. I heard. So, this is why you're back, I'm guessing."

"My father fell off the roof, and my mother is losing her mind. That pretty much sums it up," I said.

"No Peter?"

"Nope. He's the other shoe," I said. "Living with Mom for a while will seem like a picnic by comparison."

"Fucking hell," she said. "Sorry, Wen."

"Not half as sorry as yours truly," I said.

But then, another rank of nearly-dead war heroes emerged, among them Sam's grandfather, whose motorized wheelchair carried himself and two carry-ons. Clear tubes snaked from his nose while a garrison cap tilted rakishly from his bald head. When Coco spotted him, she began scrabbling furiously against the constraints of the bag until finally she freed herself from Sam's grip, launched herself to the floor, and bolted down the carpet, leaping into her owner's lap, her leash trailing behind.

"Hwar, hwar," Sam's Grand blurted.

Laughter joined the airhorns and the barking and the general din of a happy return.

"Fucking hell," Sam said again. "Fucking little fuck-turd."

• • •

Did I mention that in the first year of our marriage, not long before the Russians, the duplicate sets of books, and the bottles, Peter brought home a five-pound female puppy of indeterminate breed? Saying it was for me? No? I was turning twenty-seven, in the throes of my dissertation, and he had seen a box of free puppies across the street from Powell's, and he assumed that a dog would keep me from being depressed in the evenings.

"We'll be able to tell," he said, "about our fitness."

"What are you talking about?"

He winked at me. "Being parents," he said.

"Maybe we ought to work on being married," I said. "Make sure we've got the hang of that first."

"Sure, sure." But I could tell he was not to be dissuaded. "She'll be great when you need a break from reading or writing. Nothing better than seeing your puppy become housebroken."

"And you know this from what experience?"

"I've had dogs since I was ten. And now you have a dog."

"Your *parents* have had dogs since you were ten. You were just another member of the litter."

I have to say that this was one of the things that had caught at me when we had first started dating—Peter's parents and their indifferent regard, as though he were another in their herd of Irish Setters.

"And," I said, "who says this is 'my' dog? I didn't sign up for that."

"Don't be like that."

What he didn't like was that I hadn't fallen all over myself for his gift of a free dog, and he especially didn't like that I made it clear that I was having nothing to do with the care, feeding, or training of said dog.

"Let me know when you have her sorted," I said, "and I'll reconsider."

Peter started gamely enough; I have to say that much for him. He walked Portia morning, noon, and night three days in a row but then started to miss his appointed rounds. He signed Portia up for obedience lessons and managed to show up for the first one before there were schedule conflicts. He bought food and bowls and puppy pads, balls and chew toys and jerky snacks, but he found it difficult to pick up the puppy pads when they became soaked, and he forgot to refill the food bowl at a regular time. She chewed the baseboards and clawed the doors. I found fingers of poop behind the couch and on the bathmat, but I let them lay where I found them, waiting for Peter to notice.

Peter lasted ten days altogether. The restaurant got busy. He was distracted. Cash flow problems. It was raining. In Portland, go figure. While I wrote about Hadley's devotion toward her younger, unfaithful husband, Portia stared at me with reproach, and when she wasn't staring, she was barking to let me know that her pad was soaked, her bowl was empty, or that the wind was blowing the rain against our windows and the sound frightened her. I wrote, feeling angry and guilty in equal and alternate measures. But I wouldn't be coerced, and the anger won. One day I came home, and the house was quiet, and three days later Peter admitted that he had taken Portia to a halfway house for mop dog rescues—it was Portland, after all, and yes, there are such places—and while he had felt heartbroken to say goodbye, he knew she'd have a better life than with those who were unable or unwilling to care for her.

"Don't put this on me," I said.

"I'm not." He sat at the kitchen table with his head in his hands and was as glum as I'd ever seen him. "I'm just so sad," he said. "She stared at me with those button eyes, and I felt awful. Like a failure. A terrible dog owner and a complete and total failure of a human being. Bad, bad, bad. My parents would be appalled. They're terrible people, but they know dogs." But that's when he brightened up and told me about the restaurant's new investors. "Our money worries are over." So, if the Russians were the beginning of the end, then Portia was the end of our beginning.

• • •

Before I left for college in Eugene, my father sat me down in the den. I was afraid that he might feel obligated to have some sort of serious talk—about men and women, about sex, about alcohol and drugs, about responsibility and safety; he was, of course, a motorcycle cop, and he had only survived the dangers of his job by virtue of his hypervigilance—but instead he wanted to know whether or not I planned to attend any of the games at Autzen.

"Your mother and I might come if you can get us some tickets," he said. "If you don't mind your parents being underfoot for a weekend."

"You don't need an excuse," I said. "I miss you guys already."

I was telling the truth at the time. Even though every day of that last summer I felt the tug of a new life and a letting go of the old, I didn't realize how quickly everything would change once I hit campus. Is there anyone more self-absorbed than an eighteen-year-old freshman girl, away from home for the first time?

During the week of freshman orientation, I met Peter. He had a red halo of hair, full lips, and a way of talking to strangers as though they were cousins newly revealed. He was Peter, and I was Wendy, and I thought I had met my soul mate. Silly me. I didn't realize that his Neverland was loneliness. His parents lived in Eastmoreland with their kennel of six setters, and that was my first exposure to dogs as an anodyne for meaningful human relationships. Peter's father taught philosophy at Reed, and his mother was on seven different volunteer boards. In her spare time, she raised their Irish Setters, those overbred dogs who are as neurotic and skittish as they are beautiful. She spoke to them as though they were her confidants and then locked the kennel gate, leaving them with their own company.

I met his parents that first Thanksgiving rather than go home to mine. Their dinner was prepared by a private chef and looked like a magazine layout, but nothing was as expected. The turkey smelled like fennel and the sweet potatoes tasted like cherries. Peter's mother drank Chardonnay before and throughout dinner, and by the time dessert was brought from the kitchen, her head was on the table. His father disappeared before the pies could be cut.

"Are you hungry?" Peter asked.

"No," I said, although I could have murdered a bag of tacos.

"I'm sorry," he said. "They don't go out of their way to be nice."

"No," I said, "they're awful people, but it's not your place to tell them."

We left the next morning and were happy to be back in our respective dorm rooms and eating institutional food with others who had nowhere else to be. I realized that by meeting his awful parents, I had somehow made an unspoken commitment: to see how awful they were was to be enlisted in Peter's support team.

On the other hand, we spent Christmas with my parents, which was easier, except that my mother was already beginning to show signs of the deterioration to come, and my father had his reservations about the boy I'd brought home.

He pulled me aside one morning before Peter could make his appearance from the guest bedroom. "I like him, don't get me wrong," my father said, "but he's a little bit soft at the center. Like, you push too hard, you might make a hole." His forehead was creased; I could tell he was concerned that he might have said too much, but he was only saying what I already suspected but hadn't yet put into words.

"His parentals are nuts," I said, automatically assuming my role as his defender. "They're smart people, they know everybody important, and they have loads of money, but they're assholes. His mother treats their dogs better."

My father, who didn't approve of swearing or otherwise harsh language, winced. "They can't be that bad," he said weakly.

"They can, and they are."

That was when we heard my mother keening in frustration from the kitchen. She was sitting at the table attempting to refill the salt shaker without taking off the top.

"Mom," I said, "what are you doing?"

"Sweetheart," my father said, taking the box of salt and the shaker from her. "Let me give you a hand."

We never managed to finish our conversation, and that night Peter and I made love for the first time. It did not go any better the first time than it did the last: so clumsy and inexpert and needy as to qualify as accidental coupling rather than intercourse. I'd had better experiences at high school keggers with a dim-witted football player from Clovis. At the time, I blamed the ambiance of the guest bedroom, and the ruffled shades on the end table lamps. But that was just me, beginning a pattern of rationalization that would last for years, and like my glimpse of Peter's parents and his childhood, this only seemed to be one more bond that would keep us together rather than send us on our separate ways. In the morning, he seemed to believe that the experience had been transcendent rather than the travesty it was, and he would have been more than happy to talk about it.

"Nope," I said, refusing his offer of a discussion. "Not my thing."

He was clearly disappointed, and I was clearly a slow learner.

We lived together for eight years, we were married for another five, thirteen years in unlucky total, but it took my father's death and my mother's unmooring for me to make a move

· · ·

In the front hallway of my parents' house, an étagère—that signifier of middle-class establishment and pride—features a series of photographs: my class pictures from elementary, middle, and high school. Since my parents had only one child, they evidently decided to people the house with a kind of time-lapse multiplication. More noteworthy, however, are those portraits of my parents at various police department events, my father in his uniform, my mother in either cocktail dresses or ball gowns. It seemed they never stopped going to proms, and if I were the jealous sort, I might see in this my exclusion.

Which reminds me that, while growing up, I used to measure myself against her, but the comparison was always unfair. How could my lank ponytail of mousey brown compare to my mother's highlighted Farrah Fawcett layers? When I was in high school, she borrowed my clothes as a matter of course; they looked great on her and better fitting than they were on me. She offered me hers, in turn, but we both knew I'd never wear them, bookish, flat-chested thing that I was.

What I wanted throughout elementary and middle school was a dog. I begged her for a dog, which was the least that my parents could do, or so I thought, since I had no brothers or sisters. By high school, I'd given up, but in my sophomore year, she brought home two kittens, a male and a female, in a Del Monte box filled with newspaper strips. They had been abandoned by their mother at such a young age, their eyes were only half open, and they mewled and bumped into each other.

"Cats," I said. "Why cats?"

"They're independent," she said.

"That's why you're feeding them with an eye dropper?"

"They will be," she insisted.

She purchased all the necessaries—formula, bottles and nipples, a heating pad, pet carriers—and she fed them round the clock until they became fat young things. All was well for several weeks, and my mother doted on them, her zeal for the kittens displacing her Pilates routine. I lent a hand now and then, but they tended to bite anyone other than her, and my sympathies did not extend to the puncture wounds their teeth inflicted or the inflamed stripes their claws left.

"They're kittens," my mother said, "and that's what kittens do."

But even her sympathies were tested when one of the kittens dropped a hummingbird carcass into one of her pumps, and they lost their ally entirely when both began to claw the sofas and armchairs, leaving the fabric in threads and shreds. They looked at their claw post as though it were an amusing idea imagined by an idiot.

"That's it," she said, "we're done with this."

She put them in their respective crates and loaded them into the back seat so I could ride shotgun. She carried them to a clinic she had found in the phone book, where a veterinarian looked at her strangely but did not say no when she explained what she wanted.

"You won't be able to let them outside ever again," he said.

"Of course," she said. "I can handle cat litter, but I will not be party to the murder of innocent birds, nor will I condone the destruction of personal property. We will make do with their presence indoors."

"Fine," he said, clenching his jaw before he took them to the back of the clinic. "So long as you're sure."

"What's with him?" my mother said. "I'm only asking him to do his job."

"Maybe he's having a bad day," I said. "Maybe a horse died."

"Or maybe he's just an asshole," she said. "Just because you love animals doesn't mean you're a good person."

When we retrieved them several hours later, they were still tottery from the anesthesia and cowering in their crates.

"They'll be fine," my mother told me.

"No," the vet said, "they are not fine, and I am not fine, as I have participated in a mutilation at your behest."

He went on to describe the details of the procedure, the amputation of the tips of the toes, the cutting through of ligaments and tendons.

"They are in pain," he said, "but your furniture will remain pristine so long as they don't urinate on your couches in revenge."

"If they do that, buddy, you can bet I'll be back," she said, "but then we'll be discussing the final solution."

She paid, and we walked to the car, the kittens rolling this way and that inside their carriers, making small terrified sounds.

"The nerve of him," she said. She adjusted her sunglasses, pulled down her visor to block the midday glare, and started the car.

But when we pulled to a stop in the driveway, she put her head down on the steering wheel and wept. "I had no idea," she said. "He could have told me."

Those cats lasted for sixteen years, and she was right in one sense: they were independent, they wanted little to do with anyone other than themselves, and they asked for nothing except for food, water, and a litter box. They slept for twenty-three hours a day, blending in with the furniture they once tried to destroy, and were as useful as two extra throw pillows. They shed drifts of fur at regular intervals and hocked up hairballs in front of the television. They lasted for sixteen years, and I suppose they had a fine enough life, all things considered, but that afternoon, my mother brought them home and then went to bed for the next forty-eight hours convinced of her own wickedness.

• • •

So, my father was notable for his caution and prudence, and his lifetime habits were undone by one moment on a rooftop under a hot sun. My mother, on the other hand, was known for a flightiness and a changeability of mood that over time turned into anxiety and then paranoia. Before her dementia became clear, she was prone to sudden and obsessive bursts of hobbies and interests. Watercolors and community theater one year, the saxophone, woodworking, and diesel mechanics the next. She outlined a novel about Chinese missionaries and the opium trade. There were the cats. "Your mother is a woman of many passions," my father was fond of saying, although he conveniently omitted Bill from his list. "She's color and noise," he also said, by which I understood him to mean that, though colors can be beautiful in certain combinations, they can also clash in others, and while noise can be music, it can also be sound and fury with all its attendant nonsense.

On the other hand, I left home for college, returning only infrequently. After graduation, I allowed myself to become trapped, inured by another person's needs, spending the next thirteen years living with the consequences. I wrote a dissertation on Hemingway's wives—all of those enablers, trophies, and bank accounts—and then got halfway through an expanded, more commercial version, but the woman I should have been writing about all along was Zelda.

• • •

On the third morning that I was home, my mother was nowhere to be found. Her bed was rumpled, the bedspread on the floor, but she was not in it. Three days at home, and I had already lost her. Panic grew. I finally found her in the downstairs guest bath, the one with the embroidered hand towels and dusty decorative soaps that no one ever uses. She was standing in the dry shower in her nightgown and robe.

She turned to me as I opened the door. "Do you know," she said, her eyes vacant, "what I do next?"

"If you're talking functionally, then take off your clothes and turn on the water." I held her hand and helped her from the shower. "But if you're talking existentially, then I'm not sure I'm the one to ask."

I have no idea what possessed me. It certainly didn't help either of us.

"I love you, Jane," she said, speaking to me as though I were her sister-in-law and this was years earlier, when she had behaved badly. And then her eyes searched my eyes, and something clicked into place. "Wendy, I mean," she said. "Wen, something bad is happening, but I don't know what it is."

"None of us do," I said. "None of us ever do."

· · ·

The sun sets behind the haze and mountains to the west, and twilight begins, the sky an arc of reds, pinks, and shades of blue from the palest cyan to deepest Delft. Our sky in summer is often best described as dirty and gray and nondescript, cloudless but without sun. Heat and dust, smoke and smog conspire. But evenings can be magical. A red sun, a breeze. The parade of dogs and dog-walkers. Our neighbors lurch behind their collection of retirement dogs. Leashes cross, legs are tangled, and seventy-year-olds perform a complicated ballet: pirouettes and arabesques with their furry, beribboned partners. My mother's arm is trapped securely beneath my own, and we walk slowly in tandem, a choreographed pair, one more part of the parade. We greet the DeBennedettos, the Hasletts, and the Guidrys. We bend over and pat their little dogs while they gnaw our hands. We say good night and move forward, one step at a time.

Attachments for the Platonically Inclined

I'M NOT GOING to sugarcoat it or try to explain it away. I acted badly. In this era of the pandemic and social distancing, she was cleaning as a way to keep busy, use the time, and be productive at home, but I should mention that nearly every bad thing I have ever done happened when Francie was cleaning, even in the best of times, because, for her, cleaning means disposal rather than scrubbing or dusting or washing. Sometimes the frenzy becomes too much for her. And me. This is a fact that must be acknowledged and, in my case, accommodated. Over the years she has thrown or given away many, many things, but the castoffs for this particular moment have been especially telling: clothing (the plaid sport coat I wore when I received the Jablonski Prize as a high school senior); kitchen appliances (my George Foreman hamburger grill); and sports accessories (a Roto Grip bowling ball, with which I bowled my only 300 game). Don't get me wrong; she gets rid of her own things as well. These are merely the latest examples of the hundreds of items that have made their way to Goodwill, the Salvation Army, American Veterans, the hospice thrift store, not to mention our local landfills, and I name them only because they were once mine and I remember them. Sometimes with fondness, sometimes with regret.

The fury of her cleaning and disposal makes me nervous for reasons I don't entirely understand. I'm not threatened by the loss of my material possessions alone—I hadn't worn that jacket in nearly fifty years, for example, so its time was clearly past the expiration date—but I am threatened by what that loss represents: the memory of what lives within those objects and the sense that history is being scrubbed free of the presence of my past.

"Who could forget you?" she asked. "I mean, really. You're sixty-five years old, and you're in all the yearbooks, but for a man you make a good drama queen. You act like the child who hasn't been chosen."

"Oh, sure," I said. "Easy for you to say, Miss Easy Come, Easy Go. Little Miss Sophomore Girl."

I happen to know for a fact that she has jewelry she wore when she was ten. It's squirreled away in a bag at the bottom of a cedar chest, and she would no more wear it now than she would wear Mickey Mouse ears, but it would break her heart to see it go.

Maybe, though, maybe I take this too much to heart. We get stuff, we get rid of stuff, stuff is not us. I should be able to turn the page, right?

• • •

So, the Jablonski Prize. Named for Morton and Wilda Jablonski and endowed by their children with proceeds from their estate, the Prize honored the high school senior deemed to have the most promise. The Jablonskis performed together for forty-five years in our local community theater scene. They owned Morda's, half theater space, half restaurant, neither of which was very good. The prime rib was overcooked or gelid, the drinks were weak, and the theater consisted of drawing-room farces and scripts considered racy in 1936, but they were a generous and warmhearted pair. As I say, Morda's was nothing to get excited about, and it only became worse under the ownership of their children, who saw it as their own private slush fund, but it was a local institution and its time could be dated from the speakeasies. One more reminder that longevity can make up for any number of deficiencies. That's true for individuals as well as institutions, and I am a case in point.

I know most people point to junior high and high school as a gauntlet of zits and hormones, public awkwardness and romantic devastation, but I found a home there among the socially frightened and the intellectually callow, a home that I never found so accommodating again. Academics came easy, student government v is a natural, and a spot on the football and baseball teams paved any number of bumpy interpersonal paths. I might as well have had a key of ownership since I was there each day and for longer stretches than the janitors. At the end of each academic year, I was up and down the stairs, to and from the stage, picking up my annual graft from the principal and the other too-eager-to-please faculty, as though the plaques, ribbons, medals, and certificates were my right. All of those ended up in a trunk in my parents' garage, and when they died, the trunk migrated to the attic, that cave where it has remained in hiding from Francie for the last fifteen years, awaiting the recycling bin and its final end.

At the end of my senior year, when I stood up at the awards assembly to accept the Jablonski from Morton and Wilda's oldest daughter, my plaid sport coat led the way. Pretty splashy, I was; I could have had a job at any used car lot in town at that moment, but I had bigger fish in mind. College, for one thing, and a bigger town in which to shine. That I went to college but then came back is part of the story; that Bernadette Jablonski, then in her forties, handed me my check and kissed and kissed and kissed both my cheeks, leaving lip prints all over my face, is another. The moment gave me ideas, ideas that were no more sustainable, as it turned out, than they were original.

On the other hand, Francie didn't have it so easy; I have to admit that. Her parents split up when she was fourteen, and she was forced to witness all the shouting, money-grubbing, and vile adult behavior that ensued. Dishes were thrown, glasses were shattered, and murder-suicide threats were a daily occurrence. She lived on the other side of town and on the other side of the high school from me—it might as well have been the other side of the moon—and she was the oldest of seven, so she was constantly responsible for cleaning up somebody's mess. Sometimes it was one of her younger siblings who had thrown up in bed from the stress, but sometimes it was one or the other parent who had drunk too much the night before and was the culprit. She made breakfasts out of the demolished boxes in the pantry and dinners out of air. Given her circumstances, none of the teachers at school were surprised that Francie Peck didn't have her homework done, her assignments read, or her papers written, nor were they surprised when she showed up for tenth grade with her hair dyed green, black widows tattooed on each wrist, and her jaw clenched so tight that her lips didn't show. What that meant, I understand now, but then, given my own self-absorption, she was merely intriguing. As exotic and dangerous as one of those carnivorous plants.

So of course I asked her out that year. I was a senior and she was a sophomore, and while I might have had the edge by age, she was by far the cannier of the two of us.

"You're kidding, right?" she said when I said we should do something, just the two of us. "You think I'm dressing up for you?"

"No," I said. "What makes you think that?"

She held her arms out as though inviting inspection. "Take a guess, Mr. Hot Shot."

She was inviting me to look at her T-shirt with its baked-in-the-dryer soup stains and her paint-spattered blue jeans, all of which could have used a wash, and as oblivious as I was, I knew that the subtext was: (a) she had no better clothes than this; (b) even if she had better clothes, she wasn't about to put on anything finer just to engage in hand-to-hand combat in the tight back seat of a Camaro; and (c), what could we possibly have had in common?

I had no answers to either (a) or (b), so I answered (c) instead: "I'd like to get to know you," I said, which was equal parts evasion and truth.

I convinced her to go bowling, thinking that such a neutral activity would raise no objections, but I would be wrong. We had just gotten out of the car in the parking lot of Rodeo Lanes when she stopped and crossed her arms over her fifteen-year-old, less-than-imposing chest.

"Nuh-uh," she said. "Nope."

She pointed to the bag that held my ball and shoes. The bag that I had pulled out from behind the driver's seat and now held in my right hand.

"You have your own ball, and you have your own shoes. You're going to make me wear those red and green clown shoes worn by Grandma Moses and Mother Jones and make me stick my fingers in holes where who knows whose boogers have gone, while you wear deck shoes and use a ball that you clean on every other throw? And you're going to say we had a good time? I don't think so. No thank you."

"I've been in junior leagues since I was seven," I said. "Is that my fault?"

"Take me home," she said. "I knew this was a bad idea. The last time I went bowling, it was someone else's birthday party when I was ten, and they put the bumpers in the gutters so we wouldn't cry."

"Look," I said. "I'll rent the clown shoes, I'll use a house ball, and I'll ask for bumpers if you want. If the lanes are quiet, they might even turn on the disco ball and the strobes."

"Don't be ridiculous," she said. "Put the bag away, and we'll call it good."

I did as I was told: put the bag behind the front seat, wore the rentals, and rolled the Fred Flintstone ball with the holes made for sausages rather than fingers. I didn't bother to keep score since she said it wasn't important. That hurt me, but I did as I was told, and we got along just fine, even if it wasn't the game that I knew. We got along just fine for the rest of that year as well, even if now and again we retreated to the back seat of the Camaro.

· · ·

I guess what I'm saying is that I had it easier than most, easier than my wife for sure, and if I have my periods of regret it's only that I wish I had worked a little harder to earn the respect of others. I went away to college with my five hundred dollars of Jablonski money and the blessing of my parents, who underwrote the rest.

Francie came to see me the day before I left. She brought me a handmade card that said "Go ahead, take off, you jerk!" on the front. On the inside, it said, "Many, many happy, happy returns!" and then in smaller script, she had written, "assuming you come back, at all, that is." We had talked about this, and we knew that I was going to college while she was going into her junior year of high school; we had seen such relationships wither and die in the space of a month or two, so we had agreed we wouldn't put ourselves under that kind of pressure. Make a clean break of it, we said. Use the year to start over with new friends, and in a year or so, when we'd caught our breath from everyone and everything new that we'd experienced, we'd see where things stood. We were very proud of ourselves for being so mature.

I went to college as a math major, but thanks to Bernadette Jablonski, I thought of myself as an actor. I had played bit parts in school productions, but that last summer, I played Kolenkhov in Morda's production of *You Can't Take It with You*, and I discovered that after graduation I wasn't done with applause or attention. Oh, no. My Kolenkhov was ripe with Russian alveolars and guttural disgust, and I enjoyed the process of dying my hair as black as Raskolnikov's heart and attaching a beard with spirit gum. I bellowed my part with gusto. If anyone had asked what the play was about, I would have said that it was the life and times of a displaced Russian ballet instructor who happens to meet an everyday American family. I was that much in love with myself and prisoner to the idea. If I were honest, however, I would have had to admit that I could never wrap myself inside the character, no matter how much spirit gum I applied, how much volume I used. I was too worried about forgetting my lines. Francie came to see my star turn twice, and both times she had to hedge her assessments.

"Well, that was interesting," she said the first time. "I'm not sure the beard is you." And, "You were very consistent," she said the second time. "Your beard stayed put both times." Not exactly the heartiest of endorsements.

I didn't let her reaction bother me; Bernadette had already cautioned me about critics. She said I was to pay no mind, which I didn't because she said this as she was taking off my beard with dabs of rubbing alcohol and cotton balls and touching me in places where my beard had never been. Besides, what would poor little Francie know about theater, she of the benighted family and unenriched life? She didn't even know how to bowl.

Bernadette had cast herself in the role of Essie Carmichael, for which she was clearly too old, while her husband Walter Schneiderman played Grandfather Vanderhof using an accent straight from a Down Easter's lobster boat. At one point in Act II, I was meant to hoist Bernadette-as-Essie in a lift, but she proved to be a little too heavy and I proved not to be up to the challenge, so we played it for laughs. Night after night, she fell to the stage in a whirl of silk tights, translucent panties, and a cartwheel of pancake tutu. Her legs stuck out like Raggedy Ann's, and she swore off-script, which made the laughs from our know-nothing audience that much louder.

On our closing night, Bernadette cleaned my face of beard and then delivered me from high school inexperience in the women's restroom of the middle school theater where our production had wrapped. She locked the door from the inside to keep any latecomers at bay and then hopped onto the ledge of one of the sinks with a nimbleness that belied her supposed gracelessness on stage. The ups and downs of her tutu were as exhilarating as they were frightening and mysterious.

Her husband was, at that moment, striking the stage, and we could hear the sound of furniture and backdrops being loaded onto dollies.

When we were through, which took about as long as it took for my pants to drop, she removed her stage paint and touched up her shellacked hair.

"Honey," she said, "there will be others, but you'll never have better."

A lie wrapped in a truth, but I didn't know which was which, and that was as frightening as anything. I could replay what she had done, but I couldn't bring myself to use the words with which to name it. Was it any wonder I had to go to college?

• • •

I didn't get my degree in math, and I didn't go on stage ever again despite my many auditions, and I could feel my star fading by the minute. College was a time of discovery, and one of my biggest discoveries was that not many cared what happened to me, award assemblies of the past notwithstanding. My high school teachers continued to award prizes to younger and younger students, and they no longer seemed to think much of my promise if they thought about me at all. They doted on the next years' crops instead like faithless lovers. So I became an English major with a teaching credential on the side, and I returned home like Ulysses without the fanfare or the slaughter, only the resignation of a sunbaked oar. Rather than the conquering hero, I was just another wet-behind-the-ears new hire with a less than exemplary degree. My chemistry teacher from five years earlier shook his head, and his eyes and his words betrayed his judgment. "English?" he said. "When you could manipulate differential equations? You could have worked for NASA."

"Well," I said in my own defense, "these things happen."

I could have kicked myself for not having something wittier to say. He was no summer's day, of course, while I had a true mind, and there was no impediment in my way of the truth of the human predicament, a truth that no number or derivative or launch angle ever could find. That's what I wanted to say, but I didn't because I didn't entirely believe it, even if the space program had come to the end of its Golden Age.

Even Bernadette Jablonski didn't seem entirely happy to see me on my return.

"You," she said. "Aren't you supposed to be making the world safe for technology?"

"I'm teaching now," I said, to which she replied: "Oh, my god. That's what they all do, isn't it?"

I had gone to see her at Morda's since I had heard they were rehearsing one of their chestnut revivals. She had cast herself as Aunt Abby in *Arsenic and Old Lace*, a role which was at least a little closer to her own age, even if she was clearly targeting the high schooler she had fingered for Mortimer Brewster. I no longer fit her preferred demographic, but given the number of her former prizewinners manning the other male parts, I could see that I was entirely outside her circle of admirers and no longer particularly welcome.

As if that weren't enough, I had lost touch with Francie, who was nowhere to be found. I heard from others that she had dropped out her senior year, then got her GED, and after that, left town with a bus ticket, no firm plans, and barely a hint of a goodbye. Who knew? I came back to resume my life only to find that nothing was different but everything was changed.

I threw myself into teaching since I had nothing else to do, and if I wasn't very good, I could organize my students into lockstep and make them march through the curriculum like a brigade of shell-shocked survivors. Discipline and attention to detail are not substitutes for charisma and love, but they will suffice for a paycheck and job security and statistical result. I wouldn't let the adolescents in my charge horse around with *Romeo and Juliet* any more than I'd let them off the hook for the correct use of there, their, and they're, and if I refused the invitation to teach the seniors, that was only due to my knowledge of what disappointments lay in wait for them. I gained a reputation, just as I gained a wife, a mortgage, two sons, and Caesar, the dumbest of dumb Labradors: slowly and over the course of years. Brick by brick. But then, just as quickly I lost it all.

• • •

I blame the George Foreman grill.

And, yes, as silly as it sounds, the truth remains: without that grill, I might still be with the woman I met at church, the woman I married because it seemed the right thing to do, and I might still be father to the sons I sired. Houses can be bought and sold, and a Labrador is befuddled on the best of days, but I rue the loss of brick-and-mortar and swirling drifts of black fur as well.

The grill, well, that is gone now, too, the recent victim of Francie's most aggressive purge. She had nothing against it personally, except her general principle that appliances should be useful seven days a week and not just for the occasional one-off. And, for the record, they should also work.

"But I cooked on that exclusively," I argued. "For years."

"It's dead," she said. "And you clearly needed new recipes."

"Who needs recipes?" I said. "I got you. With all apologies to gender roles."

"Huh," she said. "I'm here now, and I've been here for years and years; the grill can go. Keep this up, and I'll be the one to leave."

The outside of it was black and scorched, the cord frayed, the wires exposed, and it had lived in the garage with the cobwebs and mice for thirty years or more; I never intended to use it again. I never could have used it again. I had kept it as a reminder of how tenuous life can be, but I guess such *memento mori* are no match for spring cleaning in a quarantine.

But I need to backtrack a bit.

Not long after I started teaching, I met Tiffany at church, one of those hotel convention center monstrosities at the white north end of town. I'll spare you the name and denomination in order to protect the innocent and the meaning-to-be-well-meaning. In my own mind I called it the Cheez Whiz and Lard Tabernacle, since that's the way the name of the Almighty sounded coming from the mouth of the pastor who had made his bones in Texas; he tended to get worked up at the conclusions of his sermons, and when the spit began to fly and he invoked the name of American undigestibles, we knew we were near the end, with the mass hysteria of the altar call soon to follow. I had gone there thinking that, in the absence of Francie, looking for love might be best fulfilled by numbers, and since this church had no shortage of single women, I wasn't far off in my estimation. What I hadn't expected was the kind of women I'd find. Very earnest, they were, and very quick to offer praise to the Lard. It should also be noted that the Tabernacle was something of a track meet for dating, since the most attractive of the single women got snapped up by the age of twenty-one, and they weren't shy about asking their prospective suitors for a resume and a paystub, if not references.

I'll say this for Tiffany: she was something of an outlier within her spiritual circle. She worked for her father's advertising outfit, and she made three times my teacher's salary; that, by itself, could have been a disqualification. Unlike the majority of her evangelical sisters, though, she liked wearing J. Crew to work more than she liked wearing sweatpants at home, and she wasn't interested in nesting the moment she got married. Our wedding was a destination affair in Carmel, the décor was Martha Stewart, and the honeymoon was a quick four-day trip to Cabo because she had meetings the following Wednesday in her father's office, and, as she said, she had to be about his business. So she was all the more surprised when the pregnancy test came back positive three months later. She was more surprised than I was since, one Friday night after a few too many drinks, I knew we hadn't been as careful as we might have been. I had been expecting the result and she wasn't, which meant that I bore the brunt of her anger.

"How," she looked me in the eye, "did this happen?"

"I think," I said, "that you know how. We did this, and we did that, and there you have it."

"I mean," she said, "how did *you* let this happen?"

So it was my responsibility, and once Brandon was six weeks old, he was off to daycare half an hour before my first period at school, and I picked him up each weekday afternoon at five. I learned how to carry all the equipment and baggage that infants require these days, and I became as adept as any circus juggler with bulky bags and the brevity of time.

And then, it happened again; Tiffany accused me of irresponsibility, and we had Kyle just after Brandon turned three, and the luggage I carried became heavier and more elaborate while Tiffany's work days became longer and longer, which tempted me to think that she wanted to get away from me and the boys. The school year was complicated, with its drop-offs and pick-ups, and I can tell you that getting work done around the corners of baths and feedings, playtimes and bedtimes was a challenge. We managed, albeit barely. But when summer came, the boys and I found ways to enjoy ourselves in spite of their mother's absences. Her clients were mostly agricultural interests, and she was up and down Highway 99, along with the long-haul truckers. The food processors and pesticide manufacturers got a kick out of seeing her pull up in the BMW and get out wearing white while the dust swirled around her in their graveled parking lots. They were eager for her encouragement, and she prayed with them as often as she gave them new marketing strategies and advertising campaigns. Her clients swore by her, she spoke their language, and she was a fundamental feature of her father's overall revenue. She returned home late at the end of each day and peeled off what became my next day's trip to the dry cleaner.

We were happy. Happy enough. Or so I thought. Until that day in July when I sat down on the couch to watch the Giants lose a Wednesday afternoon game to Cincinnati. Brandon was playing with Duplos while Kyle rattled around in one of those roller contraptions with a seat and a tray and a circle of wheels that kept him upright and, as it turned out, too mobile. Caesar lay under the coffee table and drooled on the carpet. Hamburger patties were cooking in the grill for Brandon and me, and I must have fallen asleep to yet another Giant inning of anemic offense when Brandon grabbed my nose to get my attention.

"Daddy," he said, enunciating as well as a child twice his age, "Kyle is coughing."

"Okay," I said, coming to consciousness as slowly as a boot wades through mud. "Okay."

Caesar was barking in idiotic and frantic confusion, and I couldn't hear a thing. I looked this way and that from my place on the couch. On television, Candlestick looked like a ghost town surrounded by drizzle and fog, and I knew that on the radio Hank Greenwald would either be quoting Twain about the effects of a San Francisco summer or making another comment about fans disguised as empty seats. I didn't see Kyle or his roll-around chair. Not until Brandon pointed to the foyer with its slick terrazzo tiles and the potted silk plants in front of the entry way window.

He was coughing all right, and his face was red, and if he was banging his tiny fists on the tray table in front of him like Ginger Baker on drums, he also didn't appear to be breathing.

I did everything a parent is not supposed to do in such cases, but I think I might be excused if only for being under the influence of fear and adrenaline and the useless energy of panic. I picked him up, pounded his back, felt around in his mouth, which is when I touched the feathered end of one of the little plastic flower stems from the silk plants by the door. I contemplated tweezers as though they might be forceps. I kneed Caesar away whose help consisted of jumping as well as barking. I dangled Kyle upside down, hoping to dislodge the obstruction from his airway, and then I pounded his back again until he suddenly smiled and opened his arms to be hugged and said "Da, da, da, da," which to my frightened and now relieved ears sounded like Goddammit, Dad.

I should also mention that somewhere within that sequence of events—the feeling inside his mouth, the dangling, and the pounding, Caesar's barking and jumping—the smoke detector in the kitchen had begun to wail, smoke was billowing everywhere from the electric grill, and the air in the house had turned greasy and brown.

"Jeez Louise, and all the saints," I said. I held Kyle, who was now breathing like a yogi, while I ushered Brandon and the dog outside. "Stay here," I told my older boy, for in those days before cell phones, I either had to pound on a neighbor's door or go back inside to call the fire department. The fear of embarrassment told me that breathing a little smoke was just the thing for a Wednesday, and the 911 operator, after getting the street address, mentioned baking soda once she heard the words "electric grill" and "fire" and "grease." So, with one hand, I held Kyle, who was pounding me in the ear, and with the other, I dumped the Arm & Hammer on the grill and the fire, and then found a way to get the plug out of the wall. If the order in which I did things was backward, I still count it a victory and an achievement to have had the presence of mind at all.

Tiffany pulled into the garage just as the last of the fire trucks was leaving. The boys, the dog, and I were outside on the front porch waving to the firemen. She got out of the car and joined our little tableau.

"What did you burn down?" she said.

"You might well ask," I said. "But there won't be hamburgers tonight."

"I see," she said.

"And we need to give Kyle a heavy dose of sweet potato."

"I see," she said again, even though she didn't.

I had talked with one of the firemen who was also their EMT, who suggested that the more mashed food we fed him, the sooner we'd find the plastic parts in Kyle's diaper, so when I explained that to Tiffany, she held her head in both hands and took a deep breath and said, "I think you need to go."

"What?" I said.

"Go," she said and pointed toward the garage and my twelve-year-old Escort. "I can't have this anymore."

"What?" I said again. "What can't you have anymore?"

"This, this chaos," she said, even though we'd hardly made this any kind of routine. "I can't have it."

"So, what am I supposed to do? I live here," I said, since stating the obvious seemed my best line of defense. "I live here, you live here, and so do the boys. We're a family," I said. "But maybe that's not true anymore."

"Maybe not," she said. "And maybe if you leave, I'll be able to breathe again."

And here I had thought I had been the more beleaguered.

• • •

I packed my things that night and went to a motel, and over the next couple of weeks, I moved the rest of my accumulated stuff, including the grill, which I had rescued from the trash out of some perverse notion that if I could fix it, I might be able to restore my marriage. I am not especially handy, though, so the outside of the case remained blackened by grease and smoke and flames, and the cord remained frayed and the wires exposed and broken, and my marriage remained equally kaput. I saw the boys and Caesar on weekends until Tiffany met the owner of a plumbing supply company, who was also likewise divorced. And when he decided to move his operation to Arizona, she and the boys went with him, no matter what that meant to her career in advertising at Daddy's firm. I guess it wasn't that important to her, after all, and she turned her affections toward real estate. I could have fought the move, but I didn't have the heart, and when I attended their eventual graduations and weddings, neither boy had much memory of me except as a well-meaning stranger who showed up at appropriate moments with a card for the occasion and a check for less than they might have expected or hoped to receive. Kyle has no memory of silk geraniums, and Brandon does not remember eating hamburgers night after night. I should mention, they met at church, Tiffany and her plumbing mogul, just as we had done, but it seems to have been a better match; their every Christmas card and newsletter displays a larger and newer and more featureless house in a newer and more featureless suburb. On the other hand, the grill moved with me from apartment to house, from box to garage, a charred and guilty reminder of a former life.

If I now resist Francie's call to eradicate these objects of the past, it is only for the benefit such reminders can bring. To know that our imperfections and flaws have made of us who we are. Which brings me to how Francie and I met. Or re-met, as the case may be.

I taught my classes through our separation and divorce, and since Tiffany no longer trusted my fitness, I no longer had responsibility for our boys, and my schedule had hours open that I was unused to filling on my own. I went back to the bowling alleys of my youth and signed up for three leagues a week, one of which was stocked with former pros and those who were hopeful of becoming so. Crankers, strokers, and full rollers, you name it, we saw them all. Everyone had an idea about how to get the right path to the headpin.

One night I could do little wrong. I ended the first game with a 248 and five straight strikes. The second game I strung all twelve together for my first and only 300 game, and then in the third game I threw three more strikes before I left a seven pin in the fourth frame. The feeling was other-worldly: my feet, my arm and hand, the ball, the pins—all were connected and in harmony with each other. Twenty straight strikes. When it was all over, I sat in my spot on the molded plastic seats, held my head between my knees, and wept. One of the former professionals came by and put his gloved fist on my head and said that the first one was always special, but there would be more to come. As right as he was about the experience being special, he was that wrong about the 300 games in my future. There were close calls, but no others, and I had to content myself with that memory. The memory of a game and the memory of that moment in my life when I caught perfection in the midst of losing everything else.

That night was also the first time I felt what I would call a disturbance along my right shoulder blade. A week later a lump had formed. I felt it, spongy and hard, every time I rolled over in bed, and a week after that, I began to run a fever. I lasted another week by taking Ibuprofen by the shovelful, but then one night at midnight, I could no longer lie on my back or stay seated in a chair; even the slightest pressure was uncomfortable. I went to the emergency room, knowing that my case would no doubt be among the lowest of priorities, since I represented neither gunshot wound nor heart attack, broken bone nor stroke.

A bored receptionist took my information and insurance, and a bored technician took my vitals, and only my temperature of 103 provoked anything beyond mild interest. That was when Francie pushed aside the curtain and stood next to my bed. She was wearing blue scrubs, her hair was orange rather than green, and there were three rings looping through her left nostril, but I immediately recognized her and then confirmed my recognition by seeing the tattooed spiders peek out at each wrist underneath her long sleeve shirt.

"You," she said. "Joe College has returned."

"Me," I said. "Where have you been all of my life?"

"Here," she said, "working my ass off. Community college. Getting my RN and FNP. Where have you been?"

"Back at our old stomping grounds."

"You're kidding." She used a light to check my eyes and pointed to where I was to look.

"Nope, no kidding. English. Grades nine, ten, and eleven."

"Small world. We're what? Ten minutes away from each other, hospital to school?"

"I guess. How many minutes is that in life experience?"

"Light years," she said.

"Look," I said, "we can call the world big or small, but I think I have a tumor or an alien life form as parasite."

"Really." She told me to roll over onto my stomach and pressed on the slug-sized lump. "Does this hurt?"

After I came down from the ceiling, I said, "Yes," before I could begin to cry in earnest.

"Try having a baby," she said. "You big baby."

"You have kids?" I said.

"Are you kidding?" she said. "I know what's involved. Why would I do that to myself? But I've delivered my share, and I know who deserves my sympathy. Sit up."

I did as I was told. "I suppose I have back cancer," I said, "and I have two months to live. You can tell me."

"Don't be an idiot," she said. "It's no big deal. A sebaceous cyst, but I can only guarantee you one more hour of life. Because that's how long it's going to take to get this thing addressed."

She was going to have to core it out, she said, but then she'd bandage me up, put me on antibiotics, and send me on my way. If I got hit by a bus after leaving the ER, well, that was on me.

"I'll be sedated, right?" I said.

"Don't be a weenie," she said, cruel girl. "All you get is a little bit of lidocaine," which was when she pulled out a hypodermic that looked to have been made for animal husbandry, and then watched me faint away.

• • •

I have no illusions regarding my pain threshold. If pain is a ladder, I won't make it past the first rung. I whimper *before* bad things can happen if I see them coming. I fainted when I saw the needle, and then Francie went to work. She hit me four or five times with the lidocaine in case I woke up, and then she got busy with the scalpel, opened up the lump, and then squeezed until the infection and the white, waxy gunk were gone. From what I was told, the smell was bad enough that patients three beds removed were complaining. If they didn't get some fresh air stat, they'd rather have their heart attacks at home, thank you very much. That's what they said, or so Francie swore.

I woke up while Francie was packing the hole in my back.

"I can't believe you fainted," she said.

"I get a little wobbly around blood," I said, "especially my own. And pain. I'm not a fan of pain."

She shook her head. "You probably shouldn't drive yourself home, then. Who can you call?"

"I'm woozy and in no mood for existential questions. A cab?"

She rolled her eyes. "You're lucky it's a slow night. Stay put and get some rest."

She woke me up at six, and then we walked to her car, one that was even older and dirtier and more dented than my own. In order to sit down, I had to scrape the sandwich wrappers to the floor with the Diet Coke cans and the Doritos bags.

"And to think," I said, "that our health care professionals are the ones advising us on diet."

"May I remind you," she said, "that walking is not out of the question?"

• • •

She took me home, we shared our contact information, and a week later she called with an invitation.

"I'll bet you haven't gotten that thing repacked yet, have you?"

She had given me the address and a phone number of a wound clinic, but I hadn't yet gotten around to doing anything about it.

"No," I said, "but I was planning on it."

"Uh-huh. I didn't think so."

Her invitation was this: she'd pick me up, take me to a clinic where she had privileges, dress the wound, pick up my car, and then we could go out.

"The two of us," she said. "Like old times."

"Sure," I said. "What do you want to do?"

"Bowling," she said, which was the second time, and certainly not the last, that I caught a glint of cruelty in her eyes.

"Okay," I said, "but you know that I'm injured."

"You're scared of bowling a girl," she said.

"No," I said. "I'll have you know that I bowled a 300. Recently. A month ago."

"No," she said. "I didn't know, and I don't believe it. Bring your ball."

It turned out that she had begun to bowl in earnest not long after she got her first hospital job. She did it as something of a joke, in memory of our first date so long ago, but then she discovered that she had a competitive streak, one that had resided within her all this time, albeit dormant and untapped; when she let it emerge, she also discovered that she had to govern the impulse to yell "fucking hell, you son of a bitch" whenever she missed a spare or to kick the ball return when she left a 4–10 split. So we did as she suggested—or, should I say, I did as she directed—and we were bowling at Rodeo Lanes at ten o'clock on a Friday night. And if I tell you now that I lost to her 212 to 204 because I didn't pick up a simple 4–7 spare in the tenth, would you be surprised? Or that by the time we were done, I was sweating and my back was throbbing once again? Would you be surprised if I told you that one thing had nothing to do with the other, that I will not make that particular excuse? Even though my ball, which had been so accurate only a month before, slid past the four-pin by a whisper. Even though when that had happened and she had won, Francie yelled, loud enough for everyone to hear despite the crashing and banging going on around us. On the other hand, the wound packing that Francie had done two hours earlier was leaking, and not in a good way, so we made a return visit to the ER so she could pull out yards and yards of putrescent gauze. She cleaned me up once again, but this time I did not faint, hero that I was, no matter how nauseated I might have felt from the odor of mortality I now had opportunity to smell.

We got married a week or two later because we were both in our forties with no need to wait, but we mark our anniversary from our second date at a bowling alley rather than the date of the civil ceremony with cake. All of which is to say that I had my first adult sexual experience in the women's room of a middle school theater, and I met the wife who divorced me at church and the wife who stayed with me when she stuck a knife in my back, and all of that is a reminder to me that nothing is ever as it is first reported.

Not long after we married, Francie changed jobs when the nurse's position came open at our high school. She got it, and of course the students loved her. They loved her hair and nose rings, and they loved her tattoos, and they love the way she can put them in their place with salt and sugar in equal measures. She makes them feel safe and special and smart, and because she was there, my stock rose, and when I retired, they pretended to love me for her sake. When she saw the job announcement, she said she was going to apply because why should I be the only one with a summer? But now I'm retired, so my summer is the rest of my life. And now, we are living and working at home, and no one knows what day of the week it is, much less the month or the season.

"Get a grip," Francie says, when she takes a break from Zoom faculty meetings and chat sessions with students who have questions about venereal disease. "Get a grip, and help me clean out the attic."

I had something of a temper tantrum, I admit it.

"This is my life," I said, or at least that's what I think I said. I went outside of my head for a time as I saw the objects departing, presumably never to return. "It's my life and you're trying to get rid of it, one shadow at a time."

There goes the plaid sport coat and the delusions and hormones of my high school years. *Poof!*

And there goes the George Foreman grill of my ill-fated first attempt at marriage and family. *Psst!*

But I balk at the thought of the Roto Grip leaving my life, no matter if I haven't been to a bowling alley in the past ten years, the victim of bad knees, the evolution of our interests, and the fact that she was beating me two games out of three when I quit for good. Still, when I look at it, I can't help but be reminded of perfection when perfection was difficult to find. And impossible to hold onto. Reminded that there are moments when everything works as it is supposed to, a harmony beyond applause or appreciation from others.

"Look," I'll say. "I'll trade you one bowling ball for a footlocker's worth of certificates of achievement. Who knows? When this is all over and we walk outside again, maybe we'll go bowling. It could happen."

She will sigh, I can hear it now. She will tug her long-sleeved T-shirt over her wrists, and she'll mutter words to the effect that she has been saddled with a drama queen of a husband, and of course, she will be right.

ACKNOWLEDGMENTS

I'D LIKE TO thank the editors of the journals in which these stories first appeared, some in different forms:

"Spies," *CutBank*

"Coincidence," "Fire," *Glimmer Train*

"My Life as a Mystic," *Image*

"O Perfect, Perfect Love!," *Idaho Review*

"Christmas in Jonestown," *Jabberwock Review*

"The Volcano Lover," *The Massachusetts Review*

"A Tale Told by Rube Goldberg Begins and Ends with Dogs," *The Packinghouse Review*

"High School and the Mysteries of Everything Else," *The Pinch*

"The Nothing between Us," *Prime Mincer*

"Retirement Dogs," *Prism Review*

"Next Day," *Southern Review*

Twenty-five years since the last book . . . is that possible? Apparently, it is. Children grow, parents die, careers pass. Pull out the scrapbooks, and watch the years go by.

I am indebted first to Steve Yarbrough, writer-friend and fellow football fanatic of the past thirty years, whose encouragement to send this manuscript to Wyatt Prunty was the kickstart and goad I needed. My gratitude is boundless, as is my expectation of future discussions of Munro's sneaky use of point of view and Belichick's enthusiasm for two tight end sets.

To those individuals who have read many of these stories in their various iterations— James Coffey, Deb and Greg Lapp, Rick Garza, and Ric Dice—my thanks for your patience as well as your forbearance. For all of my former colleagues and students, as well as the staff and administration at Reedley College, you were the embrace of home for thirty-six years; I can't tell you how much it meant to have a place and a community within which to work and live. For the support and breakfasts with the Green Valley Writers Group—Syd Bowie, Paul Kaser, and Tom Tyner—the next one's on me. For the recent rejuvenation from the members of the Enclave Writers Group—Jim Brennan, Jill Kapinus, Deb Lapp, Howard Rappaport, Ann Shortell, and Nancy Spiller—stay enthused and keep the work coming.

I am likewise grateful to all at Johns Hopkins University Press: series editor Wyatt Prunty, who accepted this book and brought me and this collection into a fold of writers and titles I've admired since graduate school; Catherine Goldstead, who has gracefully shepherded the process step by step in the midst of pandemic and other turmoil; and Hilary Jacqmin, whose incisive and attentive copyediting made for a better conversation than any author has a right to expect.

My family—my wife, Deb Everson Borofka, and our daughters Katherine and Kristian—knows the selfishness and preoccupation of writers all too well; I am fortunate that they likewise know the power of forgiveness. This book is for them.

Finally, I also have to acknowledge writers and friends no longer with us: Brad Watson, whose death came much too soon and surprised us all, and David R. C. Good, whose mentorship and insight I have missed on a daily basis for the past seven years. Amen.

DAVID BOROFKA'S first collection of stories, *Hints of His Mortality*, was selected by Oscar Hijuelos as winner of the 1996 Iowa Award for short fiction. His novel, *The Island*, was published by MacMurray & Beck.

His stories have appeared in *Image*, *Massachusetts Review*, *Southern Review*, *Black Warrior Review*, *Missouri Review*, *Manoa*, *Gettysburg Review*, and *Shenandoah*, among other places. He has been the winner of the *Missouri Review* Editors' Prize, the Charles B. Wood Award from *Carolina Quarterly*, the Emerging Writers Network Award, *Prism Review*'s fiction prize, and *Jabberwock Review*'s Nancy D. Hargrove Editors' Prize.

A member of the faculty at Reedley College from 1983 until his retirement in 2019, he has also taught on assignment for the University of California, Los Angeles Extension Writers' Program, Fresno Pacific University, and California State University, Fresno. He and his wife now divide their time between Clovis, California, Ashland, Oregon, and any place where the fires aren't burning and the virus numbers are low. May the earth and humanity heal.

Guy Davenport, *Da Vinci's Bicycle*

Stephen Dixon, *14 Stories*

Jack Matthews, *Dubious Persuasions*

Guy Davenport, *Tatlin!*

Joe Ashby Porter, *The Kentucky Stories*

Stephen Dixon, *Time to Go*

Jack Matthews, *Crazy Women*

Jean McGarry, *Airs of Providence*

Jack Matthews, *Ghostly Populations*

Jack Matthews, *Booking in the Heartland*

Jean McGarry, *The Very Rich Hours*

Steve Barthelme, *And He Tells the Little Horse the Whole Story*

Michael Martone, *Safety Patrol*

Jerry Klinkowitz, *Short Season and Other Stories*

James Boylan, *Remind Me to Murder You Later*

Frances Sherwood, *Everything You've Heard Is True*

Stephen Dixon, *All Gone: 18 Short Stories*

Jack Matthews, *Dirty Tricks*

Joe Ashby Porter, *Lithuania*

Robert Nichols, *In the Air*

Ellen Akins, *World Like a Knife*

Greg Johnson, *A Friendly Deceit*

Guy Davenport, *The Jules Verne Steam Balloon*

Guy Davenport, *Eclogues*

Jack Matthews, *Storyhood as We Know It and Other Tales*

Stephen Dixon, *Long Made Short*

Jean McGarry, *Home at Last*

Jerry Klinkowitz, *Basepaths*

Greg Johnson, *I Am Dangerous*

Josephine Jacobsen, *What Goes without Saying: Collected Stories*

Jean McGarry, *Gallagher's Travels*

Richard Burgin, *Fear of Blue Skies*

Avery Chenoweth, *Wingtips*

Judith Grossman, *How Aliens Think*

Glenn Blake, *Drowned Moon*

Robley Wilson, *The Book of Lost Fathers*

Richard Burgin, *The Spirit Returns*

Jean McGarry, *Dream Date*

Tristan Davies, *Cake*

Greg Johnson, *Last Encounter with the Enemy*

John T. Irwin and Jean McGarry, eds., *So the Story Goes: Twenty-Five Years of the Johns Hopkins Short Fiction Series*

Richard Burgin, *The Conference on Beautiful Moments*

Max Apple, *The Jew of Home Depot and Other Stories*

Glenn Blake, *Return Fire*

Jean McGarry, *Ocean State*

Richard Burgin, *Shadow Traffic*

Robley Wilson, *Who Will Hear Your Secrets?*

William J. Cobb, *The Lousy Adult*

Tracy Daugherty, *The Empire of the Dead*

Richard Burgin, *Don't Think*

Glenn Blake, *The Old and the Lost*

Lee Conell, *Subcortical*

Adrianne Harun, *Catch, Release*

Claire Jimenez, *Staten Island Stories*

Pamela Painter, *Fabrications*

David Borofka, *A Longing for Impossible Things*